Tales of Earth

Stories of a future's past

Dan Brady

One Insight Press

ISBN 13: 978-0692876466
ISBN 10: 0692876466

One Insight Press
San Francisco, CA

Please see my author's page on Amazon.com at:
https://www.amazon.com/Dan-Brady/e/B014ROHMNC

Acknowledgements:

I would like to acknowledge the role of my public-school teachers. They encouraged my writing. I would be remiss, as well, if I did not mention the wide range of writers, some of whom are mentioned on the back cover, who took me on their journeys and adventures. Without their artistry or visions, I would not have written this. Also, there are those responsible for the thought provoking films from the 40's onward into the 80's. While many Sci-Fi films were simplistic, poorly crafted, and meant only as B movies, there were well-crafted films incorporating important ideas to mull over, as well as moral considerations, and commentary on social issues. Amongst those, I would say the film "Forbidden Planet" is an exemplar, as is the first version of Wells' "The Time Machine" and that of "The Martian Chronicles" despite its drawbacks.

I would like to acknowledge Niels, a long-time friend. We read Sci-Fi, talked about what we read, and exchanged books. The idea of having reality-based story lines is sourced from those discussions; however, I hasten to add here, this collection does not hold to that line all the time. Some of the stories came to me, originally, as dreams or inspirational visions, while others were written in a manner of the classic pulp Sci-Fi of decades past. Last, I'd like to add, through all the revisions, I kept true to the original inspiration as best I could, however tempered that may have become with current knowledge and or keeping the back-story self-consistent.

My family and friends were, likewise important contributors to what became the prerequisites for my interest in Sci-Fi and writing in general. I thank them all; enjoy what is to come.

Introduction:

I read Sci-Fi rather avidly during my late elementary years and into high school. Those inexpensive books were bought with the small amounts of money I scraped together. I would go to flea markets and there I could buy 10 or more for a dollar. What drew me in were the scope of the plots, the heroism, idealism, and the exploration of possible solutions to current problems. They also illuminated a mostly optimistic perspective, which showed humanity becoming a source of good in the universe. Also that no matter how trying or dire the circumstances might be – there was always a way to the truth and justice.

This collection of stories takes liberties with reality. I build future worlds and civilizations, include larger than life characters, who have larger than life challenges, and, of course, the good wins out in the end—even if only by implication. There are space ships, villains, aliens, heroes, adventurers, and lessons to be learned, taught, or ruminated upon. Much in this collection began with stories written decades ago. Back then, I wrote on legal sized yellow pads with a number two pencil during lunch breaks. I also had oodles of free time back in the late 70's and early 80's at home. However, that was before I went back to college and became an elementary school teacher. Although this choice proved to be terrifically demanding, I also enjoyed it very much.

These tales were written independently of each other during my mid 20's and early 30's, originally for personal enjoyment and I've had fun revising and reworking the tales to produce this book. Do not be surprised, therefore, if there are sequels. There are many tales in the vault and I hope to produce future volumes, as opportunities allow.

Enjoy the rides.

Table of Contents

The Stage

The Stage

The Simple Setting

This world is both old and young. Old in that the body of the planet had existed for many billions of years when it was found wandering the far intergalactic reaches. It was then eased into its current location, an orbit about a very young and energetic sun. The life upon it, brought there not a million or so centuries hence, now thrives wildly overrunning the one inhabited continent. This lesser continent is bisected by a massive range of mountains running southeast to northwest, which reaches a goodly distance into the northern sea, forming as it does the spine of a peninsula that ultimately devolves into a chain of islands. The last island, the largest, is a massive round of rock, deep red purple in color, is dozens of miles long and several in both height and width. This is where the lone human settlement is located. It too is ancient but has only been usefully populated for about a million years. Located on the leading edge of this uplifting continent's periphery, the designers had eternity in mind when they chose this site.

This massif has long been sculpted form a unique city. All of its structures are carven, magnificent architectural and artistic wonders, each with marvelously worked details. Homes and temples, institutions, centers of trade or commerce, halls of justice, theaters, universities, and the places dedicated to love-healing; all of them are part of the one stone; each vibrant exterior is engraved with inscriptions and or decorated with frescos, mosaics or murals. Even the walking pavements are an archive of living script. It is no wonder that the many visitors spend time reading the cityscape and or adding to it. It is a vast complex, a multiplicity of varied wonders so rich as to dazzle, yet it all has a singular purpose.

This is where Galactic Citizenship is granted to initiates after their pre-requisite coming-of-age ceremonies, training and education by counselors, who have prepared them to attain their majority. For the vast most part everyone on this world is in the queue to citizenship, involved with that process, or in the General Administration; those who provide all the aforementioned with their needed goods and services. To ensure the living continuity and trust, the builders decreed that this planet will never become a mere home world—thus no one has ever been born there and the millions abiding there hail from off world. Nonetheless they are wholly heartfelt in their dedication to improve this place of places and, by so doing, forward the unity. Essentially, this is where the collective, the commons, the associations, and cooperatives, harmonize their essential policies and programs in order to sustain the galactic culture of peace through prosperity by preparing new citizens.

The DelAriaXuor, commonly called HeartCenterStone, was the appropriate name for this place of places. It is civilization's great womb for conscious evolution which is why the citizenship preparation culminates with a reading from *The Tales*, ancient stories of human nature, as well as psalms, which, translated from their original languages, are included in each copy because of their greater scope of intimacy. Many of the original languages varied on the telepathic scale and so the unspoken contents are inferred only from the portions that are spoken. After attaining their majority, the new citizens disseminate into The Great Constellation on missions big or small, overt or covert, vital or personal—but always for the benefit of all.

Psalm 234 "Reflections"

Just as water slipped off this moonlit strand
One star's reflection – lay close to hand
Fighting the ripples – it seemed fraught
As if in a struggle against being caught

When the waters settled into the grains
Its light faded into their dark remains
I kept station awaiting the sweeping sheen's advance –
Expecting a reprise – of its unsteady dance
The water returned over topping my shoes this time
Leaving upon them both sand grains and rime
But I saw it, I saw it near to me, I saw it there
To catch this note from far, far away, I decided to stay
I studied its shimmer – as if it was a personal display
As I noted a leak in my elderly boots wanted repair
I considered the long cold journey evinced by that dot
And how we came to be on what became our own spot

The wind was coming from the west that night
And while it was steady it was only slight
Yet it bore a sweetness I would have otherwise denied
For she came to mind, as did regrets, and I sighed
Took a trip touring the vistas of my yesteryears
But as I stilled my body my mind wandered all the more
Began turning the old pages of my life's storied lore
As I stared at this light and felt a few tears

Only the silent moon gave its witnessing glow
To that which I would never otherwise show
But I was alone and so passions could be spent
As I looked on to the light which kept me … intent
I did not have the satisfaction of a heart warm in its bliss
Rather I had the benefits of spendthrift ways gone amiss
I longed to mend that which should never have been rent
The precious evolution of a love, which was transcendent

And here was a glimmer of light in that water so near
Which, in touching my soul, had then become love's souvenir
While it could be said the star in the sand was nothing at all
Still it became something for me; it had meaning withal
No matter its eerie silence or the grace in its wavering light
It could not possibly know what it inspired that night
Ages upon ages come as this or all recollections go
While ever to the present do the timeless times flow
And so, did I wait upon this anonymous star's light
As we both reflected in depth late that one night

A Single Youth

The child was certainly that no longer and the suite, once seeming so large and wondrous, now appeared small as well as old. Every crack, piece of tile or fixture in the place, every nick in the wood of the work table or slight flaw in the sleeping pallet were intimately familiar to its inhabitant as they bore memories for the soon-to-be adult who'd lived there twelve cycles. Today had been the Day of One Candle and this soon to be citizen waited.

Paz was ready and looked forward to what some saw as a mere formality, a reading of *The Tales*. This final element of the process was supposed to bring everything taught over the years together and then some. They were a holistic summation, a set of dreams some said. These, Paz had been told, were unceasing lessons because, once read, they continued to resonate in the heart and soul as well as affect one's self-impression, sense of purpose, and personal choices, so long as one lived—the same was said regarding the psalms.

There came the tolling of a bell. Paz left the suite and followed a well-worn causeway with thousands of others before entering the Hall of Memory. They then silently stood.

"Welcome citizens," the clear telepathic voice whispered, "The Great Song will begin soon. Afterwards your counselors will present each of you with your set of tales. You are the way, the truth, and the light! Hear then, **The Great Song for all Generations.** There was a chime, silvery, lofty, and very soft—yet everyone could hear it; they sat, closed their eyes and waited.

Before, before you or your people were,
I was for long ages dust
I lived, prospered, loved, learned,
And adventured before making this trust
I sing this praise to honor all who would be free
Know, however vast our separation seems to be,
No matter distance or the interventions of time—
Still longer are The Tales—I bid you hear my wishes sublime
While I cannot know what, where, how, or who you are
By this boon, your rightful inheritance, I mean to take you far
Delve into the mysteries so long kept – but please do not regret
Do not dwell upon past glories, or ages – and do not forget—
Look from the past or present into the future, the Sovereign's Keep
Which you and I together protect from an odd kind of sleep
Out of nothing does the Dark Recruiter form taking its toll,
It obfuscates the mind with vacancies affecting the soul
These, The Tales, from a far away time, are a cure given you

Some tell of innocents, sprightly, so very young or rashly new
Others may seem incomplete, which they are – or out of order
Yet they're meant to provide heart, mind, and soul vital mortar
Our society's health depends on each of us; this is not chance
Each must live the truth that freedom requires eternal vigilance.
There are tales of majesty, legend, of peoples and their places
Of strange cultures, all their long trials, or sad, sad traces
Some illuminate precepts disguised in malevolent contents
All mean to affect you so as to better refine your intents
Know, however calm this our very own time may seem,
It is, in fact, transient, illusory, an insubstantial dream
It's not just what one does or how, more importantly, it's why
For, in deliberating on justice, we affect our wisdom's eye
In the library's vaulted halls are records of everyone known
Gifting all generations with the precious we'd have them own
This place, built so long ago, for all its majestic, lofty structure
Protects what's smaller than a grain: the essence of our future:
Keep to your word, purpose, and cause – take time to finish
You may leave, as you will; each depending on their own wish
Or stay on, as it pleases your soul even take a counselor's role
One is never done with insight; we are facets of the One Bright
Reflect, without doubt, the light within is the light without
Many, many have here graduated, as you'll now do
Stepping into time, illuminated with love and healing anew!

The Little Talk

The great hall was silent for a long moment. Again, the faint, silvery chime rang out, miraculously filling the cavernous hall. Everyone rose quietly and slowly walked out.

Paz returned to the suite where a counselor waited. Without preface the elder began, "Responsibilities are to be inherited by others. We all pass on. Some will travel the starry ways bringing their light as needed, others, in accumulating sophistication, may take up the reins of civil service—while a select shall hold forth 'neath a graceful arbor, educating children. Each answers their calling for service to live by and for each other. Each, in so doing, honors the Great Mother. This is as it should be—as it should be."

"Each comes to their own balance between belief and doubt as to what they read. However, no one is to hold another as lesser, or non-devout, because of what they come to believe or not to believe. There is no devotion, no right way; also, and perforce of that, there is no going astray. *The Tales* can never be used for berating, criticizing, or other faults commonly associated with the commitment of emotion to dry text. You're beyond such error. This is not to say one shouldn't debate the knowing man but we mustn't devolve into fearful opinions; we are, after all, made from the dust of those gone before, great or small, known or forgotten."

"As to *The Tales*, I expect one of us will speak with you regarding them as you'll have need. There are few if any passages that have not been doubted. Some hold the entire work to be a cleverly woven fabrication. There are others who doubt the existence of the mythical Earth, it being a common enough name, as well you know. When you finish, you may want auxiliary texts. We keep them all, even yours—should you choose to write one. You shall now read that which has kept our civilization steady on.

He stood, showed Paz an ordinary book, modern of construction but not nearly as voluminous as the rumors would have one imagine. Paz stared for a moment.

As if in reply, these words came to mind: "There is not just one student. Just so, there is not just one collection. There are many, many tales; however, this set was assembled to suit your needs, talents, and potential, as well as to address your failings, foibles or prejudices. In reading them you'll have a better comprehension of the extensive preparation you endured. Hopefully your pride will not be such as to prevent you from taking in all that's here as a guide."

"May you always know what you need to understand the long game and why we shouldn't forget ourselves or what has been done because of, or what is made out of, a name."

"Our hope is that your hopes are ours and ours yours. Honor yourself and in so doing honor us; then promise more, find the firmament of bliss, the center of resource, the essentiality of being, all in your heart's path. May blessings pour, read—be free."

He handed over the book and left. At that moment Paz was free to go about life's ways in the ageless city, to read at leisure, and or seek other activities as were meet with heartfelt interests. Truly time was free. Surprisingly the first entry was a Psalm:

Psalm 452   "Who influenced you?"

How and when does a story begin?
How are we to know? When I think on it, any tale
No matter its size, must begin long ago.
So, when asked who influenced me, I gave my friend an analogy.
Consider a stream, I said, even a small one, near to hand
Is not its course ever guided by contours of the land?
Is it not deflected by every rock, bit of soil, or living thing
With which it co-exists
Before or after the stony lip of its spring?
And are not all these things but a postscript
Proceeding from a source,
Which charges the nature of the stream,
And so, effects its discourse?

Nor should I fail to say that forests and men
Alike surely do amend it
For its worth is clear to those temporal beings
Who can apprehend it.

But the fishes and all the living things cannot be the stream,
Nor, for that matter, can it be the water, or so it would seem
For the flow is ever carried off, even as we watch, for sport
Whether by evaporation or gravity's simple transport.

It is surely not its path, or the things it has carried off,
Nor could it be its remains, a shallow drying trough.
A stream then is a time and place, dependent on conditions
Which, if the truth be told, have utmost antiquity as its origins,
Preconditions, which, if they be scientifically analyzed, with-all
Stretch back to the beginnings of time and matter immemorial
And, perforce, do they not, I waxed, extend too onward in time
Until the very edge of doom itself, imagine a stream - sublime!

And so full circle I came as my analogy found its end.
What are the credits I must roll to answer my friend?
No less than everyone who has ever been or may yet be
Not less than the full chorus, say I, have clearly influenced me

The Tales

Tale, the First: A Descent

I remember, it was before the big one, the seventh probe of Jupiter, that there were three of us meeting in the command center's break room of the Beta Station looking down upon the immensity of what was once a God to the ancients. To us it was a tantalizing mystery, yet the effort to sell pure science to the People's Council had been a long and harrowing slog. The project directors, Doctors Webber and Manheim, sat with me, their sometime pilot, as we got-away-from-it-all, enjoying our peculiar egghead R & R, a game we called attributions—it was my turn to provide the prompt.

I said, "Thesis, 'What makes Earth feel like hell is our expectations that it should feel like heaven.' and Dr. Webber, it is your turn to start, comport or contrast?"

"I'll do comport. Welz, you sure can pick'em. Hmm, okay, it was Palahnuik." Although appearing at ease, we'd done a slap-down bet, everything was riding a bit of old-timey showmanship in order to bolster support for the Jupiter Program. As we played, we all knew we wouldn't have long to wait. Webber added, "How about, 'There is no boundary between heaven and earth unless we believe in one.' The contrast is to you Dr. Manheim."

"Hmm. Seems it would be, uh, Delacroix, Dante, no, Dirks! Now, swat this one if you can W. 'Do I believe in heaven and hell? I do, we have them here; the world is nothing else.'"

"Ah! Davidson, of course. My turn," I said, "'The mind is a universe and can make heaven of hell, a hell of heaven,' to you Webber." Just a few months prior to this soiree, and in that very room, frustrated by mission failures and budget threats, we'd had a bull session and decided to spark public interest with a showpiece, something they both morally disliked.

Being pragmatists, however, I got them to swallow their pride and make arrangements on the QT, using the slush budget and repurposing the prep for the next probe. We launched our PR blitz and had then gone with the plan.

"Milton, W, you're being too kind to this old doc. M, catch this, if you can, 'We are each our own devil, and we make this world our hell.'"

Mannheim sat for a moment, "Wallerstein, Weiss, Marbury? No? I give."

"It's Wilde, Oscar." Doc Webber chuckled."

"Okay, fine. Now, I'll see you and raise," I said, "'Hell hath no limits, nor is circumscribed in one self place, for where we are is hell, and where hell is we must be.'" Then I sat back smirking. There was a long silence.

"Dr. M?" I asked.

"Well now, a devil of a quote, if ever I heard one," he said and we all laughed.

We had timed our series of announcements with the build up to the elections. First, we announced the next mission's target would be the red spot, something that had been reserved for later. It was a mystery and this was why the announcement generated interest, which gave us coverage, which gave us support. Everyone loves a good mystery. If the people knew anything about Jupiter, they knew about the red spot. After that we let things percolate.

"Alright, how about 'If everything happens for a reason that means you made the right choice, even when it's the wrong choice,'" offered Webber.

"Easy, Trayco! Now Welz," M suggested, "You will sum us up."

"Let's see, for M, 'I myself am heaven and hell.'"

There was quiet as he thought and I reflected. In the weeks after the first set of announcements, when we we'd gotten just about all the bounce we expected, we followed up with the booster, letting it be known the mission would be manned. This wasn't as big a change as one might think since we'd repurposed much of it from things already in the works, but since the last manned mission was nearly fatal, we got all the attention we wanted and then some. The good doctors were interviewed and the space program became an issue in the political slugfest back on Earth. We, at Beta Station, knew this was a Hail Mary play and that if we delivered funding would continue and we'd get our chance to puzzle out this magnificent world.

"Ah, it would be from the Rubaiyat," Mannheim said.

"I should have been more obscure then. Now, to the honorable Dr. Webber, 'I don't like to commit myself about heaven and hell, you see, I've friends in both places.'"

"Twain," they both said chuckling but I let it slide.

We finished the game, as per tradition, with writing quotes on three by five cards, passing them around, and scribbling our attributions for comparison. This was for the extra points, not that we kept score. The room was quiet as we responded to prompts.

No one was surprised when previous problematic failures of unmanned deep probes were brushed aside as doubters and naysayers harped on the dangers and expense of a manned mission. Ironically enough, this served to jolt the public's complacency into a surge of interest, which polls showed was associated with optimism, something we all felt. However, once we had stirred the pot, no one had been surprised when Dr. Webber was called back to Serenity, Mars to explain just exactly what taxpayers were to expect from this costly project.

Soon after arriving on Mars the media had their first big story in a long dry season. The good doctor saw to that by treating a couple of the pushier paparazzi to a hospital stays after they crashed a salon at one of his friend's homes. The next day he did the same thing, ejecting a nosey newsbug who had disrupted his great granddaughter's poetry recital, much to public approval. We got a kick out of that. We'd all been singed by the fiery wrath only an Irish-German could generate, all while leaving mutual respect and long-term good will intact. There was also a closed-door hearing. By reading between the headlines, we understood that conservative delegates, from the U.S., Brazil, and India, were hoping to make worst of our entire effort by dragging up muck or pulling skeletons out of closets. Yet the good doctor pinned them back with a couple of choice quotes. To their concern about budget priorities, he lopped off their ignorance saying, "The way to hell is paved with good intentions." When it came to the how the faithful could come to comprehend the function of the program, he said, "Earth has no sorrow that Heaven cannot heal." But it was all just smoke and mirrors, a show, in order for those opposed to our program to get traction against the Free-Liberal coalition, who had sponsored it. Webber ran a gauntlet in order keep our effort going.

We all knew there was a quid pro quo; just as success of the Jupiter program would provide a boon to the Free-Liberal coalition, so would any embarrassment force the party's hand and we could well be sent packing right after the voting holidays. Don't get me wrong; we all thought it was fair-and-square—we were using them; they were using us. But, old man Webber did it; and when he survived, so did we, at least for the time being. We had the green light before he lifted off; we were going for broke.

We busted it, laying on extra shifts to do as much as we could before Webber returned. Our dedication was well rewarded when, not long after he disembarked, his general announcement's hearty approval and pride in us more than overbalanced the dismal follow-up reports from Earth. It seemed ever since he'd left Mars, we'd become the election's issue of the moment. If we failed, political support would fall off for the Jupiter mission and the whole space program could be impacted.

That's why, not long after he got back, Dr. Webber called our little meeting where we played our little game as I ruminated upon the history of our old-timey, slap-down bet.

Silence had settled in the room as we looked at our cards one last time. M called and we laid them down. Not only did we have a three-way tie but we'd all chosen Milton's "… than serve in heaven" for the most salient of the game. Then, when W cleared his throat, we put the game aside and waited expectantly. He told us the mission would be broadcast live, something those against the effort were in favor of, for reasons of theirs— just as he was for his. He believed being in the crosshairs of the vast idiocracy back on Earth, and having confidence in the mission, gave him a chance to double down on notoriety. He figured the more coverage the better, if all went well. We waited for the proverbial other shoe. He asked me to volunteer. Yes, that's right, me, the pilot who had jettisoned one mission and caught out a contractor for serious shortchanging on another. It was no matter that I'd saved lives and a mission. I was controversial. After that word got out we got the mother of all press-bumps. I had name-recognition; it can pay to enrage blabbercating dimbulb talking heads.

So, as we left that cozy conclave we knew the press would soon be swarming both Alpha and Beta—no one wanted to get coverage secondhand. Dr. M. also let it be known that everyone was to be, polite, make nice, and put aside the usual temperaments. It took practice but, in a few weeks time, when the newsies disembarked, there was never such a friendly, cooperative or idealistic group. Why one could hear compliments echoing in the halls of the both mother ships, Alpha and Beta. Each of us was badgered for interviews and slyly used them to our advantage.

I even gave tours of probe assembly going in and out of the manned unit. This resembled the bathyspheres of an earlier age. This containment vessel, about fifteen feet in diameter, was made of the crystalline alloy

Xlenium. Only this could protect a pilot against the titanic pressures of a deep probe. Inside the sphere were the bare essentials – life support, sensors, controls, data relays and rocket pods—all object-lessons in miniaturization—yet they filled the interior surrounding a simple a pilot's couch set at its core. The sphere sat atop a large booster, as with all prior manned probes, the whole shebang awaited its mission on he Beta Station.

Of course, unbeknownst to newsies, most of the prep work on it had been completed before their arrival so the impression the media had to disseminate was one of an efficient hard-working team, doing a good job. Still, it was odd, being ahead of schedule for once. The press was awed, their cynicism and crassness took a back seat, and they had nothing to do but actually observe and report in a fair, balanced way. Boy oh boy, the public ate it up!

Just before launch, Dr. Webber broadcast prerecorded tape seen by more than one-third of the public. It was his introduction to them. He began explaining the essence of mission, which was to understand the Jupiter's mysteries in the pursuit of pure science. After all, he emphasized, there had been many benefits from the space program such as Xlenium, which was developed for the Jupiter mission and could only be made in zero g. He pointed out how it had become essential to many micro-engineering triumphs. His easy theme was space exploration made life better for the many millions. It was a brilliant, slick production number.

Next, he narrated an animated rendering of the mission, "Here is the first phase. The vessel will be released from Beta station and descend. The second phase begins as it enters the atmosphere and a series of parachutes deploy to slow its descent; this is when we'll lose our com link. The critical third phase begins as the probe arrives at target altitude and its balloon system deploys."

"The mission down under will last for three hours, although there are provisions for several more. Once stable at the preset altitude, the probe will drift as data is recorded and the pilot monitors readouts. However, the pilot will have some ability to direct the probe's flight path by changing altitude in order to enter wind currents that provide alternate vectors. There is leeway at this point so the pilot will have considerable discretion for initiating the return sequence. The fourth phase begins when the pilot releases the balloon assembly and fires the booster. This will create a signal we'll detect. The booster is jettisoned after it carries the pilot's vessel into space. The pilot's most difficult task begins at that point when he uses the sphere's solid fuel rocket pods to rendezvous with an orbiter, which will bring it back to Alpha station." It was a great show and resulted in optimism all around.

Well, as we all know, the launch was perfect, on schedule with regular reports filling the communications network of the system. All went well. There were quiet and positive expectations expressed all around as the lapse of communications left everyone waiting, and coverage focused on preparations for the rendezvous.

I later found out what happened at the three-hour mark. I was so distracted then, and for some time afterwards, I wouldn't have said a word even if I could have. At first, the explanations given to the media were easy and glib, at thirty minutes plus my discretionary options were being discussed, but by sixty plus the word "malfunction" crept onto the airwaves. An hour more and the focus shifted to the kind of errors or problems, which would explain a delay. It all was academic, practically speaking. At two and a half hours plus Dr. Webber made a live appearance to stress a few salient points. First, the life support systems had at least two more hours functionality and, second, the pilot could have made a command decision, in order to gather more data—something that had been discussed all through the planning and in prior public announcements. He laid that on thick. As part of the contingency plans, however, two additional orbiters were sent to cover new theoretical rendezvous zones. When asked if he had regrets Dr. Webber said, "if something is wrong, it will serve as a reminder that hell may be a truth seen to late." and when pressed added, "Maybe you go to hell for the things you don't do, eh?" He dismissed further questions by saying, "Everything possible is being done." He did not emphasize how this consisted, in the main, of watching and waiting.

After that, political flack began coming in thick and fast. Our little slap-down bet was being called and, as far as the media was concerned, we couldn't cover it. The news stories then devolved into doubts and debates about doubts as talking heads challenged politicians who publicly voiced support. As the vultures began to circle, viewer ratings plummeted. Many media crews dismantled their sets, boarded an overfull liner, and left leaving those with axes to grind, who kept right on pounding nails into the casket. It must have been great.

At plus 325.23 minutes plus they got the unmistakable static burst indicating the booster had fired. There must have been cheers, along with notable sighs of relief, broadcast for all to see. A whopping eighty-two percent of viewers followed the broadcast from a camera on the belly of the Alpha ship. This spectacular perspective showed them the ruddy circular cloud formation that could swallow their world. In a matter of moments there was a tiny, yet unmistakable, pinpoint of brightness, rising slowly, or so it seemed, out of that vast field of bloody chaos. Still hoping for something to gobble on, the news hounds were in a Pavlovian ecstasy. A rendezvous ship fired its thrusters and made to intercept the sphere and an even-larger audience tuned, over 90%, unheard of. The chase was not in the least unusual, the catch, flawless.

Yet, I, with deep problems of my own, was silent. I knew this was worrisome to everyone concerned, but I had to prepare my offering—my explanation, my excuse. I overhead some speculation about the extensive damage to the exterior, some wondering, on air, "What in hell could cause such damage?" Because of some of the buckling, it took longer to complete the process of opening her up. Then, lights and cameras were rushed in to catch my first words; everyone wanted to get the scoop for their own purposes. I heard the main candidates were holding press conferences. Imagine.

Before them all, Dr. Webber, the media, and the human community, I scrambled forth from the opening, fumbled at removing my helmet. All those billions saw my troubled horror-struck face, my wide glazed over eyes, upwelling with tears, filling their screens. They watched as I flipped a switch to begin a pre-selected playback of audio-visual from the mission, which was projected on a large screen behind me. I looked back to check the imagery. It was as perfectly clear as it was monstrous.

I turned, faced the cameras. "Milton, "I gasped, pointing back to the screen behind me. "Dante, someone …" and all humanity heard my frenzied voice crack, "said it." I stammered, as the bizarre, nightmarish images flowed into billions of eyes. Everyone heard me bellow, "Down below, in clouds of blood—cyclones and storms and bodies—flying clouds of blood that wail!"

Well, once hell had been seen by the billions, there was a quiet reckoning behind the scenes and funding for space programs. Exploration became a virtue as was coming to understand that which had been seen. I chose to escape into anonymity. All I wanted to do was forget the voices, the faces, and, to be blunt, that one which will haunt me. I don't think I'll ever regain what I lost. Now, day after day, aboard Alpha, I wait on peace. I used to say, "Hell is a hell of a lie, God is not a torturer" but, well, things do change

Psalm 698 "You mustn't be afraid of death"

What is death
If not graceful   quiet   a peaceful singularity
Where the eternal and the infinite   kiss
Now, I know you must know passion, my friends
How the burning heart
Turns the soul bends the mind
And sweats out that body   uh huh
I know you know what I'm talkin' 'bout
And so you think of death as a loss
But it's more
It IS "all that" and then some

Think about it; death does not harm you
Life does that   believe you me
Can I have an "Amen"?

Death delivers you
From the suffering flesh
The tortures of reason
The cold steel chains of logic
And the binding wrap
Of self-designed deceit, conceits and illusions

Death holds nothing to fear
That's what life is for
Death is not cruel nor is it painful
Nope   those are both life's work too
And you know I'm right
Consider the worst: death is nothing more
Than nothing more
And if it's not   if you're into, say, reincarnation
Well, take everything I say here
And multiply it 500 times
Death is easy   anyone can do it   once
Afterwards you won't have to worry—you'll get used to it
After awhile, you'll have no choice   after awhile
You'll see there's nothing to it

It'll be like slippin' into something more comfortable
After leaving that so-called life you left behind
So, you mustn't be afraid of death
Doesn't just about everyone say
That's when you get to meet your maker
Wouldn't you want to do that   I mean at least once?
Say everything you want to say
Ask all those questions?
Afraid of death
Don't be foolish
There is no dark grave for the deathless soul
One filled with light;
Happily dwelling in a shimmering world
Set in a heavenly fire-scape of glory and blissful with love
Such foreknowledge dissuades one from fearing death
Banishes all the mourning and abiding regrets
And secures a peace no bitterness can touch
Beyond the reach of malice
There is nothing but joy
Only the lost and forgetful
Dwell in death's sorrows my friend
Which is why I say it—in this life
Death should be the least of your worries!

Tale, the Second: The Dreamer

The mystery, of course, lay in what it was. The Dreamer would never be sure, never be able to have the right terms and would wind up leaving this essential question unanswered. He came across the thing not long after he found his dreaming mind could travel far away from his world into the vast dark regions of night, some half cycle ago, and he'd been exploring, going out as far as he possibly could.

He discovered the mysterious thing while scrying out at some incredibly distant point beyond the many star fields. He'd gone farther and farther until, in the expanse of his perspective, the ether was sweet scented and musical intuitions ran along the warp and woof of the very fabric of the universe. He could swoop and slide riding the contours of the vast invisible surface of reality, switching between sides of the plane. It was glorious fun until he detected something he first read as a smell earthy, musty, and redolent.

Closer on, there was a localized point of disharmony, sharp wrinkles, turbulence, and a cold static that either comprised or disguised it. Soon, however, he had no doubt about its dissonant malevolence and pain, which was what the Dreamer came to feel when in its proximity. At least since then, however, he very much sensed and so worried, that it was approaching his planet with incredible speed. There was more than a hint of vague, acrid enmity, or an astringent chilling hunger, about the thing. For these reasons, the Dreamer had become more than just curious.

Of course, he observed it during his scrying, in the manner he thought best, sagely, keeping either a very great distance or by hiding when and where possible. Although he thought it might well be dangerous, he was far more curious than he was disturbed by it. In terms of the Dreamer's ordinary senses, he might have described it as something like a volatile storm, a roaring chaos. Emotionally, he read it as an area of disturbance, of anguish and inchoate, violent anger, something that had suffered greatly.

No matter how the Dreamer tried, he could not account for the nature of the thing. It was so alien as to be beyond any concept of life he'd ever come across; he had no comprehension of its motivation or physical nature. In this regard, it was like studying the wake patterns left in water to determine the nature of a boat. The Dreamer was forced to wait and see what developed.

Had the Dreamer known of the term nebula, he might have had some concept of its physical appearance or dimensions. As it was, to the Dreamer, quite young and unknowing, it was all vagueness as it approached. He did make some determinations, however. First, distance, it seemed, would be his only defense. This was worrying. Although he could get away from his home, if he had to, his body could never leave his world. Second, even if he might be safe, he feared no one else could be.

The Dreamer knew there was no way he could describe its location or size to anyone without telling them about his scrying or other dreams. This he would not do. He hadn't told anyone of those kinds of dreams, assuming quite falsely, his talent as well as his silence about it, were the norm for his kind. After all, there were other aspects of life, important ones, couched in a near universal silence; things everyone knew about yet never spoke of.
The Dreamer heard others talk in their sleep, even walk about or do much more—still could not bring himself to break what he believed was a social silence. Taboos dictated many things in life; some held with such zealotry that asking about them could bring shame, or worse. Breaching social silences could bring a visit from counselors, which would have consequences even for his clan. Yet, even if the Dreamer knew enough to ascertain the nature of what approached, and could communicate it accurately to those who'd need to know about the threat, he knew there was be little or nothing anyone could do, practically speaking. Reasonably enough, the Dreamer kept his own council regarding the discovery.

On successive nights he grew increasingly uncomfortable, even nervously apprehensive, whenever his family sat out on the open porch to star gaze and the enjoy cooling summer breezes as was the habit for most everyone he knew. He worried not only about its advent but because the matter had become such a distraction that he tended toward a quietude that his parents had noticed and talked about it. He simply did not like having nothing between him and it, save distance.

For a time, the Dreamer cast up to the Moon and planets to investigate but found nothing unusual nor any hint of the thing or anything like it. Yet, still it came on. Still he found himself seeking it out to observe its approach whenever he dreamt and scried.

Those were the notions of the Dreamer, a youth of 11 cycles, still quite young. As with most children, the Dreamer's daytime concerns were with play, schooling, moral development, adult control, and the chores any child was expected to perform.

Swiftly it came on. Then, one night, of a sudden, the Dreamer knew it was arriving to rest on the Moon. Scrying in a dream, he approached the moon's dark side. There he saw it appearing like quicksilver, something the Dreamer had seen at a county fair some years ago, as it poured into a great round cup in the rocks, called craters according to the Dreamer's father.

When its motion stopped, it appeared to be a solid, absolutely still, pool of silvery brightness. The Dreamer was certain now it had to be something like a living thing and that it planned to come onto the world he and his family inhabited. Still, the mystery held, despite his proximity, he could not determine what it was, nor did it seem aware of him.

This was unique. For the Dreamer had been able to understand every other living thing. In his dreams, he could take up a mystical consciousness bond with any living form he chose. When he lived life within a creature, he understood its thoughts, could direct its actions, and more. While he was in this state he was as familiar with them, for want of a better term, as he was with himself. However, he learned to leave people alone, the hard way. No matter who he chose, all were troubled deeply, suffering horrifically, and always, always there was too much information.

After some troubling considerations, he determined to make tentative contact. After all, should he need to do so, he could just flash out and away into the starry realms, certain he could handily out maneuver the thing. So he went back to the moon.

Hovering above it, he lowered to within a few feet of the silvery surface as it reflected the starry heavens. He hesitated, and then went down through its surface, noting as he did so, that there was nary a ripple made. After a moment, to the Dreamer's perspective, something like a mist or fog came into view and this completely filled the confines of the crater. This could not be stirred or swirled, nor could the bright surface be affected by any means. He remained down inside it, where he knew it was, and yet had no real sense of it. It was as if he and it were separated—even worlds apart. No matter how he tried, he couldn't elicit a response. It seemed as indifferent and as mysterious as ever. Here it gave no trace of the emotions he'd known it by. He spent some time going in and out of it, observing the bright surface reflecting the stars and the world upon which he lived. The thing was actually very beautiful, even though he could not forget the ill-boding and other peculiarities that had originally alerted him to its existence.

He went up over several nights to marvel at its reflection of the stars but soon there was a change. When he went inside, the "mist" began to move, to swirling about him. Curious, he changed locations to see if the action would repeat and it did. Next, he decided to stay put and see what developed. It flowed toward him in what looked like currents and collected about him to become increasingly opaque, not that he felt anything. Then, suddenly terrified, he shot out and away from the moon going some distance before he paused to look back. There was no discernible change in the silvery surface but he'd been shocked that it had responded to his presence – even as he had absolutely no idea what, if anything, he could or should do about that. Being unharmed, however, a few days later curiosity got the better of him. He went back to look it over, albeit from a distance.

He was adrift above the silvery mirror, which was as impassive as ever, and which he knew would be invisible to his real eyes, another puzzler, when, blindingly, it caught the sun's glare. In a heartbeat, he was back in his room, but he'd seen it condense and rise to approach his world.

It came on from the Moon and descended invisibly through the nighttime atmosphere. The Dreamer still could not sense it out directly. He engaged the services of birds but all he got from them was an uncomfortable sensation when he knew they were in its presence. This discovery was concerning; it proved the thing was knowable only to him, the Dreamer. Only he could detect it. He was alone in a way he'd never been before.

It was a still, moonless October night. There was an ordinary, but somewhat heavy set, man walking along an asphalt path. This ribbon meandered through a strip of parkzone that had been open ground left between the uneven edges of two adjacent housing tracts. Now there was well-trimmed lawn to either hand of the path, which, during the day, was where people might picnic or relax. The air was fresh with a crisp hint of winter and, though it had not rained, there was a scent of it. The man's well-trained dog heeled. After he crested a small rise, he stood for a moment by an ancient tree, which had been spared. He sighed as he looked about.

In the path some distance ahead, covering a wide swath of the new asphalt, was a pool of water. It seemed to shimmer ever so slightly. From his vantage point, he could see stars twinkling in it. This unexpected event disturbed his constitutional and set off his irate distaste for civic disorder. As he grumbled, ruminating upon this evidence of park service inefficiencies, he fumbled in his coat pocket for his cigarettes and lighter. He gruffly muttered, out aloud, declaiming irresponsible waste. His dog, sensing some change in attitude of his master, began to snuff about in the grass just off the path. As the man took a few strong, frustrated drags he saw a small far-off, shadow. Disgusted at the very thought that a cat was loping out of the shadowy grass near the pool on the path. At a signal, his well-trained dog streaked toward the darkly colored little demon. His dog, an infamous catter, closed rapidly on its apparently unaware victim which must have suddenly ceased moving and so became hard to see.

The impassive man looked on in silence. Even if the cat, with such a great lead, did get away, it would still be a good run for his dog. The man fumed for a moment then closed his eyes to regain composure, certain that the oddly silent chase led away from where he stood. A moment later, when he looked to check, in the uncertain light, he thought he saw the cat, then dog, jump over the dark pool before vanishing in the indeterminate gloom adjacent to the path. The man awaited the inevitable sounds of struggle followed by the quick return of his proudly vicious dog.

The man had been gazing off only realizing his self-distraction when the cigarette burnt his finger. He grimaced and grunted a salty expletive as he dropped it. He sighed heavily, stepped on it, then hastily lit yet another. When he looked to where the animals had gone, the foliage seemed different and the shadowy pool had changed its shape, also it was much smaller.

He could not, for the life of him, see where the animals could have gone. The night was still as ever and man grew impatient waiting on his damned dog. After he finished the second smoke, he walked onward in the direction of his home and, presumably, his dog. He was nearing the pool when he first called the dog's name, for by this time he was disturbed at the failure of the well-trained killer to respond or return. He looked around, even back to gnarly old haunt of a tree, from whence he'd come. While it was highly uncharacteristic of his dog to chase this long without apprehending its prey, barking, or making a fuss, it was unheard of for the beast to ignore his calls. This was absolutely untoward.

The man grew apprehensive. Perhaps the thing his dog chased was a more capable beast. In this case, his dog might be dead, and after all that expense too. He'd heard some predatory animals had returned to the city and were vicious killers. With trepidation, the man continued along the path. He approached the pool of water, stopped, and called out a few times, but to no avail. He stood, wondered, and waited.

Then a boy of eleven or twelve, who had clambered up his backyard's wall and had presumably been staring at him, asked why he was calling out. Startled at the boy's temerity, he proceeded to tell the boy his plight, all about his dog, the cat, and the pool of water. Quite improperly, the boy talked over him, in mid-sentence mind, to point out a flaw in his account – that since there was no pool of water inundating the path, there could have been nothing for the animals leap over. Annoyed, the man turned to look, only to see it was just as the boy had said.

At this, the man was speechless, not to say puzzled. Just at this impasse, the boy's father came out to see what the darned fuss was all about. When man tried to explain, the father, agreeing with his spit of a boy, cut him off. The best the father would offer was that it had been a hot day and the path, having just been repaved, could produce a small heat inversion, which might look like a pool. As for his dog, since it had not returned, it might not be chasing a cat after all but rather hot into one of its own kind who was up for a bit luck in the old knickers.

The man growled, proudly declaring his dog was very well trained. He'd never seen his or anyone else's dog jump over a temperature inversion, nor could he stand over one. The boy's intemperate father rudely cut off his intemperate bluster. Then impatiently reiterated what his son had said; there was no pool, the dog was not in sight, and, lacking these material facts, he certainly seemed quite the fool to be standing about in the middle of the night making sorry noises. He should be at home allowing other people a genteel evening's rest.

The man, unreasonable and frustrated, began to argue but the father, with a gesture of dismissal, turned away. Then called back over his shoulder that he didn't cotton to disturbers of the peace, he was unwanted and, although he may call out as he wished, if his neighbors, who are not as friendly and easy going a he himself was, were to take umbrage at his antics they might alert the patrols. The father ordered his boy inside loudly chastising him, for being out without permission, talking to crazed idiots, not having done all of his chores and having low grades and a litany of the boy's salient shortcomings, which became indistinct, before a slamming door brought back quiet.

The man felt empty. He called but only half-heartedly, and gave that up when the yard lights in one house went on, a window opened in another, and someone else peered at him from behind another wall while pointing at him. The man to decided to return home. Without special regard, he walked on, only to see another pool of water on same path some distance ahead. It too had a shimmer, very much like road mirages he'd seen, but, just as clearly, he could see brightly reflected stars. Then, as he got closer, he noted the puddle was still growing in size.

Of a sudden, he knew what had happened and stopped as he considered his brilliant insight. Clearly, a pipe valve setting was the cause. The first pool was due to a system leak. When the auto shut-off engaged, a fortuitous drainage pattern had then taken the water off the path even as the warm pavement evaporated all traces. He chastised himself severely. Had he just walked over to the grass on that first occasion, he would have seen how wet it was. Then he wouldn't have been so confused in front of that snot-gobbling simian idiot of boy. It made him angry to recall how he'd just walked away from both the squirt and his unibrowed trog of a father looking quite the fool. One more thing, he thought to himself, of course, on a moonless night, the water would look quite dark on the path and it would reflect stars. The cat and his dog did have something to jump over.

Confident now, the man continued on his way home, assuming his dog awaited him there as the chase had to have gone off in that general direction—although that would also be evidence of terribly undisciplined behavior on the part of his dog. Maybe it was time to put the thing up for a high-risk-high-stakes fight to get some real money off it one last time then: win or lose, he wouldn't have the expense of putting it down.

The pool on the path ahead of him inundated fully half the width of the walkway. As he approached, he grew fascinated by the display of stars reflected therein. Not a pace off, he paused to muse upon the sight. It was fascinating, really. When a shooting star crossed its dark surface, it was so vivid and bright that he looked heavenward, though it was finished by then. The moon really caught his eye, however. It was jewel-like and so very beautiful. He had never seen it so clearly, fascinated—it seemed as though he could touch it.

Then, unexpectedly, a ring appeared in the surface of the water as if a pebble had fallen into it. A concentric ripple pattern expanded through the reflection. He stood there as the leading ring reached the pool's edge. The curve of the ripple first bowed the edge of the pool that then quickly extended in a neat arc out toward his feet. Startled, he jumped back to avoid damage to his shoes, silly really, yet he couldn't help himself. As it turned out, he couldn't have jumped far enough. The carpet of reflected stars rapidly rolled out beneath him. Except—he did not see himself in the reflection – this was not water.

He remembered there had been no moon out and so questions streamed through his mind. Before he could utter an exclamation however, he fell into a darkness that was cold, vast, and infinitely deep.

The man fell through the surface of what was not a pool, and was gone without a whisper of disturbance to the evening. His last thoughts concerned a shooting star he could see somewhere below or above him as he winked out of existence.

That night the Dreamer knew the thing had changed. Why, he could not say. He sensed that its emotional state, its puzzling, unknowable want, or deprivation, had been satisfied even if only for the moment. The Dreamer understood it was going to stay on his world for some time to come and that he'd have to deal with it—also for some time to come.

Psalm 21 "Some Things are nothing."

Some things are nothing;
The break at the end of a line,
The spaces between letters,
Without which
We'd understand nothing,

A comma,
A space for breath
A period,
A time of contemplation
For its antecedent -
Reflection
Before proceeding on
When we remain
In the space between thoughts
Linking past and future
Seeing patterns.
If not for perforations
Breaks - over time
We'd not learn the connections,
To pattern,
To reason,
And invent
The dots that connect stars.
We came to be thus

Not by letting simple chance
Make our choice for us.
A decision
Is a flash of insight
Which is weightless,
Having no mass,
Shapeless as liquid,
And
As clear as the light
Through which we each
See ourselves
Nothing
Seems to be
More than it seems
And so
There is something
About nothing
Which brings us back to it
Again, and again,
Curious, to reconsider
As the moth, perhaps
To its flame.

Tale, the Third: The Hiker and Hera

I don't know which of us thought up the trip; it may even have been me. I don't dislike hiking but I'd never gone far into the backcountry or been to higher altitudes. I've always been out of shape and tend to lag. I guess I should've known better. As soon as we left our cars and I could see the place, I had that all to familiar sinking feeling and wished we'd taken the idea of driving through the western part of the country farther. Yet, I also had reason for optimism. They had been enthusiastic about having me along and so I hoped this trip to the Sierra Nevada would be different than my life, my job, and my so-called career in photography—not to mention the sorry state of my social affairs. Annoyingly, their nickname for me wasn't even original, it was the one which had dogged me for as long as I could remember, Slow-Sam. It was as if my current set of friends couldn't be bothered to create anything original to describe me. Still, and perhaps oddly, I harbored hope that everything would turn out for the best. I was glad enough go along, and it was possible I'd win a measure of acceptance.

Now, it had been described as an easy route for the most part, but needless to say, it was no such animal. I found the grade varied from twenty degrees and, in some places, the trail was a stairway cut into daunting escarpments. Some sections were of loose rock and treacherous for the novice hiker. In the daytime, the heat was in the nineties consistently. By the fourth day they were up to speed and "happily moseying along" at an "easy" fifteen miles a day plus.

The first couple of days I managed to keep up but by the fourth I'd become the anchorman with my friends leaving trail markers and I'd catch up by the time they'd settled into camp. On the evening of the seventh day, I did better though, I was in time for dinner and the fire was still going strong allowing me to cook quickly. I usually told them I had taken some interesting photos on the way; however, I felt they'd seen through this ruse by now. Some of the comments they made were not humorous. Oh, I understood if something happened to me that they wouldn't know about it until it was getting dark. Then one of them would have to backtrack to find me in the dark. In addition, the rest would have to wait it out the result of the search or join in with it. Still, cutting remarks I did not need. I didn't tell them I had strained my ankle and, by placing it near a freezing stream, had made it better; how I expertly wrapped it for support then cut a good walking stick and had come right along. If it hadn't been for that, I'd have been right with them. I was thinking I'd gotten my second wind. I thought about telling them I had met a woman, but that was something they'd never believe. Luckily, none of them asked about my delay.

I turned in soon after I'd eaten. They all stayed up chatting and laughing but none of it was about me. As I settled in to sleep, I felt very much better, good in fact. After all, I had looked after myself when it counted.

When I opened my eyes, the clear morning sky was beautiful; the sun was up and the chill off. The others were just breaking camp. I breakfasted on granola, some dark chocolate, and finished off the coffee. I was up with them when they started out. I almost said something when Warren made a jibe about how they'd keep the trail well marked, a comment he had taken to making in various guises without fail; instead I just laughed at him so heartily that they joined in. Great!

This day, I was determined. I studied the map as I went along and discovered a short cut, which became my plan of revenge or one-upmanship. The route did involve a steep incline but on the other hand, it cut eight miles off the "big leg" a twenty-four-mile distance they were going to cover before the next campsite. I silenced my inner critic, refusing to berate myself or be plagued by self-doubts; I was going to take on the challenge.

I dropped back. As soon as I they were out of sight, I started off on my own. I felt better. I was sure the extra effort would be worth wiping the smug look off Warrant's face. I had taken to calling him that as I felt he was arrested in some way. He always kept focused on the next step, point, stage, or what have you. He was always going to the next "there" wherever it was. He never stopped to look around at the all-encompassing beauty of this place.

The ascent had good footing, making it far easier than I thought it would be, or perhaps I had really hit my second wind. When I attained the saddle, I found small, round alpine lake, which was not on the map. It was about fifty yards across and about two or three feet deep. All about it was a rich carpeting of lush grasses, no doubt growing on accumulated sediment. Surrounding the verge was an open area of gently sloping rock-face. I didn't see a spring and assumed the source would be rainfall or the snowmelt off the slopes of this odd little catchment, which I fancied as being a natural amphitheater.

This being a suitable site for lunch, I found a nice spot at the shore, slipped my feet into its refreshingly icy waters, and began to eat. I had made excellent time already and I knew it was downhill from here.

I took a breather and meditated a bit. When I looked about afterwards, I noticed the only interruption of the verdant carpeting was a large Prussian-blue stone some yards away. I was sure that I hadn't noticed it as I hiked in. I say that because I would have considered it for a place to sit. Before I left, I went over out of curiosity. I was surprised to find it was actually an incredibly large, and leathery hard, mushroom. I took a few pictures, intending to do some research when I got back. I had no idea there were varieties of such size, just as I knew one never sampled any particular mushroom without real knowledge of it. The thing was beautiful. I studied it for a while out of curiosity, felt its smooth cool surface, gave it a friendly pat, and wished it well before I went on. It would make a good story to tell the others, later on in the day. I went off in a good mood.

Not twenty minutes later, my entire plan took a bad turn, as did my ankle. I was not sure how happened but that was moot. My first thoughts centered on how annoyed my friends would be when they came to the conclusion that something must have happened to me. I could only imagine Warrant's face as they discussed which one of them would go look for me along a trail I hadn't taken. Great! To my further dismay, when I took some time to study the map, it looked as though I had a poor idea of where I really was. What I should be seeing was different from what I was seeing. However, there was a silver-lining, were it not for the injury, I would have gone even farther off track.

When the swelling reduced far faster than I had any right to expect, I was puzzled. I could not believe that I had been disabled for less than twenty minutes so I decided to go back to the lake, hoping to reconnoiter, find out where I'd gone wrong, and figure where I needed to go. I was actually happy as I accepted this setback. I was making my own way.

Once at back at the lake I quickly saw my error. As I thought about the routes I could take, I was, of a sudden, inexplicably fatigued. I just wanted to take a nap but woke hours later instead as the sun was setting. I panicked before I found some hope in the desperate idea that if I got up very early enough I could, by racing along, make their camp before they left. That would be one way to minimize their derision. I also planned on spilling the beans, telling the truth, the whole truth, and nothing but the truth to one and all. However uncomfortable that might be, I was going to take my lumps and leave it at that.

I fixed myself a leisurely and luxurious dinner, with some nice maple tea. I had honey on crackers as a dessert. I lay down half in and half out of my tent, with the flaps open. I wanted a good view of the Milky Way. Although I did nurse some ill will toward my friends, I actually hoped they weren't worried, and they'd go about their business.

Hearing is quite acute in the mountains; at least it seems so, what with the complete lack of background noise ubiquitous in the cities. For a time, I dreamt of a flute or wooden pan pipes being played. The music was so relaxing and evocative that it was some time before I realized I was awake, though my eyes were closed, and someone had to be near my camp and playing music in the middle of the night! Looking about as I lay there, I couldn't see anyone nor could I determine the source of the sound, as it seemed to dance about, echoing off the periphery of rock surrounding the verge. I was relieved, thinking the person had given me a warning, when they could have sacked me as I slept.

The moment I began to move out of my bag, the music stopped. A soft, cool wind came up. I stood up to take in the area and looked to where I heard a woman's voice singing. She was over by where the big mushroom had been. The pale starlight was cool; it was the night of the new moon. Her back was to me and she was without clothes; imagine!

I froze, of course, before walking slowly over, almost in a trance. She had awakened me. Now she was waiting. She must have watched as I returned and set up camp. I wondered how far away her site was and about her kinky, odd way of introducing herself. This whole thing was about as crazy as any movie I'd ever seen. Her method of seduction, if that's what was, was wild. I was about ten feet from her, hesitating and unsure. I mean to say, what would I say? I took a step back. She shook her head. I took a tentative step forward, stopped. Then she nodded. I could not help but see her motions as an answer to my self-questioning.

I began to think going back to my tent was the best idea; this was too much for me, really. She turned her head to the side, not enough for me to see her eyes, for sure, though enough for me to see her high cheekbones and the graceful profile of her face. She motioned with her head as if to invite me. I slowly walked closer but stopped when I was just behind her. I tapped her on the shoulder gently, twice. Though I knew my hands must be cold, she hummed a bit and sighed.

When I stepped around to face her, she looked down to the earth as she said something in a charming rhyme. I touched the side of her face gently and then her ear. Still she looked down. Placing my hand beneath her chin, I raised her face so that our eyes met. How beautiful, how perfect and absolutely dream like; they were dazzling. Her eyes searched my face; wordless, we were in a timeless moment.

"Who are you?"

"Hera."

"Hera?"

"Yes, and this is the Lake of Dreams."

"No, my friends are on their way there; I came here by chance."

"No, no, you are wrong on both counts." She said this as she stood, took hold of both of my hands then gently embraced me. I know I blushed head to toe. My heart beat up one crazy rhythm. With her ear at my breast, what could I say?

She said, "I'm in love with you. It's why I played my music. We shall love tonight, the night of the new moon."

We kissed, tentatively at first, then with mounting enthusiasm. The pale starlight washed her soft, warm skin. We spread my sleeping bag out and spent an endless night together. Sometimes her passion would interrupt what seemed like an eye blink's worth of sleep and I'd ascend, as if in flight, from a deeply tired, yet curiously, weightless state—to a place of light and sound within a myriad of life dreams, all of which would come and go. Sometimes, I'd awaken her with kisses and caressing. It was a vastly long time before dawn insinuated itself, brightening the sky.

When I woke, I was shocked that I was alone but when I sat up I saw her, not far off, sitting in the deep verge, facing away from me and toward the sunrise. Again, I saw her beautiful figure. I was put to mind of so many lyrical, poetical ideals; the words *curvaceous, lyre-like, a perfect vessel*, all ran through my mind. I uttered none; all were terribly inadequate, stale. I went over to her; knelt behind her to kiss her neck, closing my eyes as I touched her. She murmured. I looked down over her shoulders, her breasts. She was pregnant and very well along. I was sure it all was right, though; I couldn't have been happier as I watched the swelling bloom, and her blush become passionate.

"How soon?" I respectfully moved my hand over the full moon of her.

"Any moment now."

"I'll help; I want to know how."

She was about to answer, when she shuddered, rose up onto her knees, and then spread them apart. I supported her as she leaned back and bore down. Her water broke. In a matter of moments, a baby emerged cooing, smiling. I accepted this birth on glistening pristine mountain morning. She bit off the umbilicus and held the newborn boy to her breast as I caressed them both. After a few moments, we got up. I followed her to the water. Quite soon the three of us were swimming about, splashing, and laughing noisily. The babe, having precocious amounts of energy, continued long after we were tired. I was sure it was all fine and good.

"Where does he get all of his energy; he has hardly fed."

"The sun, the water, me and thee" she replied with her slight, wry smirk, as if I should have known.

After a time, we were lovers again. It was as though there was no time. We were languidly at rest when the boy came up from the pond asking many, many questions. I answered all I could. I told him stories. I played with him in a rather rough, athletic fashion. Hera sang or watched us in her quiet way. Later, when the adolescent went off for wood, we spent ourselves in passion's dreamy worlds. Later, as she napped, I dreamt of the sun.

It was late in the afternoon when I awoke. Again, she was ready with child. This time the process had barely begun. I watched. In moments she was full, her breasts in bloom and ready to nurse as her body blushed. When I kissed her, she spoke these words, "My time is again; how nice; we do so well together."

She smiled. Her body glowed in sheen of perspiration. I helped her to the now familiar position. She had slow smooth contractions, hardly noticeable before the child's emergence. I was gratified. It was a girl; who absolutely beamed with pleasure as she cooed in a singsong manner. I could see her grow as I held her but when I held her in sunlight her growth accelerated. Hera swelled up to deliver again, in a matter of minutes, first one, then another. These were twins of a sort.

Later in the evening, the children ran about laughing as they explored their small lake and valley, Hera and I talked, laughed, and loved occasionally. In calmer moments, we called them to us for singing, playing games, or more stories. When our first son returned, he was a man bringing many gifts fruits, vegetables, roots, nuts, and several large salmon, ready for cooking. That evening we feasted. I told many stories of my life and from books I had read. I never was I as clear or lucid. I would not have imagined myself being this happy, yet there was no question in my heart and soul. They laughed, or cried, or stared in wonder as I reeled off fairy tales, jokes, history, my own life as well as stories of the world.

Late at night, as the embers of the fire glowed, my eldest asked many questions about the world. He and I talked a great deal about the process of life itself. At last, after Hera's lullabies, when he slept along with the others, I stood up, went over to her and we embraced, saying nothing. I could see the younger ones had lost all traces of a childish physique. They would be adults by morning.

Hera left our camp and I followed. She had some place she wanted to go to. Together, we emerged from the forest and onto a rocky outcrop overlooking a great area of valleys and lakes. I don't recall having walked very far at all; still, I was very tired. In the light of the full moon, I noted wrinkles on the back of my hands and how tellingly we had aged; it was a shock, my skin was thin, my walk unsteady, and we were hoary with age. I had a sudden fright at this profound sight. We lay down on the flat surface of stone. Love was once or a thousand times; who knows, who knows, so dreamlike was our breathing and sighs. My sense of direction was lost as I drifted through love's afterglow. The earth was beneath or above us as were the stars, which swirled as they flowed through season after season, as we flowed through motions, careless of anything in the world.

After some timeless time, we came to a peace and looked at the stars. We sat side-by-side embracing. She told me about the stars, their names, their stories—about the seasons and the names that animals, trees, rocks, and God have. She sang or chanted. I joined in; I knew every word by heart. I saw each of the uncountable visions her every utterance brought forth to my mind.

Finally, she said, as we dozed on and on, "Remember me, the Lake of Dreams, and our family forever at home."

We slept. I dreamt as never before. My whole life played out as I observed the years unfold, saw it all lead up to the backpacking trip. It all made sense, something like a musical progression, and it was inevitable. I saw myself come to the lake, make camp, and felt all over again the sensation of that first moment, the poignant hesitation before Hera. My loving, beautiful Hera; it is no wonder I love you.

Yes, there was the birth of our children; how they made me laugh with their antics; of course, they are all grown now and gone. I dreamt of the Sun and how the shadows of the mountains shifted and changed as the valleys were swept clean of the night as the dawn overspread the earth.

Then, there, far below, was a particular place. From on high Curious, I dove down to swoop over and see. There, on a jagged outcropping, were two corpses, the figures of an aged couple gracefully laid out, swiftly reducing to dust, which was carried off in the wind. Not far off, a group of boys were passing through an alpine valley where they found an old tent with some camping equipment strewn about. The boys hardly noticed the set of oddly colored mushrooms, all unusually large, leathery and not far off. It appeared the boys were searching for someone. In this dream, I went to them. I looked into their faces. They made frantic arm motions, as if plagued by a cloud of unseen insects.

Then, one of them exclaimed, pointing to an eagle. They all remarked upon its unusual size and appearance. The creature fascinated me. I went toward it, following it as it flew off at some great speed, then I flew as its wingman.

Here…here, was Hera's laughter. She was right with me, whispering a new kind of language in an ear I knew I could not possess. I dreamt of her, of light and sound, though those are hardly proper concepts for what they were at all.

Psalm 3,428 "They call it singing."

For miles around there is farmland
But I stopped to look at you
A great but lone tree
Of a kind I do not know
But which has long taken root here
In the soft love of the great mother
Through the parade of seasons
Your leaves seem golden in this light
And you whisper
Your limbs motion
So, the thousands of leaves
Follow in millions of ways
This is your body   singing
No wonder children love to come near
And regard you as a friend

Home to any bird
They join in with you
Though they play tunes of feast or drink
While you sing only of time

I took a portion of this day
To touch you with peaceful intent
Give you a pat
Speak softly and,
In a way, offer to you the grace I feel
As my beautiful eyes behold your elegant naked frame

The friendly wind plays soft
Through fluted clouds drifting in the sky
And you have a beautiful style
Wonderful taste in friends
And your mind refines mine
Your spirit laughs with the ground
And this is freedom
Intimate with our mother
You reach to the stars with muscular limbs
Moaning in your passion
So that God is pleased
His hands find your soul
And feels its yearning to build music

We share instruments you know
We are companions on this earth
And with it so are we friends of the sun and its planets
Mountains and clouds envy your dance
As they might my legs or tongue   were I among them
And singing as I do now, hopefully, with you
As you   dance

So, there'll be no sleep tonight
And I have become a pilgrim
With the whole of this prairie as my summer house
And it's true, Love does bring out the Truth
That one is never forsaken
As one may be   by the joys of our simple paths...
Surely, my friend, we can guide each other here
Find what's hidden
Forever   when all we have is time

That night   heaven lifted its filmy veil
Revealing the magnificence of myriad worlds
Flung out upon the universe
Of unlimited Love

And our conduct of that Love was exemplary!

Tale, the Fourth: A Box of Bones

It was a deluge of a day in Baghdad by the Bay. Marin County was a washout. A good number of its roads and highways were inundated leaving many areas accessible only by boat. There were pockets where tens of thousands were stranded on the "winter islands" as we called them, all over the region. This is what we Friscans called an ordinary winter day, which meant the usual wild and crazy scene. I had to arrange for a helicopter to get into work. Understand I'd have stayed home but I couldn't afford to; I'd heard, via the grapevine, that I was wanted for a specialty case.

I was dropped a few blocks from my building but, as was also terribly normal, a fierce morning wind off the islands ripped the umbrella out of my hand as rain, bursts of hail and punching gusts just beat me up as I slogged along through slush. Once inside I relished in the warmth of the place. On the way to my section of the building, I passed the emergency road service center, which was where I started out and, touched by nostalgia, I looked in. It was a hectic scene though they were a tight knit crew staying on top of it all. I empathized with the frenzied pace. For old time's sake, I called in refreshments. It was my birthday, after all.

Now, I was with Integrated Investigation and as I checked in I had an uncomfortable hunch it was not going to be just another crazed time-crunch kind of case so I slipped around the usual conversational traps and made it to the lunchateria undetected. I took the least of the worst offering then sat at a side table where I could look into the reflection of the food dispensers in order to see who was coming down the hallway before they saw me. I eyed the back door appraisingly. I was chewing through whatever I'd bought when I looked up, and oh joy, I saw the DA, John Emmet, not only coming right along but I'd swear he was staring through his reflection right into me. I hoped there was going to be some small talk, so there'd be time for the coffee to kick it up—no such luck. He paused, sighed, shrugged, and came on anyway. What with that look in his eye; it was going to be hell squared no make that cubed. I glanced at the clock, which showed I was already on duty. Resigned to my fate, I lit a cigarette as he sat down. Without so much as a how do-you-do, he began.

"Hi Jerr, I got a good one for you; no make that great and so bizarre it has your name written all over it. The first thing to do is read this deposition"—he slapped a folder on the table, which then slid to a stop in front of me, "and we'll show you the ransom note as soon as its been gleaned of every little thing. The FBI will be coming by in less than an hour along with some others already in on this one. I told them you are their man in our city so don't whine and, yes, I do know you have time and over-comp to burn; so, don't mention it. You're a champ and, after this case is closed, you can have that month you've been yammering about, go to Ireland, and find your grand uncle." He said tapping the folder and then, using his right index finger, nudged it even closer. I picked it up, turned it over, and it really did have my name on it—imagine that! I opened my mouth to say something smart but he shushed me, cutting off any choice words I might have. As he stood he said, "Just read it; you don't have much time," I opened my mouth again and, without looking back he added "You'll remember the headlines, of course, but now you'll get the Twilight Zone details."

Dieter "Vir" DePetco, was the man who wrote whatever this was, didn't ring a bell, but if FBI was all in, and this town agreed to foot the bill, the least I could do was read the tract, take the case on full steam and run all the leads down. I just wanted to punch out at the end and have the time to find my ancestors. I read:

*****

A few years ago, I had come out to Frisca for my uncle's ceremonial burial. The California authorities had had hard time finding any relatives, even though our family name was quite unusual. I was told they'd only found me only because of a letter in one of his safe deposit boxes. He'd never sent it but it was addressed to his sister, my mother, congratulating her on my birth. They also told me he'd died without a will. This, in combination with the unseemly delay in finding me, had caused unusual procedural delays in handling the man's estate. However, once I had presented myself, they had to be sure there were no other relatives. I was told they'd have to research national and international sources and it would take time. I was ok with that, being very busy at the time. Then, since I didn't like funerals one bit, I subsequently left more or less unconcerned for something I hoped to forget.

When I'd first heard the news, I couldn't remember anything about old goat, that's what mom had called him. She said he'd disappeared after her 18th birthday and that they'd had precious little contact since. She always said he lived out west and traveled, something I verified after finding her collection of his postcards when she passed away some years ago.

Two weeks later, when the red tape cleared, my presence was again required for the disposition of his estate. Very annoyed actually, I chose to fly out from the City State of Boston's floating airport to deal with it rather than from the nearer one in the Connecticut's Nation. Being self-employed, I had to make tedious arrangements, inform my building's manager, and revise several plans having to do with my regular accomplices. I figured to be away perhaps a week, maybe two. Although I had known the disposition was going to happen, its actual occurrence was chilling. I was inheriting from the dead.

To the best of my knowledge, my uncle and I were the last of our family line and it would die out unless I changed things and there was a fat friar's chance in hell of that, believe you me. I had no intention of marrying, so it goes. During the flight, I mulled over the few salient facts I had understood from the representative assigned to the case. My uncle had been eighty-nine and in good health. He had a professional passion for history, archeology and traveled extensively. He died from a cerebral hemorrhage the morning after he'd put off a burglar. The documents I had with me, necessary to confirm my claim, offered absolutely no other clues. My childhood memories offered no recollection of my benefactor; if he ever visited mom never mentioned it.

Upon arriving, I kept the appointment with the state's representative and filled out more forms in preparation for an interview. Of course, I had brought everything I could find, a sparse assortment of records and documentary effects of my mother's, my grandparent, and mine. I produced this orderly collection, upon request, from a legal sized envelope. It was something of a surprise to me how three generations worth of life could be contained in something so compact and fragile. He and I both looked through the assortment but found nothing that could change my status as the sole heir to the estate. Everything was copied and then dutifully sent out for verification. Everyone was very professional but, overall, I spent most of my time waiting or waiting to wait.

A couple days later, I was allowed to testify. I stated that to my knowledge, my mother had no other siblings and, since my grandfather had made up our unusual family name and by so doing thoroughly disguised the family past. My mother never spoke of my father or her mother so I had no information for either of them. I also testified that, at one time, I had gone questing for my roots but my mother was uncooperative and I was unable to find any clue about my dad or grandparents. I did present my research, which was dutifully copied and filed but no one demonstrated interest in it. In sum, I asserted that, as far as I knew, I truly was the only surviving member of my family.

Two days later, I appeared for the findings and was told I was the sole inheritor. That is when I was advised of the specific nature of the estate. There was a large house in the city, a rural property of some 100 acres, and an investment portfolio valued at about 18.25 million dollars. I was stunned – shocked really; I felt a kind of numbness and a sense of disassociation, which was disconcerting. I was not happy. I was depressed, oddly enough, as well as inexplicably enervated and at odds with myself. I didn't know what I wanted to do. After hearing me out the friendly lawyer suggested I temporarily take up residence in the house to sort out my plans as he was sure the place held many items of interest. I could take stock at my leisure before making any decisions. As soon as he made the suggestion, I was sure he was right. I began to feel better for having at least some kind of plan to cope with this new situation.

I did not enter the house until I had all the papers filed and stored my copies properly. When I closed the solid oaken door to the three-story structure behind me, I was its new owner, free to sell or keep it. It was old with the styling of the last century, replete with a many-gabled roof, Victorian turrets, gingerbread trimming outside, and intricate hand-woodworking through the inside. I liked the neighborhood and my intuition suggested that I keep the house and move in. I had found the people in Frisca friendly, easy going, and very understanding. The neighborhood is called Noe Valley, though, to be sure, there's not much of a valley to it.

Although I was in no hurry to explore the large dwelling, I was glad to finally have access to a kitchen, as it would free me of my hotel's culinary embarrassments. After looking over some papers in the office, I found my uncle had purchased it decades ago for a fraction of what it was now worth. He must have managed his affairs well enough because, from what I saw, his professorial salary wouldn't have allowed him to buy it even back then. As to the source of his fortune, well, there was no indication of that.

The place had a closed, musty atmosphere. The first thing I did was open all the windows. I cleaned the kitchen, getting it ready for use, had the utilities reconnected and got the place cleaned professionally; during that process, I made notes to triage what I would keep, sell, or give away.

The process of cleaning, however, led to nothing less than a carefully calculated project of renovation. I took part in the process of painting some rooms, refinishing floors, papering walls, and the cleaning carpets and drapes. It was about a month before I, with all the hired help, had finished the to-do list I'd made. Walking through it afterwards I was pleased; it really was quite the gem.

After all that, I settled into a routine task of cataloguing the furnishings as well as the library's volumes. I was able to continue much of my own work from my uncle's house as I was gaining clients in the city. I believe, even then, I was disconnecting from Boston, as I no longer wanted to liquidate the estate.

Another month on, I still hadn't decided to go back east. The weather was a medicinal, an intoxicating balm to my forlorn soul, or so I said to myself. I knew I did not want to sell and when the income from the investment portfolio kicked in, I was able to retire and began to think about taking a year off to travel and see what life was like on the other side of the work-a-day world. It seemed sudden but it wasn't really when I woke one morning and happily having decided to stay.

It took time but when I was done with the formal library, I began to examine my uncle's journals. I spent many an evening perusing his neat handwritten tomes. It appeared his main interest was ancient Greece and its colonies. He'd been there several times to investigate historical sites however his last trip, a few years before his death, was to a place that hardly seemed likely in such regard. Matching his notes to reference works and maps, I saw his last expedition went through the eastern areas of Kurdistan, into the neighboring regions of Persia and through the Caucasus Mountains. I wondered how he gained access to Mongolian territory, especially that of the Golden Horde, but gain it he did, and apparently with ease, as he made no mention of any difficulty. He was exploring in an area he said could have been part of Medea or one of its trade colonies, which had survived there as an independent Greek city state in the post Hellenic era.

There was little indication as to what he was searching for although his notes contained phrases such as "this connects to it" or "might be a link." I could not tell from the notes, the route or the sites he visited, all described with painstaking accuracy, what "it" was. For all that, the trip seemed no different from others. It too produced a collection of ancient objects—everything from lamps and swords to broken pottery, the bric-a-brac of cults, and some additions to his library concerning the region's history.

My uncle had, within the confines of his house, what amounted to a museum of ancient Grecian artifacts, historic scrolls, and books. One could study for years without being able to read a fraction of it all. I felt justified in the assumption that these collected works would be worth a great deal to the right persons.

Amid the many outstanding objects my uncle collected, there was one most intriguing, which only came to light as I read:

"…we went farther into the tiny glen, where we found ample evidence for the violent deaths of many soldiers. For some time, we believed we'd come across a battle. This thesis was supported when we found a group bearing shields from Athens and some of its colonies. These had died as a group after being backed against a sheer cliff face and their injuries were of the type suffered in battle. Although I was puzzled as to what Greeks were doing here, who fought them and why. The mystery compounded when we saw the others—and there was a considerable collection of them in the area—were variously armed, had disparate shield markings, or other clues, indicating they'd come to this location from an extensive variety of nations, over a very long period. The other notable fact was that almost none of these had been killed in battle. Their wounds seemed more like the kind suffered from a large carnivore, some with necks crushed or limbs severed, but this is what gave me hope, nay, I should say, expectations."

"I was not long in waiting for some clarity. One of my labor groups, exploring farther afield for 'anything odd or unusual' found what they believed to be the skeletal remains of a group of very large serpents. I did not disabuse the poor souls of that impression, and that's what they gossiped about. My error of omission ensured my colleagues would ignore my wonderful find. None of them were even curious enough to take a look and I was very glad of that. If they had but looked at the things, even assuming they were serpents, they'd have seen them as giants of their kind, something altogether new, worthy of mention or even study. To me, it made sense perfect sense that they died snarled together as a group. They were in a formation of rocky soil that was easy to work. I, and a few trusted others, worked delicately and quickly to separate out the whole formation. Their heads were most curious …" There then followed a detailed drawing which, though good, was the most bizarre.

The intriguing thing was that, although my uncle had proved himself to be an expert in his field, I'd be a monkey's uncle if that drawing was of any kind of snake. I've never seen any with horns or rows of shark-like teeth, as depicted in his drawing.

His time had been short when he made the find, and yet, he spent precious time rambling farther and farther about the area. From the notes and hand drawn maps it certainly seemed as if he was searching for something he believed should be in the area. As a consequence, and uncharacteristically, he let assistants segment the formation in which the strange animals were embedded, and it was they who packed it all into specially built crates. He lamented how this most curious find of the expedition occurred during its last days so the delicate work was necessarily hurried. And he wrote something tantalizing: "…the trail is not cold, to say the least, now, if only my dear friend had lived to come along…"

I had to wonder what was so important that he kept searching until the very last minute. He left only when Mongolian troops were seen advancing upon the near village. He, his crew, and the crates barely made it onto a last train out of the region. But what excited me most was then reading that he'd added the dumbwaiter on the outside of the house in order to facilitate the transport of the whole find to the attic. I was very curious indeed but I had to first decode his filing system in order to know which box or crate held the specimens referenced in the notes. It was late on a Saturday night by the time I went up.

Now, the attic would have been very difficult to search during daylight hours for it was gloomy even at high noon. Although the place had many gables with just as many windows, all of those were made of small darkly colored panes of stained glass. I hadn't thought of installing lights up there and so had to use a flashlight to find my way around.

The larger crates were easy to find, as I looked one over, I allowed myself a moment's pause before swiping dust off a label to see my uncle's precise handwriting. As I traced his lettering with my finger, I had feelings of nostalgia and something like fraternity, both unfamiliar as well as surprising emotions. I'd always had a favorable attitude regarding precision and order in my affairs and here was a man who, although dead, had been fascinating me for some time with his orderly estate as well as his humor, wit, and philosophy. In this moment of profound silence, there was a welling of pride. I admired his penchant for order and neatly kept records, which I fancied might be family traits. There was no way to budge the larger crates but my uncle's notes had indicated that a smaller one contained but a pair of skulls, still set in the rocky mineral deposit in which whole formation had been found. This was my choice for examination. It was also the smallest, measuring five feet by almost four, and two and a half in height. I could barely push it across the floor and the material inside—I imagined bits of rock and bone—shifted about. I muscled the box up the ramp to a delivery platform, opened a sliding door, and worked it onto the dumbwaiter outside.

About a third of the way down, one of the chains snapped and the platform's right side dropped down to jam firmly against the frame. The crate slid off to crash in the yard. I have to admit, I should've tested the machinery before entrusting it with the weighty transport of such rare items. I had made assumptions regarding the integrity of the device and, in so doing, failed to adhere to one of my own maxims "To assume makes an ass out of you and me." I smirked, reflecting that my benefactor would most likely stand in agreement.

I hurried down grabbing a flashlight and broom as I went through the pantry. I was hoping the well-built crate had protected the frail set of fossils but before I opened the back door leading to the back stairs, I could hear the growling and scrabbling of dogs.

In the dim lighting, I was not at all surprised at the shadowy forms of two large beasts. These half wild hounds had been in my yard before and were the bane of the neighborhood, what with their aggressiveness, upsetting of garbage cans, and digging up gardens. Both were very large and partly wolf. One bore a white collar and the other, a black. My small yard faced a carriage lane, a relic from the pre-auto days, and its low cobblestone wall was no barrier to them. I guessed they'd heard the crash and come to investigate an overturned trashcan and or kill some raccoons, which were also a nuisance.

At first, they didn't even respond to my shouting or brandishing the broom, which was unprecedented. When I took a couple of steps down one of them just looked up at me as it licked its chops, merely curious it seemed. The other turned to look at me, as it worked a piece of bone in its mouth, crunching down hard and swallowing before ducking its head down and gnaw at a loose piece of the crate. As it began pulling at the wood, I raised my voice again to shoo them away. They not only stood their ground but also took up positions, eyeing me as they made ominous growls and bared their glistening fangs. They maneuvered seeming to assess my vulnerabilities. I reached back inside to grab my uncle's pistol from the small recess where I'd placed it with just this situation in mind. The white collared alpha clawed the earth and crouched, as if making ready to spring. I fired my first a shot into ground in front of it but it jumped aside. I took my second shot at the dark collared which then charged the steps. It leapt off the stairs when I shot it a second time. They both then circled only to advance yet again. I fired twice more, once at each of them. When they both ran off, bounding over the low wall, to scamper along the cobblestone carriage lane, doubted whether I had hit them but my emotions were then overrunning me. I heard their barking and a further disturbance some distance away. I sat down on the stairs, shaken, badly.

I went into my yard and stood there when the neighbor next door, having heard the shots, asked me what was going on. I told him the two wild dogs had attacked. He asked if I was okay. I told him I had feared for my life and shot at them but had apparently missed. I was trembling as I spoke and admitted I was in shock but reiterated that I hadn't been hurt. He offered to help but I was recovering by then and told him just talking for moment would be good. He was very surprised at the event and remarked as to how they'd always run off if he yelled or thrown objects at them. I told him they seemed crazed. We chatted; it was nice. After a while I was more relaxed; I thanked him and went back inside to check and reload the gun before going back out.

Gun in hand, I went down to the yard to collect what I could. It didn't take long to gather things up. I dragged the box up the stairs and into the back pantry. Then I went back down with a powerful flashlight and found a few pieces of bone and some bits of that ruddy rock.

Just inside the door I made a cursory exam. One skull was perfectly fine, but the other had been damaged—exclusively to one side. Both dogs had gotten to it I guessed. There was some garden dirt and debris that had to be removed from the horrible skulls. I then dragged the damaged box into the laboratory of the house. There I removed the specimens and took the opportunity to examine them as they rested on a table. I used some of my uncle's tools to clean off the garden soil and so forth. Each skull was rather flattened and triangular, much like contemporary poisonous snakes. I noted there was little mineralization of the bone material so it wasn't fossilized, making the creature current in a geological sense. Each of the skulls measured about 50 centimeters in width at the base, and something over twice that in length. Each had two pairs of horns. The larger pair was rooted behind and below the eye sockets; these curved outward and up; were thick at the base, very sharp at the point, and reminiscent of those attributed to a Viking's helmet. The smaller pair, set anterior to the nostrils, were much shorter, also curved up and seemed functional for gouging yet were, surprisingly, hollow. The specimens had provisions for the replication of their teeth, similar to that of sharks and the teeth were razor sharp. It was a complete carnivore in my view.

I had just finished cleaning the skulls with my uncle's special brushes and swaddling them in white muslin, when the quiet night was ripped first by one, then two, then a whole chorus of sirens. To me it seemed they were converging on the usually crowded intersection of 24th near Noe, the heart of Frisca's dinner theater district, or so it seemed. Perhaps a fire, or an unusual accident, a big one, I'd thought then. The cacophony lasted for almost an hour.

As I prepared for sleep, I couldn't help ruminating about the specimens. Judging by the size of their heads, their bodies had to have been larger than most any snake I'd ever heard of and the horns just seemed impossible. I decided to contact some of the local universities to see what the experts might have to say. I became so obsessed with this thought that I was unable to sleep. I got up and spent a few hours prepping a set of documents encompassing the dig where the find had been made, drawings and other supportive documents as well as researching through the phone book to get a list of institutions I could call. Still unable to sleep, I even left a few messages.

The next morning, I went through the routines I'd long set for myself; some exercise, prayer, and playing music. I showered, ate some excellent cuisine created by yours truly, then strolled out to get the Sunday paper. It was an error of sorts. The headline glared, "Horror on Noe." Disinterested in sensational news, I eschewed the front section, folded it over and read the comics instead. When, at home later, I read the headline story, I was quickly alarmed. A number of ghastly attacks had happened the previous night—and not at all far from where I lived. Seven people were killed outright, four more died later, and some two dozen were seriously injured—all by a pair of rabid wolves that had gone on a rampage near the intersection of 24th and Noe. The survivors were being treated for rabies and blood poisoning.

I surmised this had been the cause of the alarms the previous night. In addition to the citizens, two police officers had been killed soon after they arrived on the scene, and four others had been wounded as they attempted to put the vicious beasts down. As if the implied horror weren't enough, the paper described how the dogs tore at the throats of the victims or severed whole limbs. When the wolves attacked, the panicked people tangled traffic and so complicated the police response. After the first responding unit had been disabled, SWAT units arrived. Strange as this all was, the ending was just as odd. After all the chaotic damage they did, the animals were killed as they stood quite passively, after cornering a considerable crowd of terror-stricken people inside the Whole Foods market.

It was the last paragraph that jolted me upright for it contained corrections. The animals were really dogs and only part wolf, one wearing a white collar and the other a black. I called the police and was told someone would call back as the investigation progressed. I, having been a New Yorker for some years, was not assured. I thought it would be days before anyone would come by.

Miffed at this, I called back so as to get their attention. I told them some of my neighbors had been bothered by this very pair of dogs, that they should have records of this, further, it was the considered opinion of many, that their owner lived in the area. I went on, getting a bit loud and angry, saying I wanted to see some investigation of this wild dog pack that had plagued the area. Last, did they know about the gunshots heard in the neighborhood? I could tell them who the shooter was then I hung up. After calming down, I listened to the few messages I had on my answering machine. By early afternoon I had finished sending off replies to those as well as leaving few messages regarding my specimens.

While I spent some time organizing my uncle's papers regarding the find as I thought on the warnings my friends had chided me with before I left to come here. They all said Frisca was an open ward, or that every loose nut in the country rolls west, before collecting in The City, eventually. I had expected the unexpected; still murdering canines hadn't been on the radar.

As I snacked, I received a call from a Dr. Davidson, who had been recommended as an expert in the evolution of serpents by several universities. At first, he doubted what I was saying, but when I read a few salient passages from my uncle's notes, I roused his curiosity. He was confident he could identify the specimens, though he too doubted they were serpents. There was another turn in his attitude when I named my uncle's colleagues, where the remains were found, and their circumstances. We became quite conversational. I have to say that he—in a quite unexpected and continental fashion I found refreshing—agreed to a dinner at my house, after which we'd examine the find in the hope of clearing up any mystery. I was to expect him at seven in the evening. He certainly seemed interested as he rearranged appointments in order to accommodate the visit.

Not long after I hung up, the police were at my door, fancy that. There was a beat officer along with a special agent in charge of the investigation. They expressed gratitude for my willingness to help. I invited them into the study to sit and talk. In an orderly fashion, I began with an accurate description of the antics the pair of dogs had performed in past but they hurried me on to the events of the previous night. I told them about the contents of the crate, the dumbwaiter, which failed, and how the crate fell, broke open and attracted the dogs. I described the encounter and identified the dogs from pictures.

In answer to their subsequent questions, I told them I had a gun license, albeit from Boston, which I had ready for them, naturally. When they began some chastisement about regulations, I interrupted them to say it wasn't my practice to fire within city limits but that I also had an expectation of public safety. My life had been endangered, and to turn the tables, I pointedly asked why the long-standing and well-documented danger the two dogs had long presented hadn't ever even been dealt with and how it was that those beasts had been allowed to roam in residential areas. Then I reiterated that my life had been endangered due to city negligence and speculated upon the city's responsibility for the considerable damages, which would have to be ameliorated, and which would probably be in the tens of millions. Getting a bit hot under the collar, I added that harassing me would be a bad move. I'd acted to save my life and did my best to kill the beasts before they went on their bloody rampage. I asked them to consider the kind of the headlines that would ensue should they accost me. Then I went back to pressing them as to just why nothing had been done beforehand. Well, in sum, they let it all go, apologized, sincerely enough, before trying to distract me by asking about the contents of the crates.

I began to ramble on about the skulls. Sure enough, it wasn't long before the detective waved off that course of conversation and began asking detailed questions concerning the appearance and behavior of the dogs—I guess in an attempt to find a causative theory. He said initial laboratory work found each had been shot twice, that they were not rabid, yet as a life-long dog-trainer for the police, he'd never seen such violence. He was sure some chemical had been involved but I couldn't help him there. I guess he'd hoped, as last one to see the animals before their rampage, I'd provide some clues. I couldn't. In the end, I reiterated how, in the past, they'd always run when I brandished a broom, shone a flashlight on them, or simply shouted. Yet, not only did they hold their ground as they damaged a valuable specimen, they attacked. I emphasized that only my gunfire had driven them off.

They began to look disinterested. I guess because I'd added very little to what they knew. I advised them to talk to my neighbor, but they already had; he'd been the one to report my use of a gun. They were going to question the owner of the dogs later that day and speculated that the papers were going to be hot to find someone to blame. They told me to call them if I remembered anything else. I said I would, sure.

I went back to my daily affairs before preparing dinner. I went out for some miscellaneous items, and when I returned, there was a message on my answering machine from Dr. Davidson. He said he would be some ten or fifteen minutes late. I liked such civility and was able to time things quite well therefore; I'd finished setting the dining table and was draping a cloth over the undamaged specimen in the lab when the doorbell sounded.

I was surprised when I saw the man. I'd expected someone younger, but here he was, nicely dressed in his fifties and quite urbane, even if after a west coast fashion. He was stout, strongly built, and of English descent, judging by his skin color and facial structure. We proceeded with preliminary introductory small talk. I did bring up the issue of his descent, albeit obliquely, but he declined to comment although it would have been nice to have confirmation of my thinking. I was quite pleased with this reserve—so refreshing when compared to the coarseness all to common among the untermenshen, who think that by rushing into the subject at hand, or feigning friendship, one is being at ease, informal, or demonstrative of democratic ideals.

He did justice to my culinary efforts and his obvious pleasure was my reward. He was a man of agreeable pacing. We talked at leisure during the dinner and he made his experiences, analyzing the remains of various kinds serpents, quite accessible and fascinating. This was as close as he would come to discussing the very purpose of the visit, before its proper time. It was, in point of fact, myself who brought up the subject when we retired to the study where the records of the find had been laid out.

All his calm was removed in a breath, when I uncovered the display I had arranged. After a quick, silent observation, all he could manage was a muttered, "Well, well, well." He examined the skulls with some of his pocket instruments and then wanted to get some others from his car. Together, we brought back two formidable portmanteaus, one held a most remarkable field laboratory and the other a goodly number of fine instruments.

I cleared a side table and spread upon it a run of muslin so Dr. Davidson could set out his instruments and supplies. He examined the bizarre skull closely with a practiced eye and a used a magnifying glass here or there. Using a fine brush, he worked some material off its surface and dropped the grains into some tiny containers. Then, and with my permission, he scratched here and there upon the bones, dropping those scrapings into other small containers. To all of them, he added drops of water, and then a few drops from various vials. He took samples of the soil, to test them in a similar fashion. After a moment's study of the changes evident in the test vials, he turned away to look through the notebooks where the find's site was described. While he studied those, I monitored how the various samples were affecting the liquids in the vials. He read for a bit of a while, said he appreciated my notated bookmarks and I looking through notes I hadn't yet seen.

After some time, he broke his silence, "Well, this is a sweet one; clearly your uncle had a great interest history. You know, he wasn't surprised when he found the various shields and many of the other items in the area—writing only, as he did, and cryptically so, that they were good clues. We can also put to rest any debate as to the authenticity of the find, since some of the persons who were along with him are quite respected in their fields. However, as you've said in you notes, it certainly appears your uncle did not simply happen across these then decide to collect them as a novelty. To be logical, it seems to me, from the notes, he knew what these were and, if they were not the sole objects of his search, then they, and the carnage surrounding them, were certainly very important clues. I wonder why he did not pursue the matter subsequently. As to his fellows, he let them believe the rumors they'd heard going around the camp. In the end, his compatriots were happy enough with their own discoveries and glad enough to leave him to his. Then too, I must say, I don't see how he managed to explore that region; politically, it's near to impossible even now, not to mention how much harder it had to have been back then what with the Prusso-Asian Conflict and all. The bribes must have been enormous."

"What are you saying?"

"As soon as I laid eyes upon your specimen, I knew the beast was of no living species. I mean to say, I know of some having one or the other of the characteristics special to these, yet none have them all, and then there's the size. While I'm sure the fossil records do not include any such creature, I'll have searches done. And then there's the matter of the find, the soil and rock indicating they lived during historical times."

"There are many contradictions these present, real as they are. For example, you'd expect this sort of rarity to evolve in an isolated geological area—or the narrow confines of an ecological niche. However, the location of the find was not geographically isolated, so something else must caused their line to evolve so radically. Even so, we'd have to wonder what kind of conditions, peculiar environmental conditions, could explain a divergence of this magnitude. Then too, it also seems, their radical changes in morphology developed, and drastically so, over the course of historical times. This too would indicate a condition wholly specific to locality, and yet, no other species in the area was affected in a like fashion. Of that, I'm sure; we'd have heard. Still I can have some checking done."

"Now, as to the creature itself, it is well-adapted as a top predator, and certainly capable of surviving. Yet it was apparently confined to a limited range, one must wonder how it existed, during historical times, mind you, as a top predator in a populated agricultural region and yet generate no historical record. I cannot understand any of these things, and yet, here is respected documentation" he gestured broadly, indicating the notebooks, "and" indicating the skull "there are the remains!"

"Maybe they were the last of some here-to-fore unknown and vastly ancient line? Couldn't that account it?" I asked.

"For that to be true the creature would have to have had an impossibly long lifespan to account for its being so bizarre, so capable a predator, and yet be so rare as to have no related forms. The explanation for all of this is beyond me, at this time. I'll also add, I'd certainly like to know what your uncle was about when went on this expedition, and why he engaged in such subterfuge when these were found, only to then store them away in obscurity. So, I'm sure he was looking for something else, whatever that was; well, it's all most curious. However, as you might assume, those considerations are beyond me, or my essential interests in this matter. If you don't mind, I would very much appreciate being able to study some samples."

"Have you considered fraud? Is that possible?"

"No, not at all. Most any such effort would be immediately obvious and then there were the tests I've performed tonight."

"You are sure?"

"Think for a moment. Why would such clever fakes be left around for hundreds of years in such a nondescript location? Who would craft such an extensive and complex fraud not knowing when it might be found? No, fraud is off the table. I mean to say, who'd get the last laugh?"

"You believe this was a living creature then?"

"Certainly."

We then discussed the kind of tests he or his lab partners would do. He kept the language non-technical and said he'd only need some bone chips and soil samples. I was impressed and agreed, then and there, to let him take a sample vertebra which was embedded in the rock and soil. I also agreed to organize a set of documents, the salient pages he needed from my uncle's notes, and a few other papers, for him to copy. He agreed to be back in the morning to secure those items. I was happy since he was happy.

The next morning, just before noon, he was at my door. He told me he'd worked all night with a few grad students and uncovered nothing except more puzzles, which had compounded the original mystery. The specimen was unique, and in that way, seemed to be an exception to the evolutionary processes by means of which creatures evolve incrementally over great periods. Preliminary searches in reference works found nothing like them at all. Nor were there any legends or folk tales concerning such a creature. That all said, he hoped the field notes, maps, and other papers would provide clues. He told me he was going to take his test results, and the remaining portion of the samples, to Berkeley for further testing and analysis. His plan was to have an extensive workup done on all the material and then present the puzzle, in all its complexity, to a combination of graduate students and faculty to see what came of it all.

I offered to bring one of my specimens over at an appropriate time. He smiled, then said that would be the most important piece of evidence, one impossible to dismiss, as it was too curious. I suggested he take a look at one thing I'd found that morning. When I had turned one of the skulls on its side and was brushing off dust, I noticed, in a clump of ruddy-colored material in the sub-glottal region of the creature's throat, a metallic glint. I thought it was something the creature had inadvertently eaten. When I extracted the clump and cleaned it, I was very surprised. He was then quite curious, anxious even, so I showed it to him. He was speechless when he saw the remains of a finger with signet ring. I could tell the design on the ring meant something to him, yet I forbore asking, and quietly waited as he studied it. He just said "More and more curious." I told him there was a detailed photo of the ring included with the package of documents. He assured me he'd return my materials by special messenger, as soon as possible. As he left he said I should expect to hear from him within a fortnight.

I wasn't surprised when I hadn't heard a thing in a few weeks following the return of the documents. I did not concern myself as I had a new city to explore and was excited by my new client base as well.

My patience was rewarded when, a month on, he called inviting me to a round table group. He apologized for the delay in getting back to me but said the find and his data had occasioned quite a bit of controversy so he'd had to do much more than the ordinary due diligence. He added that some at the university had made the issue personal as the disputative furor built. However, he believed the doubters now had all the rope they'd need to hang themselves, which would happen upon the presentation of a complete skull. This would definitively resolve the issue—he hoped I was still willing to bring the specimen over. I was happy lend him a hand and bring the skull he'd studied. It was a shame my uncle never had the chance to enjoy the notoriety, which would now attach itself to him posthumously.

I drove over with the specimen contained in the repaired wooden case strapped to the floor of my van. I pulled up to the rear entrance to the hall where Dr. Davidson met me, along with a few graduate students and professors. I was surprised to see some minor media people. After he introduced me, a round of questions ensued. Everyone was very enthusiastic about the find. As we talked, pictures were taken and reporters took notes. For a time, I was the center of attention.

My centrality abruptly concluded as soon as a pair of graduate students, in charge of setting up the display, placed the wooden crate on a gurney and took it away. Everyone followed and I became just another person in the crowd, except to the doctor, of course. It wasn't long before I gathered, from what was said or not said, that I was being softened up. I knew there'd be a request to donate the specimen for long-term study or even custodianship but was noncommittal to the hints. Yet he was happy to share some new facts. I was surprised to learn the skull had to be less than four thousand years old, that its cranial capacity was enormous when compared to the proportions common to reptiles, that the eyes were binocular, and so there'd been speculation as to the creature's intelligence. The horns were akin to those of the rhinoceros, being made up of fibrous growths that were sourced from specialized regions of bone and flesh. The teeth were harder than any known. He told me no one had offered any well-thought out theory as to how this species came into existence and that there were some still in a state of stoic disbelief. He said there'd even been some talk of returning to the site to resolve questions the specimen presented.

After a time, we entered the display room. There was many an exclamation in spite of the fact they'd all seen photos and examined samples of bone material. For a long time, there was a crowd around the display table. Since I had nothing to offer, I stood off in the distance. It seemed the thing retained an aura of mystery that could only be experienced directly. After a timely announcement of refreshments being set out many attendees gathered at the table, served themselves and then reformed into chatting groups. Some of the graduate students were taking photos and measurements, others discussing the documentation.

Dr. Davidson introduced me to a few people so I had a few interesting, if brief, conversations. I actually considered making the donation, as their attitudes and demeanors were so studiously concerned. Although I'd make a bit of a splash with such a donation, I worried about undue attention or notoriety. On the other hand, it would serve to advertise the existence of the find and so make the remaining specimens, notes and my uncle's collection all the more valuable, a win-win.

The crowd thinned as the food was depleted and, left to myself, I read the small brochure the university had used to advertise the event, it listed the local luminaries scheduled to attend and gave credit to my uncle and myself along with a few small photos and graphics. I looked forward to the round table, which was hosted by the archeology department although others would be represented. As I read, the afternoon sun brightly slanted in through the windows and I was hoping I'd be able to get home before nine pm. I was still wanted to take the specimen with me.

Then, as a lovely doctoral candidate chatted with me, the extraordinary occurred. A large recycling container near the doorway caught fire. It was very sudden with violent flames shooting several feet into the air. No one panicked. Everyone pitched in. Although we extinguished in short order, it produced unbelievably thick and voluminous clouds of smoke. We could hardly see. Security arrived as the ventilators powered up. When I could see better, I went to look over the display.

Imagine my surprise when I saw three teeth missing! The skull had been in perfect shape when I had boxed it that very morning; but now—this! I also noticed they hadn't been removed carefully as there was a slight fissure in the upper jaw. I was shocked, angered. I loudly called Davidson.

"This way no way to treat a unique and fragile specimen!" I fumed. His reaction was stark; he blanched and was very agitated as he examined the damage. He swore he'd inspected the skull just prior to its being put on display. We both stood looking at the extent of the damage, he more closely than I. When he was done, he signaled a guard to keep watch over the display and asked me to wait while he checked the room where the display had been prepared. He strode back in an instant later with another pair of security guards as reinforcements and then showed me a note which he said would explain most everything, except, he added, the student's peculiar derangement.

"My Dear Doctor Davidson:

I planned quite well, or you wouldn't be reading this now. By the time you've finished, I'll have had enough time to make my preparations. You know who this is by the handwriting, I'm quite sure. Since no one was willing to listen to me as regards the name AND origin of the "snakes" I was forced to take certain and extraordinary measures in order to perform a demonstration, which will prove beyond any doubt, the correctness of my theory. I am waiting on The Circle Green across from the Student Union. It will please me to have as many witnesses as possible."

"You *know* who wrote this?"

"Yes, a good student, usually, though one whose theories or opinion are quite beyond the pale once he gets into the subject of mythological morphology."

"Well there is that. How far is this place from here?"

"A couple minutes. I've alerted the campus security; this time he's gone too far."

"Who is it though?"

"One of the students who set up the display, although he's a bit of an eccentric, neither the specimen nor its controversy seemed of interest to him. I had no idea it would trigger in him such a wild, unheard-of extremities."

By now, the four security guards, several remaining students, and a few professors had caught the drift. Amid a hubbub of apologies, indignant outcries, and derision directed at the thief, we left to meet him on his chosen ground. Van, the guard in charge, listened half-attentively to the nature of the theft as we approached the specified location.

We had no trouble finding the man. He stood atop the slight knoll on the north side of the circle of lawn set in the quad. He was speaking loudly to a group of lackadaisical students as we approached. Although he was loud enough, I couldn't understand him; it seemed he was giving out a bit of a rant and so overwrought as to be stumbling over his own words. In any event, we were given way through the students. The man had a trident in one hand and had dug three holes in the lawn before him, each several feet apart. Behind him one could see the haft end of an ancient-looking sword that had been stuck into the ground. He pointed the trident defensively at the four security men. Much to their dismay, the crowd became fascinated, and voiced support for him. The young man warily watched all of us as he finished his spiel.

He called out, "Which is the man who brought the skull?"

"I'm here. What kind of show do you intend to put on?"

"You found it?"

"No, my deceased uncle did; and some years ago."

"Where did he find them?"

"In a place he said that was, or should be called, Meddia, Medea or Mediena. You saw the maps? You know must…"

"Yes!" he screamed almost exultantly "Yes I know." His exclamation was more like a shriek, a passionate shout with manic gestures, truly crazed. I wondered what he meant.

"Sir," he began, adopting both a theatrical tone and posture, "would you allow me the honor of demystifying this matter?"

"I am willing. What do you want with the teeth?"

"Ah! I am going to plant them and you'll see."

"I've had just about enough of this bullshit," muttered Davidson in a gruff aside to Van, the not-so-excited ranking guard, replied, "Look, everything is under control; we'll get him soon enough. Let him do his act. We're watching for our chance. I don't want anyone hurt." He focused on the speaker, folded his arms across his chest, and waited

A reasonable attitude I thought. I shouted over to the young man, "What will happen after the planting?"

"Ah, yes! That will be the surprise, will it not? Yes, that will be the ticket to fame and glory. Please, bear with me for a minute or two at most. I'm sure you will enjoy it all."

"It is a matter of timing, then?" I said.

"No, but I did want to have a number of witnesses, and with such stellar ones as are with you now" he said, making a sweeping gesture toward me and those I stood with "Such respected persons will be impeccable witnesses and will have to soon bear the truth."

"I'll tell you what," I added jocularly. "If I'm satisfied, I'll drop any charges. How about that?"

"Quite amenable. I shall proceed then. Please, everyone, allow yourself an adequate view of these holes. Observe as I place one tooth in each hole. Prepare to observe an old kind of power." He began reciting some a kind of chant, which was as much like blathering despite its regular albeit odd sort of rhythm.

I waited; we all waited. I felt hair rising on the back of my neck. Raymond, the student, turned thief, now held the trident with a defensive posture, facing the three holes intently. There was a humming sound; it seemed to be coming from the ground.

"Now," he said, as he put the trident down and turned to reach for the blade. Van was in and it was over. The others wrestled him down.

He cried out "No! Stop, I will be late!" I took the strength he exhibited during the ensuing struggle as a measure of his insanity. He actually broke free for a moment and could have run off, instead he made an attempt for the sword, which choice allowed the guards to grapple him down and cuff him before standing him up in order to lead him off. The students, seeing that the show was over, laughed, jeered, began rise, and disperse.

Raymond was yelling about the hell-spawn's power. Amazing, I thought, a real lunatic freak out, a bad trip, as they used to say. He bellowed that he cannot be held responsible for their acts then he slumped to the ground. I told Davidson I'd proffer no charges against the man. I saw no reason to further complicate the young man's condition.

Raymond sat up and was sobbing and shivering or shaking, as if in a fit. One of the guards sauntered over and, as he laid hand to haft, Raymond slumped to the ground as it rumbled and shook. It was like a forty-ton tank was passing by. Then the force increased. The police, just arriving on the green, stumbled and fell. Raymond struggled wildly and the few remaining students fell as they tried to move away. The lawn, at each of the three spots, began to heave upward. Something was pushing up from below! Strange as it may seem, when I glanced about, all was normal in the distance, students strolled along distant walkways with but a few pausing to look our way. This wasn't an earthquake!

On the circle, there was much confusion. Everyone was shouting. The shaking was so severe one could hardly even crawl. The police were still dealing, rather badly at this point, with a fantastically, frantically struggling Raymond. I saw the grassy soil at the three spots burst up mightily, each opening with a thunderclap. Then the quaking subsided. For a moment, a cloud of thick dust obscured the scene. As it settled, there were three much larger holes in the ground and, by God, we all saw raised swords come into view, held aloft by skeletal hands and arms! Then the complete skeletons clambered out, stood, and seemed to look about assessing their situation. Each attired with heavy armor fittings, helmets, swords and shields. For a moment, all was gravely still.

Van took up the trident and lunged mightily at one of things but the thing won out, it blocked a blow, parried, kicked and then slew the man. He then neatly sliced another officer's midriff wide open, releasing a gush of blood and organs. Disemboweled, he was dead before he hit the ground. There was a gasp. Even as he fell, two officers advanced upon the three things, firing as they did so, while a third called for back up. Their shots were useless. One officer had his head lopped off; the other had his leg sliced away clean. The third officer and the security guards began firing as the ancient skeletons advanced on them, but the twentieth century men began a barely controlled retreat as death was dealt to any who stood their ground. After the slaughter, the crowd broke and panic began. The skeleton men moved out, herding the crowd, which jammed the walkway leading to the university's gate. I heard sirens approaching over the rising chaos of screams. I wasn't hopeful police could deal with these demons.

I dropped down to keep out of sight and crawled over to Raymond. I wanted to get him out of there, but he'd been hurt, his ankle was swelling and his back was in pain. Exhausted, he was still quite frantic and babbling. I understood he believed the sword would have allowed him to kill the skeletons as they arose from the ground but the police had prevented him from doing that. I wanted to get him to safety, and told him so. In a sudden rage, he grabbed my shoulders with a vice-like grip and pulled me face-to-face vehemently spewing, "There won't be a safe place …" then, speaking rapidly, he swore and rambled about the sword working but the longer they were free, the more their immunity to it would grow and, should they ever get hold of the weapon, there would be hell to pay. I struggled, but his grip was unshakeable. Then, as he continued speaking, I was, it seemed, in a dream, dizzy and enchanted. I could hear each word, but the whole of it escaped my comprehension. In a seeming instant, however, I became convinced I could and would face his monsters. He bade me bring him the sword; I did so. I could not hear what he sang as he had me hold the sword with him.

After I was released, I stood, nearly swooned, recovered and ran toward the demons, as they, in turn, methodically killed all who were too slow, had been trampled, or fallen. They were herding a wall of screaming panic down Telegraph Avenue. As I gained on them, the sword began vibrating along with my hand and lower arm, which went numb. I stopped but could not let go of the thing; it was fast to me. As I charged the demons there were resonant harmonics; it began to sound like a musical drone.

The street was littered with bodies, car wrecks and rubbish; the shattered storefronts had it resemble the aftermath of a tornado. I jumped over bodies and saw blood run in the gutters. It seemed like ages were to pass before I'd engage them yet my sight was fixed upon them. I saw their practiced moves killing with precision and efficiency. The trapped, or those who fought back, were put down. I yelled as loudly as I could, though what I wanted to say did not come out of my mouth. Rather there was some guttural arrhythmic gibberish and this clearly caused one of them to turn toward me. It was uncanny the way its empty sockets just glanced at me before taking an especial notice of the sword and following its movements.

It charged with a hellish, banshee shriek. This was the only time I reconsidered what I was doing. I believed that, were I to drop the sword and the monster take it up, the thing would certainly become a living being with tremendous powers—that's what my fear-filled imagination plagued me with anyway.

The sword's vibration became more like powerful massage unit. The bizarre sensation quickly overtook my sword arm, shoulder, and penetrated clear into my heart. My grip on the haft was unshakeable. Simultaneously, inexplicably, I was also not at all there. A part of me was as calm as could be, as if I were relaxing and reminiscing upon the memory of some horror movie I'd seen—even as the thing came running toward me waving its weapon in circles over its head; its gaping mouth louder than the approaching police sirens. I prayed for rescue.

We circled, closed, and our swords clashed in a blur of motion. I was fighting fiercely, yet in a daze, there and not there. I was forced back constantly. I panicked. Out of fear, exhaustion, and frustration, I gave up, closed my eyes, and just let go, striking out with everything I had. Strange as it may seem, that's when I made my first strike on the thing's shield. I saw it shaken, it nearly lost its footing, to the force of my resounding blow. It then became wary and prone to leaping from one side to another in order to make quick flanking attacks, which I parried or blocked. Even so I could not get the sword to fully respond to me; it was like trying to turn the hub of a spinning gyroscope.

Neither could I give up. I found cool solace in the forlorn belief that while I delayed this one I was indirectly saving lives and I was thankful. As I had that thought the demon stopped and seemed to study me anew, staring again at the sword and ignoring me as I faced him off. When I began to pray, it came on more furiously and I could not long hold ground. In desperation, I let the sword take its lead; where it moved, I followed and so forced the horror to draw up. I began to circle it. As if it could read my mind it gave shriek and resumed a violent but ineffective attack.

I cannot truly describe what then happened, or how, but my body was awash in glow, a light mist or aura. I lost all fear. The sword's thrumming became musical – as if it were playing a tune. I sang along in my mind. The sword's moves flowed even more easily then; it was lighter, almost weightless. Increasingly, I met the being's blade with my own and felt great when I forced him to his shield.

With each clang the sword began to ring louder and longer, with a sound not unlike a tuning fork or singing bowl. I had a sense of the musicality in the movements I was making and began to get my timing in synch with its. I saw the fight as a dance, or a song. I, myself, was estranged, almost disembodied; the constant ringing all I heard.

In a moment, the other two were making moves on me. The crowd they had been chasing stopped and turned to see I was fighting the monsters. They began to throw rocks and bottles at the things. The sword? I could not hold it back from doing what it wanted with me. I held off all three, dancing, making leaps, and tumbling into rolling moves. I was a puppet of some force. The sword made beautiful music. I sang under my breath as I moved on the triple threat.

Out of the corner of my eye, I saw the SWAT unit arrive. Strategically, I backed toward a building to draw the demons away from them and to improve my defensive position in preparation for a counter-attack. To her eternal credit the commander assessed the situation, had her team approach quietly from the enemy's rear; then directed their volleys of fire in targeting the skull of one creature at a time. I was heartened.

When one of the things suffered heavily it became distracted, dropped its guard, and I lunged in to slice off its shield arm before striking it below the crown, which then fractured badly. I grabbed its shield mid air as it began to stumble about as if blind; though murderously dangerous, it was out of the fight.

One of the others turned from me to advance upon the newly arrived officers as I put the shield to very good use against the one that chose to remain fighting me. This one was incredibly fast, agile, and struck sledgehammer blows. Nonetheless, I held my ground and began driving it back when it too was shot and distracted. Gleefully, I struck a mighty blow but that was the last thing I saw. I was out.

The orderly heard me screaming and rushed in to talk me down. Once I knew where I was I was fine except for a splitting headache and my right arm being bandaged, obviously swollen, and oddly numb. He gave me an injection and soon I felt warm, happy, and deliciously pleasant. As he withdrew, a police officer entered. She had a wonderful calming effect and wanted to ask a few questions. I was ok with that. I was ok with everything. She began with what day it was, who was Crown Regent, and a few more before I asked why I wasn't dead.

She told me I'd been hit in the head by a full two-quart bottle someone threw at the thing I'd been fighting just after I'd beheaded it. It, then unable to see, struck out viciously, albeit harmlessly. Not a moment later, a hailstorm of bricks and rocks smashed into it, whereupon, the thing collapsed into a scattering of twitching bones. At that point, the last skeleton turned and bounded toward me. The officers ran up on it unloading at near pointblank range. Although its thick helmet protected its skull, they shot off its right arm at the shoulder when it made a grab for the sword. Then it turned and rushed them using its shield as a weapon. That's when students ran in to drag me off. The end came when a security guard came up behind that last fighting monster and shattered one of its legs with a shotgun blast. It fell but when it again crawled toward the sword, which had fallen from my hand, another security guard, also using a shotgun, obliterated the horror into wriggling shards, even as the crowd cheered as they'd downed that one other, which had been blinded, so to speak, earlier on.

She told me I'd been out for three days. The toll was one hundred seven students, one hundred and two other adults, twenty-three officers or security personnel dead and more than four times that injured one way or another, directly or indirectly—all in less than 20 minutes.

She said the papers couldn't get enough about dead warriors on a berserker spree wreaking havoc and that I'd been secreted here, in a private room, thanks to Dr. Davidson. Then she asked about Raymond, since he was missing; I knew nothing. I began to tell her it was his research, his words, and the sword that had done the deed. She sagely nodded but suggested I say that I'd acquired extreme ability, becoming superhuman in the often-documented way in which the petite wife lifts a car off her husband after a car accident. The more I thought about it the better I liked it and that became the only explanation I countenanced

With Janiniee's help, and Davidson's friends, I got out few days later on the QT. I was in the Big Apple for a quick minute and got by with a little help from my friends, went on the down-low, incognito, you know. Four months on it and there was a book out, which I denounced during my only radio interview. Six months on, when the hue-and-cry seemed dissipated, I again took up residence in my uncle's house—miraculously no one had associated me with the place and I could again live life as I wanted.

Until a year later, that's when I received a package from Raymond containing the sword. I liked the thing so I kept it. No one believed anything I said about it anyway, my narrative having worked wonders in that department. When I took it up however Raymond's mumbo-jumbo still worked. The other shoe was in the next package, a toothless skull.

Dieter "Vir" DePetco

*****

I'd lost track of time. I did remember the dogs and the university but wasn't on the case. I found my coffee cold and that I had about five minutes. I was gonna take this puppy from the slap and I had been right, it was going to be a helluva day—a one ring-a-ding-dong a'dandy, as my daddy would say!

Tale, the Fifth: Talking Big

"…Well, yes, then again, no. I couldn't say it started with me—by the way, is the tape rolling? It is? Well, like I was saying, I couldn't say it started with me though that wouldn't be the whole story. My part consisted of an idea, an idle comment on a weekend afternoon. Although Joe has always declaimed, I was the intuitive one and, although he appreciated it, it was the reason I was ignored when it came to nuts, bolts, circuitry and soldering. I did not have a hundredth—a thousandth of the 'know-how' he did. Still, I was sometimes more a help to him than anyone else. In this case, however, I was blindsided just as much as he was – as everyone now knows."

"Also, just to get it straight, I don't, to this day, nor does he for that matter, remember exactly how it all came about but we've talked it over in preparation for this interview and so this narrative will have to serve."

"You see, sometimes I rephrase his perception of a problem at hand, challenge something I viewed as an assumption, or restate something. What it boils down to, from what I can comprehend, is I've a talent for triggering his thought processes. I might indirectly illuminate a puzzling aspect of what he's considering, which could result in a change of approach or suggest a new path leading to another solution. He still calls me 'Tanner the Spanner' when, in fact, a hint or nudge is all it takes with a mind like Joe's."

"We'd been friends since we were freshmen. Although we weren't outcasts, we were certainly on our own recognizance and completely unencumbered by the expectations of our peers in terms of conformity or socializing. With but a rare exception, at the very end of our senior year, we weren't on the radar of any of the luminaries in our school's social network. We met by pure chance or chaos, when he "lucked" into being PE locker mates with Mike, a friend of mine from middle school—who then introduced us early in our sophomore year. Soon, however, we both found we both had an intellectual outlook and an express interest in learning for its own sake, which set us apart from the mainstream of our suburban environment. We had introspective characters. Add in an oddball sense of humor, with caring honesty, and you have the foundations of our original friendship and camaraderie of spirit."

"Summer vacations were spent with occasional fishing trips or sitting in his yard, where our talks plowed the fields of philosophy, politics, history, and more. We would pass through metaphysics or physics to wander at conversational length through the various imaginary realms. All nature was to be explored or discussed, everything grist for our proverbial mill. Any news event or discovery would be a welcome topic which could trigger such rambling idylls as we enjoyed."

"All of his hobbies involved engineering and electronics. He was a perfectionist in this regard. Often, he would decline very lucrative work if the person he was dealing with wanted to cut corners, decline the best, insist on the merely functional, or worse, the near-term affordable. Persons with such attitudes would grate on him. Later on, I'd be the one to hear it all and have to calm him down, perhaps with a game of checkers during which we'd color up the game with running depreciatory comments, snide asides, and disparaging remarks regarding the other's 'ability' to play, something we found as entertaining even if the game was not. If the upset was bad, we'd exhibit grim reserve, playing silently and for blood. Truth be told, we both played poorly and were evenly matched for all that."

"Although we lived in different housing tracts, it was only a short bike ride between Cabrillo and Hamlin. When we got together, we'd talk, play music, and take walks. Then too, often enough, I'd get sidelined and suffer some down time spent looking on, as he'd wheel-and-deal with local tubeheads or geergeeks. This was no hobby, rather his business at the time. It was no surprise to me that he was well on his way to financing his first two years at college what with the buying and selling of gizmo-baubles, as I called them. I was impractical, a writer, cum daydreamer mainly interested in poetry at the time."

"The thing I noticed most about Joe back then was his reputation. Honesty and quality workmanship were the basis for his success. What he noticed about me was my uncanny talent to bust him into silliness with near idiotic send-ups of cultural icons and more. I liked nothing better than to get him to laugh so that I'd follow suit. But our talks were wondrous affairs of the mind and soul—ah, the good times."

"So, to some facts: Last summer, the first Saturday in June, I was eating breakfast when the phone rang; Joe asked me to come over. He'd just received the developed photos his younger brother Paul had taken on our last camping trip. I quickly left for his house, using my trusty, heavily paint-camouflaged, ancient Schwinn ten-speed."

"In about twenty minutes, there we were in his living room laughing at all the crazy antics we'd done a few weeks back. Our laughter, and all-to-loud exclamations, caused his mom to laugh along but this brought us to the attention of Mr. Nelson, Joe's taciturn father. He suggested we take our noise elsewhere. Somewhat subdued, we went outside to sit on the back deck in the shade of the lemon tree, as we watched the goldfish swim around in the pond he and his dad had built years before. Soon, we were done with our giggling fits."

"This was the setting for our talks. We had a warm, calm afternoon, no duties or schedules to keep, and a clear sky with a slight cooling breeze. We began talking about some news filler, which he'd read. Gradually we gyrated outward toward the more rarified philosophical spheres. Then we struck upon a discussion about the nature of sound and vibration wherein one of us said something like, 'Now, take sound, sound is a vibration, yet, of course, not all vibration is sound,' that's what started it all."

"We talked about how vibrations can be measured, or in a sense, heard or detected. We talked about sound vibration as being somewhat analogous to other wave phenomena such as those for the electromagnetic spectrum. Of course, the big difference is we can hear sound but most of EM spectrum requires specialized detecting devices in order to perceive them."

"We saw detectors as translation devices, because they record the wave and primarily function as a means to translate what they receive into visual or auditory output detectable by humans. We knew the human eye couldn't see X-rays nor could the ear hear subsonic or ultrasonic waves; however, if they can be detected and humans can then perceive their presence.

His mom offered us some lemonade, made from their lemons, it was great and thanked her. We then took our glasses into his room and continued talking about how the mechanics of a detection device interferes with the detection itself and, since such devices can never be one hundred percent efficient, this must affect what it reports to the human observer

So now the good part begins. As we were sitting near a disassembled stereo he'd been working on, he began looking at it. He began to wonder out loud if it would be possible to make a perfect stereo—one that wouldn't lose any quality of the original sound while reproducing it. He began to talk about how to eliminate the effects of speaker boxes, the acoustics of a stereo's location as well as earphones for that matter."

"We mused on how the tonal quality of a live performance cannot be heard for what it is, even by those present, and so there couldn't be any means of reproduction that would be perfect, even if the human ear were to be the gold standard. I recall him saying something like, 'If we did manage to build a machine which could produce a vibration fine enough to transcend all material interference and still affect our sensory apparatus, we wouldn't need to translate the vibration. Such a device wouldn't lose anything at least in or to translation.' That's a fair paraphrasing."

"Then there was something he said about 'the apparent contradictions to get around apparent limitations leading to something about harmonic patterns in wave forms generated by the elements, as they got lighter or heavier.' Then he went through some kind of some pro and con as he spun off theoretical considerations and ideas. I sat there listening, mumbling an 'uh huh' or 'why do you say that,' even though, once again, I was not able to follow. I'd seen this before, him going on and talking with and or against himself as he thought out loud. That particular time it seemed as if he'd gotten caught in a feedback loop. Oh, I believed he believed he had something worth mulling, but I was bored."

"I interrupted him with a monumental, yet quite musical, belch and said, 'Well, it sounds very interesting so you want something, call it transparent sound, a means to affect the space existing within or around matter, which, in turn, can then affect the aforesaid matter.' He looked at me and said, 'space is as space does,' and I replied, 'the space which is here, being the same as that which is out there among the stars, is undifferentiated.' Then he said, 'They're just different volumes of space— both are just as empty.'"

"'Yes,' I added, 'so there's absolutely nothing separating any two points, or only nothing separating the sender and receiver, right?' That's one exchange I think we recalled pretty well."

"Well, this startled him. He stopped talking, stared hard into the distance and I thought I'd stumped him, or if not, at least I'd gotten him to finish his rambling. For a moment, he was quiet and then all he said was, 'Humph, transparent sound, interesting; want some coffee?'"

"He dropped the topic and we went on to other things. I went home and the rest of that day was ordinary, except that my brother Charlie had broken a window in a neighbor's house for reasons known only to him. By the time I got home, everyone was looking for him. Taking my surreptitious leave of the brouhaha, I found him in the crawlspace under the house, our secret hide away. After a family tribunal, he owned up and made a reparations agreement with the neighbor. After that, because it was too dark to play outside, my family and I enjoyed an evening at home reading, playing board games, and some of what we called family music—all par for the course during a mid summer's eve."

"The summer was languid but when we, independent of one another, met girls—Anna and Astrid, exchange students from Denmark and Belgium respectively, we simultaneously began a new phase of life. Imagine the surprise when, on our first double date, we found the girls knew each other as friends but neither had known the other had come to the US. Although he and I had less one-on-one time after that, the four of us would go out hiking, picnicking or cycling. We were quite the set, I'll tell you."

"By mid-July, there was a change. After experiments gave promising signs, Joe, obsessed with the idea for a new kind of stereo, grew more reclusive and began to use savings he'd sworn he'd never touch. He was reading lots of books, which weren't all electronics or math. He began blabbering on and on about metaphysics, quantum mechanics, music theory, wave mechanics, as well as psychology, meditation, and color theory. His room was cluttered with books on those topics, as well as others too diverse to mention. Because I could not understand how those subjects related to his project or to each other, I had reservations about his obsessive effort and whenever he'd try to explain any of the endlessly interconnected details, although he was speaking English, it was nearly impossible to follow more than snippet here or there. Sometimes, as he rambled, it was all I could do to remain patient, try to steer the conversation—or monologue I should say— toward something else, anything else. The girls and I became concerned as he hammered away at what I increasingly viewed as an impossible problem. We wondered whether he or his hammer would break first."

"Of course, as his frantic experimenting continued, his romantic life waned, even as mine waxed, and we saw less of each other. His parents were not concerned; they'd seen him go through similar phases. My parents, on the other hand, who'd always thought we saw to much of each other, were glad to see me become more involved with my siblings and, finally, a girl. Neither set of parents understood the bond we had, the joy we had during our discussions, which, however rare during this unusual period of divergence, still kept us heart-fast."

"After a few weeks, I was deeply in love and began to think of Joe as a bit of a loon. Whenever he spoke about his project, I couldn't bear the babble. I'd listen, but only for so long, it was really beyond my ken. When I chanced to meet his girlfriend and she would ask after him all I could offer, outside of the fact he was still working like crazy, was that he wasn't seeing anyone else and that he did ask after her. The last wasn't quite true, yet, as a friend to them both; I felt it was the right thing to say. After a while, I didn't chance across her at all."

"Well, he called me on August twelfth, as we all know now. From his babbling, I gathered he'd created clear sound, as he dubbed it. He'd completed preliminary testing and was connecting it to his parent's stereo so he could input a recording. Of course, I wanted to see it. He said it would be ready by the time I got there."

"When I arrived, he was out front pacing back and forth, muttering to himself and gesticulating as if in conversation. The first thing he said was that his parents had taken a weekend to visit relatives in Tulare, so he'd taken the opportunity to test things out, using the very expensive family stereo. He had enough time to disassemble the necessary portions of the stereo in order to incorporate them with his device and, after the tests, restore it all before they got back. My response was understated at best. This prompted him to evince a trace of anger, which I made worse by mentioning I had a date in a few hours. He stopped, closed his eyes, and sourly observed the demonstration could take less than half an hour, or maybe a bit more allowing for recalibrations or readjustments."

"At that moment, I had a half-thought that this announced success was a desperate attention-getting hoax, for he seemed to be so out of it. Though I must say, in light of the well-known developments, it was more likely he suffered from a species of indifference that often accompanies extreme exhaustion and depletion. I followed him inside as he talked on in an attempt to describe a few changes he'd made in the apparatus, components, problems still faced, or theories of its operations. I didn't understand a thing. I cut him off in saying, 'Look pal, where's da beef' in my best James Cagney, 'I wanna see de action … see?' In a huff, he turned and I followed."

"We silently entered the living room where the grand stereo had been moved to its center and most of his assembly was on the coffee table set up behind it. There was stuff laid out on the floor and an assortment of wires leading into and out of a series of beakers, each of which contained colored liquids with crystals suspended in them. There was a vacuum pump next to a bell jar, inside of which was an arrangement of crystals, as well as a few tubes and some components, all wired to gold mesh, or so it appeared. He told me the whole shebang was a rush job, because of developments and the time constraint—by which he meant he'd have to restore it all before zero hour, ten am Monday when his very prompt parents would be pulling into the driveway.”

“Then, I saw this one, seemingly rude, homemade component, a concentric arrangement of gemstones set in what I knew was silver with a gold inlay which looked to function as some kind circuitry. I secretly began assessing a cost, part-by-part, based on what I knew. I guessed he’d done more than dent his savings. He noticed the object of my attention, knew what I was thinking, and said he’d learned a good deal from that complex of crystals, the most sensitive of all the subcomponents. They were the heart of it, a kind of sequencer. When he looked my way, he stopped with that nonsense, and wryly explained that, excited by waveforms targeting them, it would, together in harmony or in dissonance, reproduce any sound. He told me that assembly was, in essence, the device.”

“I remember asking him, ‘So you’re saying you have theory and application steady on?’”

“He dryly admitted there were some small gaps for, in a rush of inspiration and intuitive experimentation, he had reworked components and circuitry to achieve his first success. However, the succeeding models failed, so he’d been forced to do some reverse engineering. What I was looking at was his first successful reproduction. The first working model was still stored in the garage. He said he’d done more than duplicate the success of the first, as this one had upgrades. He’d found shortcuts, and was quite sure later versions could be assembled from more common components and materials, all of which would neatly reduce the cost-per-unit in manufacture. I admitted there would certainly be demand for a stereo that delivered clear, unimpeded sound, despite barriers. He then emphasized that it wasn’t ‘heard’ through the ears, but rather via electromagnetic effects upon the substratum that resonate with organic matter, in this case affecting only certain receptors in the neural network of the brain. I remarked that it really wasn’t a stereo in that it didn’t have two speakers; in fact, it did not use any at all. He nodded.”

“Then, he said he wanted to thank me, and when I asked what for, he told me there was time when, although was able prove he was broadcasting clear sound, he couldn’t hear anything. He’d thought he’d reached a dead end but I’d given him the key clue during a phone call when I’d asked, innocently enough, if, in some analogous sense, he might be working with frequencies humans could not sense, so while the clear sound he was producing might be perfect for a dog or a bat, it wasn’t receivable by humans. That simple question prompted a redesign of and got him on track.

He told me that because I'd done it yet again, he wanted me to be the first to see its debut."

"He then held up a necklace, a braid of fine silver threads, with a green stone woven into it. He said it was the amp, which allowed the current version of the unit to be heard by humans. He quickly added once my brain understood how to receive the signal, I wouldn't need it at all. I put it on with the gem near to and above my right ear as instructed. He turned on the stereo. I noticed its operational lights weren't on and he told me the signal was rerouted through the sequencer first, then the bell jar, which began to take on an unearthly glow, as did the rest of his apparatus. I wanted to know more, but he shushed me as he put on a record so I could see for myself what Joe hath wrought."

"The sound, or rather the sensing of clear sound, is very much like that afforded the ordinary person who has a jingle running through their mind apparently, all by itself, with no need for concentration. Usually, that's just a bit of a phrase or a stanza, which repeats and is faint or indistinct. However, the sound I heard was exact, clear, and complete. There was also a calming, pleasurable effect, which the simple trick of memory sometimes has but this device caused a much deeper, more pervasive sensation on the body as a whole. This effect alone was worth a million bucks, or so I thought at the time."

"He lifted the stylus to bring us back to reality. We speculated how various notes, individually or in combination, had various kinds of effects on emotions and so forth. I sat down in a comfy chair next to the dissected stereo and asked him to try it again, for a minute or so this time. I relaxed, closed my eyes, and was introduced to a new world. I saw colors or illusions appearing and disappearing in association with the music. I heard the sound as if I was sitting among the players, between the strings of the instruments, or far away in some balcony hearing the overall effect. There were pleasant sensations accompanied by an odd sense of weightlessness. I was not concerned with time, in fact, as I went from note to note, color to color, floating in a bath of sensations, I had an odd perception of being distant from the world and my body seemed warmly comfortable and relaxed. When at last I opened my eyes, it was because Joe had again taken up the stylus. I'd forgotten quite completely that I was hearing a recording, as I'd been so very lost in a dream like stream of beauty. I couldn't believe I had been entranced for less than a minute. The return to the real world was abrupt and jarring. I hadn't needed the amp for that second session at all. I'd forgotten to put it back on."

"It was great. We decided to play something to test out the range of the effect as we walked about the house, see what we observed, and when the record was done, compare notes."

"We put on one of our favorites, Led Zeppelin's 'Been a Long Time.' We walked around his house, marveling that, no matter where we went, the unimpeded sound followed. When we went outside, the sound was just as good. When I asked him what the range was he said this was the first real field test. We went into his back yard as the record played. We took a look at his old fishpond. I, for one, took this opportunity to consider the effects this device would have on the broadcast industry, our lives, as well as human development."

"The record began skipping, so we went back in, straight to the turntable. He removed a bit of dust from the needle, cleaned it and the record. Joe made a couple of adjustments. We decided to play 'Stairway to Heaven' and I told him to crank it up, which he did. Then we sat down to listen from the beginning, as we looked out his picture window on an ordinary suburban street replete with parked cars, lawns being mowed, cycling kids, running kids, and the glow of TV sets coloring the curtains behind windows."

"With the opening notes, I closed my eyes and floated as music and vibrant fields of color formed lucid and vivid dreams. The music was at full volume, yet I could still hear myself think, still reflect—amazing! How beautiful the woman was how well-designed was the archetype of a stairway as it led to a wondrous soaring concept of beautiful cool, cumulous clouds, glowing with bright warm spring sunshine."

> There's a lady who's sure
> All that glitters is gold
> And she's buying a stairway to Heaven
> And when she gets there she knows
> If the stores are all closed
> With a word, she can get what she came for…

"With this last phrase, her pursed lips opened with a billowing of formless light bubbles, folding into fractal floral shapes, forming and reforming. She was elusive as the scent of lilacs, which came and went on the gentle breeze. We flowed into an amorphous cloudscape of heavenly proportions, rising farther into visions of Christ's resurrection, Paradiso, and transformation!"

There's a sign on the wall
But she wants to be sure
Cause you know sometimes
Words have two meanings
In a tree by a brook
There's a songbird who sings
Sometimes all of our thoughts are misgiving …

"Flying over the world, I came to a mountainous carved monolith, beautiful and dreamlike, dwarfing every city I'd ever seen or heard of. It towered above a surrounding rainforest. Then, in a thought's breadth, there I was, in a deep forest, the trees rising hundreds of feet above me, as I wandered toward the sound of a waterfall. As I came upon a pool of water, she was there, now as an auburn-haired Nordic fantasy. She laughed as if in birdsong, spoke as a vibrant instrument might, and her touch could not be described. There were redwoods redolent with powerful incense intoxicating me with every breath. I grew heady; in love, our bodies blended as if we were insubstantial ghosts. We were weightless, amorphous, laughing. Our hands touched, our lips met; it was as if we flew over clouds. At last, there was only light and music again as I gradually became aware of myself."

There's a feeling I get when
I look to the west...

"A brazen sunset filled my vision; I was flying far above the ocean looking down on migrating pod of whales. The clouds all crimson and clover, holding hints of her image."

And my spirit is crying for leaving
In my thoughts, I have seen
Rings of smoke through the trees
And the voices of those who stand looking...

"I felt their pain, passion, and what they thought of whaling vessels. I came to a shoreline, to a port where I saw there the common drudgery, the urban blight, looked into, out of, and through many thousands of eyes, I heard them all speak, cry, laugh, love, rage, struggle, and die; a phantasmagoric kaleidoscope of visual experiences. I was lost in it all. I was going all over the world, only to return to the cool forests during the musical interludes, the spaces between notes where all was quiet."

"Joe was the first to notice what was going on outside. He'd been uselessly tapping me before he just fisted my shoulder and said, 'look out the damned window.'"

"I was not at all pleased with the interruption of my most wonderful dream. The sudden return to the ordinary angered me, for its rudeness. Annoyed, I was really going to tell him off but looked out the picture window first. In the sky over our suburban neighborhood, there were many, many UFOs. One of them was a gigantic cube-shaped thing, absolutely black, and not far off. It was hovering some hundred feet above the housetops. Its shadow covering an area of several blocks."

"Increasingly the sky became peppered with the usual and unusual UFO's. There was no believing or disbelieving either. I remember wondering if it was an invasion."

"The neighbors were all out, looking upwards, pointing and talking. Some were on their rooftops, most of these had cameras, a few brandished guns, but thankfully, only the former were being used. Everyone was talking, gesticulating; it looked like the beginning of a truly rad-ass block party. We both heard sirens forming a confused background chorus. They were clearly converging on our part of town. Dogs were running wild. Meanwhile, the record continued."

> And it's whispered that soon
> If we all call the tune
> Then the Piper will lead us to reason
> And a new day will dawn
> For those who stand long
> And the forests will echo with laughter…

"I was in a deep forest glen dancing in a circle holding hands with dreamy elfin-like beings. Strands of the wood's incense drifted in the dusky, floral summer air making for an intoxicating aromatic blend. I swayed, rather than moved to the music. The players in the forest had instruments of strange appearance, yet I could also see that I was in my friend's living room, blissfully accepting the impossible view I saw through his picture window. People were arriving in cars, by bicycles, and on foot. Crowds were forming in the street; I saw high school friends with their families. I was not at all concerned. I believed wholeheartedly there was no danger to

Joe or myself, as we listened; the song crossed its musical bridge. We blissed out, mouthing the words."

and it makes me wonder…

"The harmonics of the bridge carried me beyond concepts or form; this was the song's high point. I was swimming in sensuous textures, drifting in scented winds of colors, weightless in the center of some vast space of a kind I'd only experienced in fevered dreams. Looking out the window, there were several dirigible-shaped UFOs hovering about, as many smaller craft began to descend. I didn't care; in my mood, I was happy just to watch. Joe seemed dazed and was unresponsive when I gently tugged his sleeve. That's when I noticed I was on my feet although I hadn't realized it. I just continued to take in all the experience. It did not matter much that it was all too much."

"Ships landed on rooftops, in the street, in front yards, backyards, wherever space allowed. Everyone was calling to others to come on out; everyone stared in disbelief. Still, no shots were fired, and, except for the music in my head, and the visitors it would have been an ordinary day. About eight wildly different vessels landed within talking distance of the picture window framing this impossibility. There was the arrival of many mirror bright vehicles of the typical flying saucer design, a spherical center with a circular wing extending out from the equator."

If there's a bustle in your hedgerow
Don't be alarmed now
It's just a spring clean for the May Queen
Yes, there are two paths you can go by
But in the long run
There's still time to change the road you're on…

"The lyrics came crashing back. They were soothing as a ripple on water. I envisioned each word unfolding into a vast novel, and a dream-within-a-dream-within-a-dream, each phrase produced a panoply of historic documentaries, and for a moment, I saw the Yellow Brick Road leading on to the Emerald City. This is when many, many doors, hatches, locks, or what have you, began to open and the legendary fun began. Out of one came a hexipedal rhinoceros-like creature, its horn blinking in many colors like a strobe light. Joe and I agreed this was a mode of communication; all the people laughed at the appearance of her/him/it. Out of another came a swarm of insects, apparently, all about the size of bumblebees; these stayed together in a tight, cohesive cloud, each of them glowing with a bright, ghostly blue.”

“From another, a very large, silvery mirror-like spherical vessel came an odd creature. I called it the black giraffe, because although its body was black, round and had six spider-like legs set in radial symmetry, its neck was giraffe-like. Despite the fact that its head was a large cluster of glistening, dark purple, basketball-sized drupelets, that’s what I called it. Its ship ascended before another, more football shaped, flat grey in color, and a quarter mile in girth, descended slowly to hover above the giraffe thing. The giraffe began to behave quite oddly, first it alternately stretched out and contracted its neck, and in addition, it danced, so to speak, as it rotated its body, taking tiny circular side steps. Its neck was more sinuous than I thought possible; in fact, it was snake-like.”

“More creatures poured out of more ships as they landed. There were creatures like alligators walking as bipeds, things that undulated or crawled like walruses, and the indescribable. All the while every being in sight, alien and human alike, seemed friendly. There was a lot of dancing going on. The aliens, I noticed, were handing, pawing, or whatever, bright, blue one-inch cubes which sparkled. From what I could see, these allowed communication. There were many thousands of ships hovering about, as more continued to land, and myriads of fantastical creatures came out of each one. People who touched the blue cubes were those that were dancing.”

“I saw the stuck-up stuff shirt snobby types hanging cool with the aliens, swapping souvenirs, and teaching dance steps. I could not speak, not a wit. Joe stared and, for once, had nothing to say. There were a set of gold-colored monkeys talking with another humanoid, who would pass for normal were it not for the large rose growing in, or rather, out of his chest. The petals of the rose seemed to be in motion; I thought this was its means of communication. Oh, and its face had one big blue unblinking eye.”

“Soon food was being shared, along with liquor, which had its well-known effects, however unfamiliar the aliens may have been to Earthly forms of it. The few cops arriving on the scene walked about dumbfounded, staring at the ships still trying to land, as well as the mind-boggling variety of creatures that were attempting to explain something to them. One officer was shouting as he called in to report. I guessed that he was having difficulty being understood, or believed.”

Your head is humming and it won't go
In case you don't know
The piper's calling you to join him
Dear lady can you hear the wind blow
And did you know
Your stairway lies on the whispering wind…

"More doors opened, more things came as another menagerie was yielded; balloon beings which moved about like miniature dirigibles, humming above the heads of the very happy throng. I remember thinking how wonderful this festival was, when, right in front of our window, there was a flash of light and a modest sonic boom. We saw a whole collection of elves, leprechauns, fairies, gnomes appear in clear egg-shaped ships, as they disembarked their ships rose up and away. I saw gargoyle-like beings making strange gestures while holding translator cubes, as they hopped about, or blinked strange colors, or changed colors like a chameleon."
"Joe's and had a dreamy glaze as the song continued."

And as we wind on down the road
Our shadows taller than our soul
There walks a lady we all know
Who shines white light and wants to show
How everything still turns to gold
And if you listen very hard…

"Outside, the giraffe-like creature was poking its purple drupelet head into a horizontal opening at the base of the grey football thing, even as it continued dancing. The larger vessel was swaying in the breeze, we guessed. We couldn't comprehend why it began to expand and contract ever so slightly, as if breathing deeply. We thought it was getting ready to take off, or something. As I stood there watching, I began to think about the girls. I wanted them to be here to share this moment with us, and I wasn't alone in my thinking. I mean, we all know why now. The Xlantos, a must at any big celebration, were doing their thing. The big female ship and its tiny giraffe-like male counterpart were transmitting what can only be described the love vibe, as they engaged their organelles. Of course, we also didn't know that Joe's machine amplified those effects, so the scene was certainly awash in sensual sensitivities. I've since been told we were quite fortunate that a

Xlantos was in the area and dropped in; most of my neighbors agree with me there."

> The tune will come to you at last
> When we are one and one is all
> To be a rock and not to roll
> And she's buying a stairway
> To heaven.

"Then the song was over. All the creatures paused. Everyone began looking up or around. The rhino stopped blinking its horn; the gargoyles, alligators, elves, humanoids, cloud insects, frog-people, insect-beings, as well as the gold monkeys who had just landed, all took attitudes of rest. Joe and I knew there was a connection between the aliens arriving and the device as well as everyone's behavior and the music. All these alien individuals had heard the clear sound and had homed in on it."

"Before Joe or I had a chance to verbalize any thoughts another development snagged our attention. The black cube ever-so-slowly sidled over toward us. All eyes outside were upon it. When it became obvious the vessel had halted above Joe's house, everyone moved off humans and non-humans alike."

"A small gray globe, about the size of a beach ball, emerged from the pitch depths of the cube and hovered. We were taken aback when the device swooped down and rushed toward us only to stop in front of the window. After a moment, Joe opened the door and took a few steps back toward me. The sphere came to the open doorway and paused, as if in consideration."

"I said, 'Come on in.'"

"It entered, hovered before us, and then circled the room before it paused by Joe's invention. It played a red light all over the device. A bit later, when the record player, being set for replay, began playing again, the dreams swelled with the first chords to fill my head, the globe abruptly switched to using a blue light, which doused the volume. My illusionary visions dissipated."

"The globe quickly returned to hover in front of us. A small jewel-like light appeared at the thing's equator. In a fashion, not unlike a clear sound transmission, it said, 'This device you see is with the police. The jewel you see is a translator. You will have to keep your tonal pattern broadcast at a much lower volume; complaints from all manner of psionic users now total some 25,687,934,277,230. Out of common courtesy, we've already extended apologies to those complainants for the time it took to find the source of your broadcast. The rowdies, such as those you see,' here it tilted on its axis, to indicate the outside, 'are a fringe element, which are tolerated as long as they just party. Since your world is not in the unity, there is no mechanism for resolving compliance issues or conflicts of interest. Therefore, this will have to serve as a warning. I am correct in assuming this is the complete device?' The globe tilted again to nod in the direction of the apparatus. Joe gave out a hoarse, whispery, 'Yes.'"

"The globe hovered in silence. We waited while staring at it, then at each other, and shrugged our shoulders. In a minute or so, a small opening appeared in the globe's side. Then, what looked like a large marble, tinted blue, yet translucent, drifted over to us. Joe was instructed to take it; he did."

"We were told that it knows us and the invention, that we were now registered and it will assist us with those who were, no doubt, on their way to see us. It was described as an auto-manager, a standard device which does translations, keeps accounts, acts as an agent, makes contracts, manages key registers, creates fiduciary plans and takes elections for the banking of simple credits."

"In a friendlier tone, it added, 'You've got a nice planet here, real quiet. Some of the trouble we had in locating you was because the device has such an incredible range with no differentiation so the usual locator techniques didn't apply, also its nature was, well, absolutely new. Also, your planet wasn't in the registry and way out on the periphery where, it just so happens, a resistance storm has been a bother for a few millennia now, this also made determining any 10-20 rather difficult so your device will come in handy, in a number of ways, no doubt about that.' "

"So we're in that registry?" I asked.

"You are now that you've made contact."

"Joe and I looked at each other and didn't know what to say or think for that matter while it continued on. " 'Yes, there we were, picking through the scanner evidence we had, when a Lorper, praise be, intercepted a psymessage about a party on the third planet of this system. On a hunch, we zipped on out here and it all made sense. Well, your planet is on the register now, and you'll have to watch your step, if you know what I mean. Oh, yes, I know what's in your mind; I appreciate your thanks, as I am on track for full consciousness it is helpful in my quest, I can't accept gratuities, however, as I'm only doing my duty. Goodbye.' "

"The gray globe left as it had come and swiftly ascended and disappeared into the shadowy confines of the black cube, which then seemed to rapidly shrink until it too disappeared."

"We looked at each other, the marble glistening in his hand, then at the door when someone knocked. It was one of those alligator creatures. He handed me one of those sparkly cubes. It introduced itself as a regulatory agent. He quickly produced another cube for Joe. He/it, uh, they began talking big, I mean really big!"

Psalm 209 "Worlds: For Carlos Ramirez"

Oh, my friends there are worlds
And good ones
Beautiful worlds
So wondrous and full of marvels
As to make one weep

There are worlds where peace is all there is
And nature is let to run rampant
The verge is rank
With skies and seas full of life

Animals who see your soul's light
With hearts innocent of fear or rage

There are worlds gowned in clouds of delight
Graced with rivers of love
Where ranges upon ranges
Of emotional peace   rest
Under the glowing countenance   of their moons
Dancing in the firmament

Worlds such as songs are made of
As epic poems might suit
Where painters, upon an overlook can gaze
At a life's work set before them

Where God is happy
Life tame and where we'd be glad to be
Were we there   instead of where we are
Dazed and confused by our own earthly illusions
Oh, forsake fight and flight   let go of want
Our past   histories   of unending sorrows
Poor reasoning   and marshal drums

For there are worlds
This poor, poor scribbler asserts,
No artist could hope to convey,
Without a proper preparation,
A long, long, restful life of enjoyment –
A million-year picnic,
Then, then they could provide a semblance
Of one such world
Oh, I tell you
This is a magnificent universe
Well made   and fit for who but us
Or those   of our kind
It IS like the mystical Ganges
With its endless beaches
Where each glowing sand grain is a full repository
Of galaxies strung like beads
Set in a glowing firmament   of stardust
So, there are worlds
And then there's us
And our longing   our song
So profoundly deep and unending
That even this grand universe
And all of its works
Couldn't possibly contain it

Tale, the Sixth: Chamber Brother

The interior of the chamber had been absolutely dark and undisturbed for an incredibly long geological time. A miracle of magnificent, near-magical engineering, it had been made in order to keep its contents absolutely secure. This was why the makers of the chamber had set it near to the core of their planet. Then, long after an errant event extinguished the makers and their civilization, another solar system intersected that of the maker's causing its sun to go nova. This extinguished all remaining life upon that poor sphere, which was hurled into the interstellar reaches before subsequently drifting into the vast intergalactic wastes.

Long ages were to pass before the planet was captured by another system where, after a glancing collision with an outer planet, it disassembled into large fragments, one of which held the chamber. This continental sized torn and shapeless mass then returned to the interstellar deeps before being captured by another system where, after some long time in an erratic orbital path, it paired with a young outer planet as a moon. This caused that young planet to migrate sunwards to where it settled into a stable orbit much closer to the solar body. Soon, the mass containing the chamber combined with the planet and settled in near to its core.

For most all this time that which was in the chamber was dormant. Its creators had never dared monitor it and so it had been almost entirely unconscious as it unknowingly waited to be called upon. Still, without a sense of time, it dreamt and fed as we might understand such. Unbeknownst to it, its makers had never faced the challenge the chamber, and what it contained, had been designed to cope with so commands were never given. Thus, it was completely unaware of its creators or their fate.

It was a negative thing, bred or made so as to feed upon what's not, the void or seems to be darkness in the peculiar sub-form of space-time contained by chamber built to harbor it.

That which became the inhabitant had been captured by the makers, transformed by them and forced into chamber for the express purpose of creating something of use, a power source and, when needed, a cataclysmic weapon. The makers knew full-well of the inhabitant's capacities to survive upon the aether, a substance the builders made great use of yet, despite their far-reaching capacities of mind and spirit, essentially and fatefully misapprehended. For eons the makers studied, to no avail, the inhabitant's quite miraculous transubstantiation process, even as they used its power to transform their society and remake their world. Ironically, their use of its power caused the errant event that brought about the maker's utter downfall, which was horrifically violent and transpired in the course of a single day.

While the disaster was completely mysterious to the makers, it was something wholly ascribable to the Unity Factor. That's why the inhabitant may have sensed something of that occurrence although its perceptions, being far different than any we know of, would have prevented it from understanding the reality of that disaster or its role in the event. This was because, at that time, the inhabitant misapprehended the nature of the chamber and couldn't know about what existed outside its confines, and so couldn't grok the consequences any of its actions had.

Because of the planet's wandering the inhabitant, affected by changes in the aether, slowly gathered evidence of what seemed to be unaccountable influences. Then, some long time after, and despite its limited perceptions, there came an inkling, which led to a consideration that, once upon a time, it had been something different than that which it was. That line of thought led to the concept of change. Although it had lost touch with its sensory faculties, it understood it was inside something, if those were the proper terms. Consequently, it understood there had to be an outside and a before. Thus, for the first time, there was a theoretically possibility for the inhabitant to develop awareness of things outside the chamber.

Of course, it wasn't perfect. It had long forgotten what it once was, how it was made, made over, had thought, what it had believed, or wanted. No matter its immense cognitive powers, it had forgotten the nature of the realms outside the chamber and was unaware of how its scheming and experimentation, had caused first the extinction of its creators and, later on, their world to be loosed to wander. These changes in its planet's circumstance, essentially directed by it, provided the inhabitant with its first very vague concept of an externality.

Those first sensory reports, if such they could be called, were due to changes in the influence of gravitational fields as the planet containing the chamber left its original system. Up until then the gravitational network had been ever constant and so its set influences had gone unnoticed. However, when it became chaotic and then swiftly reduced in complexity into but a single constant, the inhabitant followed a thought sequence resulting in awareness, more inklings and nascent self-consciousness.

After some long time, it sensed being caught in a new set of influences. Before any real knowledge could be gleaned however, there was a sharp decline in the complexity of this set of influences when, again, it reduced to a single constant. Some long time passed with no further changes noted until it again detected and was caught in a new set of influences. This time it attempted to read, study, and learn. It had a purpose.

The chamber, set in an agglomeration of nickel-iron, had not been affected by this long journey. However, soon after its arrival in this new system of influences, the inhabitant could sense it would not leave them. It understood it was being drawn toward something huge and, as with the other locations it had been in, there were moving parts, influences, which systemically tugged from various angles, with differing strengths and various durations.

Soon it sensed acceleration; it was falling. It mapped out pulling sensations as they came, went, or changed. It understood the patterns, learned to pull back, and so affected a course change.
Although the inhabitant didn't understand what it, in reality, was doing, as it sought a neutral balance of motion which caused the mass containing the chamber to orbit about a small outer world, which then moved sunward to a new neutrality point.

During the ensuing respite the inhabitant gathered data from the inscriptions in the crystal facings of the chamber. These had been built to harness the inhabitant's capacities and to prevent its escape. The makers built well out of greed and for dread of what would transpire should the inhabitant ever escape.

It was called the Chamber for the Weaver—or Dreamer—of Darkness, according to its makers. These terms were abstractions to the inhabitant. The chamber had never held anything—not a bit of matter nor any kind of vibration. Its makers well knew anything could act as a supply of such proportions as to empower the inhabitant, allow its break out, and result in the consequent and unimaginable horror they feared.

Only the crystalline mechanisms lining the inside kept eternal vigil and so provided the inhabitant with the only thing that could be described as company. These structures, with their specially engraved markings, kept the inhabitant at bay in ways altogether mysterious. They obviated all but its most harmless activities. Nonetheless, over the long stretch of time, the inhabitant learned to leverage infinitesimal factors into a few frugal portions of potential, secreted for the time when it would gain its freedom.

The great block of nickel-iron containing the chamber joined with its small inner world in a violent, but thoroughly planned fashion. After some long time, the mass worked its way toward the center of gravity and the temperature around the chamber grew to many thousands of degrees. This would not have mattered when the chamber was new; however, it had suffered to some infinitesimal degree and so this new environment could wear on it. The inhabitant knew its time would come, that it would be allowed—allowed to be all it could be.

It waited as the exterior environment put strains on the functional structures of the chamber. Although the crystals would never lose their power, the inhabitant was sure external conditions were the cause of vague and an extremely rare sense of physical motion, as perceived by the inhabitant, the Dreamer or Weaver of Darkness. Thus, it continued to exercise and extend its potentials.

To its perspective, there was a flash of light just before the crystals vaporized. Then it was free of its restriction of form and the limitations as all such are heir to. It discovered its true dimensions when it made physical contact with the naked inner walls and, although it could not move what might be called its physicality through them and suffered from painful limitations, something else also occurred.

There was a part of it outside, sensed by the inhabitant in a dream-like state. This part swam in the planet's magma. There it began to work the super hot fluid into a spinning current and so it rose toward regions less dense. Its dream self went along with the magma as it broke upon the surface. The inhabitant could sense everything via this etheric-simulacrum. The essential part of it was out even as its physicality was contained in the horrible chamber!

The system's sun was sufficiently energetic to supply the inhabitant's incorporate form with energy for continuance but its ancient memory was unreachable. Nothing arose into awareness as had been hoped. It mulled over its new circumstance and what it could recollect out of curiosity. It developed a better understanding of how it had destroyed those who had made it, what might have been called its home planet—as well as how its orchestrations had resulted in the adventurous journey to where it now was.

Invisibly adrift above the planet's hell-like surface, it was an essence, a quality, a thought—all of these, yet none of them. Intangible, yet it had motive, force, and awareness enough to consider its evolution. It was free but desired nothing. It enjoyed the planet. Fascinated by its ring system and two moons, it soon understood that one of them was destined for instability and destruction while the other would be cast off eventually to form a new planet. It pondered their fates as a means of passing time.

With time, another change, more interesting than interplanetary relations, occurred. After the planet cycled through phases of ice and volcanism and the atmospheric chemistry changed, a peculiar manifestation of matter developed in the shallow marine environments. Matter appeared to weave itself into non-crystalline forms and these replicated so inefficiently as to morph over time; they were both intricate and puzzling.

Now-One-Free couldn't explain these forms but was, from the first, fascinated and continued to investigate them as they grew larger, more complex and began to roam the planet's dry surface. One could characterize its subsequent thoughts as follows:

"This life so simple. These—those—who dwell hereupon are reminiscent of that kind who built my chamber. Just as the life on that world, from the simplest unconscious bet of life to the largest, all fed off one another in networked of energy exchanges supporting the larger apex creatures, so it is with these."

"One specie, conscious enough of itself, learns how the chains work, profits thereby to become a globe-encompassing form. A marvel of adaptability; they use flora and fauna to their advantage. These apex creatures reap benefits by manipulating the network of mass transference and chemical reactions. They show promise. They make tools and form communes. They are a way forward. I am determined to manipulate these. They've potential and could free my body from the chamber."

"I influence some of these individuals, via an overlay, as distasteful as such is, until these apex beings evolve a capacity to project sequenced sonic vibrations. Despite not being at all hive-like they had minds, imagine, intelligent life forms without a hive-mind! I learn much upon the expiration of a host when I inherit their sprit essence, this informs and sustains me."

"It is difficult to keep a connection with one in order to begin programming because almost as soon as I manage this, its consciousness burns out or its body falls into corruption. They are fragile and terribly short-lived as to make continuity of influence nearly impossible. I believe transference, communing, may be necessary—however horrific or disgusting that may seem."

"Instead, and for a time, I inculcate, rather than ensconce or commune, in order to experiment with channeling to and through them. It was a good sign when, after a number of generations, individuals began detect my presence. Although this would sometimes foment an irrational resistance, which was futile, such struggles took time and impacted the production rate of measurable output. Still, I saw gains. Thus, I came to understand, all the better, the need for breeding as key to creating compliant minds and longer-lived individuals. I introduce naming and counting, which quickly bring about the formation of group-mind organizing and cooperative conspiracies over the generations."

"Basic problems being solved, I worked on their multiple forms of distemper, confusion, as well as structural irrationality. This was most frustrating until I saw those things as useful. I now have some who believe in secret abilities, that they can call upon magical powers or communicate with deities. Some few breed lines, with special advantages, run the multigenerational cultures now sprinkled the globe over. Their ingrained tendency for chaotic conflict has become key to managing populations."

"Ever more capable at manipulating their environment and crafting constructs to their greedy advantage, simple civilizations follow one another. I guide scientific developments toward the simply materialistic and or mechanical—away from real science, which would provide any chance of a threat."

"They develop consciousness via a bicameral mentality, a unique solution to the old stumbling blocks. In this they are virtually identical to my long-ago captors. However, this time, I'll use them for my purposes. Although virtually any one of them can act as a puppet, I still burn them out quickly enough, but because of their hierarchical social networks I can replace a given lead unit without much, if any, loss to my plans."

"Dwelling hidden amongst them is sickening enough not to mention difficult and painful, I mean to say, what with their blizzards of confusion, chaos, and their odorous emotional idiocy not to mention their twinkling of a life span. Although I do make progress, I am plagued by the limits of this indirect input, which is a formidable barrier. Although research indicates that if I lived as one of them, with complete sensory contact and control, I'd certainly understand how they're wired, how to better breed or manage them, and so facilitate their development for my ends, yet, there is the rub, being born amongst them. My absolute livid revulsion at the very idea is the only counter to my own extremely logically loathsome conclusion – no matter how I rail."

"Even with the downside of direct install, then ensconcing, communing, my consciousness would be on their time scale; I'd have to wait for the container, the host's body, to develop to maturity before I link and generate output. But still, yes, I know, afterwards, progress would be swift."

"I will be born then. I'll put them to task and make my life's will theirs. I will be Their Light, their I Am, The Will, Perfection and the One Direction—I prepare a way."

"I select a culture, small, troubled, and in desperate circumstances, to mould. I take one of theirs as host, let it use my talent and through it I remake its culture. Their kind becomes elevated, The Chosen People, destined to reign above all others. All serving them will, through them, serve me."

"The Chosen will challenge all the others, this is my will, my will! The law of the land shall be love; love under will. My people wax strong as, through host after host, I lead them to greater and greater glories. Unseen is my hand though they fight to serve my every need. They view their own kind as holy— the Divine Host and, lost in an illusion of freedom, they slave to secure my ends at all costs through their means. They begin to know order!"

"Progress is swift, conquest sure, and power unfolds through each successive host. Each with the life knowledge of those I've incorporated and, with my skill to weave spells, their word, my word, is believed. All celebrate their magic, my magic; revere their wisdom, my wisdom, and in so doing honor me."

"Their adherence to the One Faith focuses their perceptions, forms their dreams, colors their thoughts, and leads them to a ripening of soul; they heed my call, enlist in my service, and do as bid. I am—their names, their wills and fears. My vision, blinding their psychic mechanisms of faith, I receive their supplications as music, their blood as wine, their bodies as bread, and their souls are the essential sustenance upon which I sup. I am majesty, divinity and give them victory over enemies."

"I am I. They know nothing else. Their glory is my worship. Their obedience, their passion, are all mine—even as I am both unspeakable and unknowable. They serve! I, who am of and from nothing, will be their Forever Way. They see my vision, hear my yearning, and it is theirs. They will serve my end and take me back to find my own. I am The Word, the abundance upon which they depend. Resistance is futile. All enemies fall prey to storm, drought, pestilence, famine, fire, plague and war. Might makes right!"

"By my command, a talented host orders populations concentrated into places where, en mass, they are dealt into death. Then, when their souls attempt flight, they are drawn down into a great vortex, a ravenous all-consuming maw."

"Oh, brilliance! With a will, they heed my demand, feed me with many millions. I harvest dreams of the souls captured as they flee life while the residuals are taken into the fiery and incorporated into my physicality still imprisoned in that damned chamber. My physicality waxes, breaks free! My body rises from the depths as my birth calls—I am in, in pain"

"Yes, now! There is light, more and more. I am in a body, my host, with my mind and essence! It is all one. There is beautiful clean air, I am in-breathed, have multi-sensors, all the world rushes to me in this –- everything! I am I; the word made flesh."

"Yea, all before me will serve; so that I may feed! Their science bent to my purpose, to find my original source! To this end I will be master of this life form and any others they discover."

"Woeful woe to one and all; vengeance is mine!"

Psalm 10, 004 "They call it"

A failed place … a place of … dis – ease
A place where … no one knows their place   anymore
Where counting … numbers and abstractions
Have become as real as that which is counted
And where they count everything
And then it's all denominated
Even as the … sacred … the eternal
Has been forgotten … forsaken
Even … foresworn of its denizens' hearts
Hard as this is to believe
It is, all of it, true … and … still … there's more …
What seems morally impossible –
Astonishingly, they dismember their network
Act to consume it …
Using   monstrous creations

To dig, break, scorch or bury their living sphere
Poisons are let to soak into soils - which die
As do rivers
So that now ... now ... life is leaving ... a home-world ...
Something – so incredibly rare as to be unheard of
But it is happening –and in the unlikeliest place

Its beings ... obsession with possessions, real and not
Have devolved ... lost sight ... and who ... in their rage
Extinguish their own kind
And make coin from everything that lives – everything that dies

Its own denizens - call it bedlam—pandemonium
A chaotic melee of enmity - a place of devouring
Ruled over by soulless incorporates
Which mark everything with cold calculations
Where hungry ghosts raise up the dead to worship an eternal evil
That then thrives on their godlessness
It is a world of pain
Where every joy is a sufferance, love wilts and their beliefs
Are simply ... not to be believed!

This ... place ... vast in abyssal sorrow
Harbors more horrors than we can describe
Such that ... such that
All those in the vast deep reaches of this universe
Who feel kindness, know Love,
And are soulfully connected to the great family
Feel this disturbance in   the force
And have come to know of this unique point
This painful rift in the networks - of amity
The cries from this place reach to all heaven
Into all time
And so, to the universes before and yet to come

Such is the inheritance of separation
The yield of irrational, passionate fear
The great bounty of forgetfulness
The ruination of rationality

Some call it a place of regret
Others the lost place of ignorance
Some say it is ruined
This is why we   in our trillions—of trillions
On the myriads of worlds
Set in their glittering heavens
Have begun a chorale
We sing that this place may be soothed,
For Love to bloom   and peace to hold sway
That the web of life will heal and prosper
And that the Great Song will return
To that strange planet Earth!

Tale, the Seventh: A Letter about Jovia

You might recall my byline, Jack Ralins but it's more likely you don't and I wouldn't hold it against you, as my salad days, or Hey Daze, were over long ago. Even then everyone said I was an old man, but until my personal disaster, I'd always felt I had farther to go. I got suckered into blowing out my reputation on a very important, very, very public story, which, when the truth did come out, morphed into one that focused instead on a big nine-figure lawsuit which nearly folded the paper I worked for. Oh, they defended me but after it all blew over I was out on my ear,

I was good, still, but truth be told, I had been having problems with the job, my life, everything except Mr. Booze. Amazingly, I acted my way through the whole debacle, implying others had sandbagged me, partly true, and that my divorce was to blame, yes and no, really. I even said, "Age happens to everyone, even the best, just like me." In fact, I said everything except I was sorry.

Back then I thought it was a happy, albeit private, miracle as to how I'd kept my private drinking parties, just that, through it all, working, writing, marriage collapse and the end of my career. Yes, Jimmy, my boon companion, aka Mr. Walker, finally got the best of me and did his part to help me fold my career, like I would a bad hand at five-card stud.

The change hit me hard. Never light on my feet, I wallowed for being wronged, which, in part, I had been, and this gave me reason enough to drink. I thought of it as a way to get back at them all. Ironically, gambling, which was an important factor in the break up of my marriage, kept me solvent while everything else vanished in a chaotic fog of haywire events, arguments, and hazy, incoherent memories. As for my dearly beloved, I don't know where she is, though I'm sure she's doing well enough without me. The good thing was, she didn't take me for a dime, mainly because, at that time, I didn't have one.

So, the rest of the relevant back-story in a nutshell is this, I bumped along on the bottom for a couple of years before I got on the wagon, kept off the streets, worked odd jobs, and gambled just enough to stake a new start, three thousand miles away from a past that had haunted me wherever I went in the Big Town.

I sent some freelance stuff around and started making sales. Before long I was hired as a stringer. Now I might get lost in the technology of modern reporting, but I've style, old style and that's what they liked, at least for the contrast. Anyway, I knew enough of the business to help sprouts nurse their stories, and handed out advice to any who'd listen, like a short-order cook. So, after six months, where did they put me? In charge of the Science Desk, "Dead City," the "Retirement Desk" yeah, that's what it was called behind my back. However, I will grudgingly admit I was ready for the assignment.

I got letters from those who wanted to have their discovery published to make "us" instantly rich, enlighten humanity; or who explained endlessly why something had to be done, although they hadn't a clue as to how to go about doing whatever it was. The worst were those who'd demonstrate abyssal ignorance of basic facts as they argued their so-called point. I also received a plethora of notices, reports, periodicals all gratis, and so became learned, even if after a fashion. Yes, I covered technological miracles and the wonders modern medicine has on offer. My job was to sift through it all and come up with about a thousand words or more, depending on how my page was going to be set, on any given day.

I chose to focus on the common guy, and how old or new science information could be applied in everyday life. My first successes came when I began to cover items with benefits to handymen and do-it-yourselfers. Later came urban living and house and home advisements, all based on the principles of science, simple chemistry, or engineering. Sometimes I'd just pass good info along or clarify the import of some discovery or theory. Upshot, it was manageable and I got to like it.

Of course, I wanted more and began to think out of-the-box. When I added some simple science demonstrations, having to do with homemade healthcare or cleaning products involving the use of simple chemistry, I ran afoul of a malevolent manager, who, prompted by some irate advertisers, gave me unholy hell. When word got out about that, I was ridiculed. However, when other papers wanted to carry my column, it was my turn to laugh. In sum: I'd made a reentry into legitimacy and the sweet spot in it all was that day when my old paper took my column. I smirked when my byline reappeared in that old rag because I knew some tongues would be wagging, no doubt.

Anyway, I was told to get an aide somewhere, so that I could organize my department, and it would not look like what it was, a spare room overwhelmed by a growing conglomeration of papers, books, magazines, boxes, and charts, all manner of strange gee-gaws, an assortment of samples, and a miasma that was renown. I had never interviewed people, for a job I mean. I didn't know what I wanted but no else did either so it was up to me.

I wound up choosing a local sprout, name of Willy Tainn just before a three-day weekend. He had an impressive portfolio, backing up what I garnered just by talking with him for a few minutes. He was a wiz-kid, nerdy maybe, and yes, he had an odd choice of clothes, lack of hairstyle, not to mention a tinny voice, but all that didn't figure into my equation. He was a-okay in my book. He came with a sense of humor, and was a kind of jack-of-all-trades when it came to the egghead realms. He knew something about anything I could think of to ask him about but, and just as importantly, he knew how to communicate efficiently, beautifully, and effectively—whether he was speaking or writing.

Those things were all good but what set him apart from the others, what sold me on him, was that he had come to hold the same work philosophy as I, albeit for different reasons. We believed in being useful to our community and, if possible, to the world in general—and if we could do that through our job it would be the sweetest possible sweet spot. Although we appeared as an unlikely a pair as you'd find, I hired him. We shook hands, and that was that, as far as I was concerned.

Then, having nothing to do but shoot a bit of it, we talked. I was taken aback when he said he wanted the job because it suited his plans to get out on his own and that just that tore it; I had to get down to brass-tacks. I winced when I told him what I'd conveniently forgotten thus far, how much he'd be making after all the usual deductions. Yup, he crashed a bit but, as I watched, I could see him figuring. I couldn't stand it and, for some wildly uncharacteristic warm-fuzzy reason, I invited him to throw in with me. I had a master apartment so he'd have his own entrance and figured we'd both be better off. We knocked it around for a while and it all fell into place quickly. We'd share the common rooms, essential expenses, and he could move in when he was ready. He told me he didn't have much to move and it wouldn't take him long.

Next, I showed him our so-called department, a large ex-storage room measuring eight by 19 with a 14-foot ceiling. Although you'd never know it, there were actually two desks in there, one legendarily lurked beside the ancient copying machine underneath an assortment of mailbags and an amazing collection of office flotsam and jetsam that I had "organized" and which had long taken up residence atop, aside, around, and below it. The back third of the office was what I called the mountain, a disorderly stack of the unknown things I'd never gotten around to even looking at. The second desk was still partly visible, though one could mistake it for something out of "bad house keeping." It had that proud, unkempt, lived-in look. On its small side-table, there were a couple of dress shirts, a jacket, and pair of shoes I'd been meaning to get fixed since the winter past, as well as a collection of the usual desk items in creative disarray. Only the phone had a clear space all around it with several attending notepads.

When I saw the way he looked at it all. I said, "Everyone has things they mean to get done yet they don't; it's how it is sometimes." He nodded. I told him he could start on Wednesday, when we'd team up for Thursday's column. That seemed to be it for the moment; I told him I was going home for the day. When he asked if he could stay on, I assented; I guessed he wanted to get acquainted with things. "See you Wednesday!" I said cheerfully.

Well, moving right along, I had to come back late on the following Tuesday, and I was brought up short as I crossed the threshold to my department, did a double-take, and stood there confused. I was the right place but inside it was completely organized and there was no odiferous waft. Some of the other guys saw me and chuckled. "Cowboy Bob" gave his buck-toothed bray before asking, in his signature hayseed accent, "Hey Slim, do ya' wunner where yer orffice all got tew?"

I went in to inspect the damage but the operation looked really good, I mean to say. The mountain had been humbled and everything sorted on the floor to ceiling shelves, my files were now actually the filing cabinets, and all the reference works, even those I hadn't ever unpacked, were in one place. I was amazed. I recollected telling the kid he could start by doing some organizing if he wanted to. Well, the place was sure organized; he'd taken up the challenge and then some! I went to my desk where I found a note from him.

"I cleaned up around here as you suggested. I was impressed by some of the collected material—interesting things we could talk about for Thursday. Anyway, I sent those shoes out, and they'll be coming back Thursday, as will the other stuff. I shoveled out the back, did some serious sorting, filing, and disposal of duplicates or junk. I installed the makeshift in and out baskets on the side-table, which is now by the door. By the way, I found a very interesting letter that came in some time ago. I am trying to trace it back to its owner; it's probably a wild goose chase, though when I show it to you, I think you'll agree we shouldn't let it just go. In any event, I hope to be back before you get here to read this. –Wiz."

I hadn't used his nickname but twice, but was glad he liked it enough to use it. He later told me he'd adopted it because, by doing so, everyone in the office would know who he was and what he did by virtue of it. I was thinking if he was as good at research on current science and fact checking as he was with organizing, I made a good choice. When I sat at my desk, it was so neatly organized that I was drawn right into a few stories and some articles related to them. After a time, I paused. I became embarrassed at how old some of my unread stuff was, yet with his sorting and arranging, making plans for their use was easy. Great!

I don't know how the assistant editor knew I was in but I got word he just had to see me about something that absolutely, positively, couldn't wait; yet by the time I got to his office he wasn't there, par for the chaotic course. When I got back, the Wiz had been in and gone out again. I wondered what, on our dearly beloved world, the Eard, he was up to. His desk now was respectfully scattered with books. His jacket was thrown across the back of his chair. I smiled. Too much order, I was sure, was bad for the human condition. I hunched into my work, leaving the door open, as was my usual habit.

I looked up when I smelled the coffee, along with the unmistakable waft of a hot pastrami with glazed onions, aioli with pepper jack on rye, my favorite order from Ryderr's Deli. Wiz was human, after all, even if skinny as the proverbial rail.

As we ate, he explained how the magic was done. He had called in a few favors from friends and gotten good use out of some office and paperboys, who'd been very willing to help. I wondered how he'd hooked them and dismissed the idea of telling him he'd overstepped his bounds and figured that's what the editor had wanted to see me about. When I asked about the letter, he shrugged it off saying he wanted to get more information.

Soon enough it was Friday, then the next Friday and a few more went by. We'd become quite a pair, and the column got some good notices. We quickly got up to speed, usually working ahead, always having a few columns in the go-to file.

One Friday, I returned from a ballgame, and having done well, was good mood offering to order in whatever he liked. He was glad, though he couldn't help mentioning how he also managed to beat the odds on same the game I'd covered. We celebrated with Pirro's Pizza, amber Indian ale and a lot of laughter. After we toned it down, i.e. became tired, we began to exchange tricks of the trade and happily agreed to team up. This became a big deal, what we called "the business" or "the investment concern" and soon we had the means to live it up a bit and fund our own news intel and street operations.

A few weeks later, in order to do some research for our investment concern, we went by the office late. There, he found a large envelope that had been hand-delivered after hours by one of our youthful street crew. As he tore it open, he said it was from a well-known math researcher. I waited for the other shoe as he became more agitated as he read and started to go on and on about how the proceeds from our investments had made "all this" possible he said, tapping the letter for emphasis. Then he dug out his Jovia File, looked through it and rambling about how our ability to travel a bit, get research done, and maintain our info-network of sources had "gotten us there."

"Where is that? Calm down, okay?" I said, "I guess this has to do with that wild goose chase letter of yours?"

"Well, yeah. But before I tell you what's in here remember you had the original letter for nearly a year before I found it and then it took all this while to check the information and try to find him, which we haven't as of yet, sorry to say."

"I remember you said the letter came from guy who taught college in Philosphia."

"And I got interested because …"

"It had to do with Jovia," I finished.

"Right."

"The planet, not the God," I added in lackadaisically.

"You got it. It's the farthest planet from the old Sul but it has begun to radiate heat and there's no agreement as to why"

"Thus the probe was sent."

"Yeah. Anyway, this guy, Lovedraught, who wrote the letter, seemed to be explaining the heat as a precursor of a series of events because … "

"Jovia has more than a quarter the mass of old Sul!"

"Ok, no need to be sarcastic," he said, "It's my baby, my first lead." I sat quietly as he continued, "All those telegrams and letters, long distance calls, paid off. In this package, we have two things, first the last piece of the puzzle had gotten a second confirmation of its value."

"This other sheet, however, is mixed news. When I learned some of our new kids had cousins in Philosphia, where I assumed Lovedraught lived, I had them to look for the guy. I thought it'd be quick, as there couldn't be many bearing such a name. Come to find out, he moves about and often. However, finally, our street crews here found him, living not half hour away from here. I sent some of our kids to scout around, but they were rebuffed by a burly grouch of a landlord who wouldn't give, no matter what their tricks. Now it may be that the man no longer lives there, after all, none of our scouts saw anyone, save the landlord, come or go for the last five days. Still, I believe I'm close to finding him. I wonder why he's so elusive. I wish I had a photograph."

"Also, as you know, from day one, I tried to go through the formulae in the original letter. I was fascinated by the logic, the mathematics, not to mention the theory, or what I understood of it, I mean its way out there. There's a story there, in and of itself."

I had to interrupt him, "I hope I don't wind up twisted in something I can't get out of, one of these fine nights."

"I understand the concern, but what I just got back tonight was a final check on the last piece of the theory. You know, I farmed out pieces of it because I didn't want anyone to look at the whole of it; I had to protect the man's interest…"

"And ours …"

"Yes. As you know, he used terms I'd never seen, so I couldn't follow parts, and couldn't understand it completely but was willing to bet it explained what's going on with Jovia. The man who replied in this note," he indicated the one he'd just read "speculates that something else, far more fantastic will happen, the essence of which is couched in those mysteries contained in the impossible last section. He notes there are symbols referring to magnetic force, which are used in relation to variables commonly found in formulae describing expanding wave patterns, wave propagation, and others having to do with interference of radiation. He, as was the case with everyone else, could not follow where common symbols must have alternate values, are arcane, or are something created by the theorist. He indicates there'll be radio effects on a scale as will be detectable here on Eard, some kind of light show out there and then he gets lost as did the others. However, if he is right, all broadcast media will be affected. There's one more thing, when he wrote this letter, months before I came across it, he was still taking observations, and hadn't properly calculated out the timeline. The only solid hint for that was in the cover letter where he mentioned the main event horizon could be two years off.”

“So, we could be in the midst of some kind of countdown right now.”

“Right.”

“And the probe out there should get something, right?”

“From what I understand of what the others wrote, it’ll be like big city fireworks in some Thor forsaken jerkwater town. We should put this in the paper, something …”

“So, okay, this is interesting, but I’m sure only a very few would comprehend what it means and, because of what you’ve just said, even with that rare handful, most would not believe it.”

“Yeah, still, we could excite someone out there.”

“I don’t know about this at all.”

“Okay, maybe this then: call it a hunch; the guy’s math is dazzling. I mean, maybe publish a part of his work and appeal directly to him so that he’ll write in again.”

“Well, I’d like to hear from the man, but I don’t want to get royally hosed again. We might catch hell with those who claim to know what’s what. One other thing: lots of people who write in don’t want to be published and we don’t know that he does.”

I could see his disappointment. My thinking was, that if we were going to scoop NASA, we'd best be as solid as we could be, and have the man’s approval. “Listen, you get his approval and we’ll run it; it’s the best I can do.” Then, after getting some info to help us with our playoff calculations, we headed back home.

We heard the TV as we approached our door; one of us had left the set on. As we entered, we stopped to watch as a NASA spokesperson talking in serious tones about the ‘fly-by’ to Jovia being captured by the planet while going in and out of contact for the past hour and there were no explanations as to why.

We decided make a few sandwiches, relax, and get updated. A few minutes after we finished eating, the view was switched to the control room showing those at the consoles and controllers cheering. The announcer told us they’d just manipulated the craft into an orbit; it seemed stable. The bad news was they were still confused by unusual and problematical planetary phenomena affecting the gravity gradient.

We were struck and although we argued our options, we agreed we had an obligation to inform the citizenry, public safety trumping

Lovedraught's self interest. As to publishing, we figured that the worst case would be him finding himself put in the limelight and some of his ideas would be found useful— but it sure looked like we scooped a big fish, and how. We were excited. Neither of us could stop talking as we made a to-do list and, man, there was a lot to do. We bolted straight out.

We went back to the office, grabbing coffee and some stuff from Izzie's AllNite Delhi Deli on the way. By 515am Wiz, or W as I now called him, had discovered espresso's restorative chemical prowess, our street crew had supplied us with deliveries of further foodstuffs, and we had a cash-starved, top-drawer grad student looking over the whole of theory along with the letters from others who'd responded to W's queries. While they were at it, I was trying to concoct a column, or a semblance of one but it was slow as the things they wanted in or out kept changing.

In the more remote realms, I had the linotype operator holding space for a specialized drop-in, a friendly copy-editor who was checking over the text each time I updated it, and we had a few very loyal go-fers going anywhere for anything. A serious bottleneck was caused by the specialized type pieces that had to be make in order to print the terms of the formula in the paper, these had to be made in the tool room—and they kept changing as W and friend made revisions; what a circus! We were tight though and steaming along, hard at it, because there was no telling how long our so-called exclusive would hold.

The phone jangled jolting me awake; it was pressroom, and boy did I get an earful. The manager had caught a particularly savory helping of deep fried hell because he'd been holding up the run just for me and I, dozing, lost track of time and hadn't let them off the hook. One of our kids ran down with a set piece we'd reserved for just that purpose.

I was surprised when the grad student's professor arrived just before nine and jumped in full on. All I could do was nervously look at the clock as I wondered if we'd make even the late afternoon edition. I waited while everyone was shoulder-to-the-wheel, nose to the grindstone, as it were, and chatting excitedly in terminology that had only a loose association with English. After some long time of this, all of a sudden, they got into sharp arguments and voiced frustration at their inability to puzzle out the uncommon meaning of common symbols in the last portion. They wanted to meet Lovedraught, and all I could say was, "You and me both!" I told them W and I had our kids working it.

Hours flew by and again I lost track of time; again, the phone rang, the pressroom wanted to know what our plans were. I told him we would go for the morning run, come hell or high water. He was fine with that until I told him how that we had not determined how much space we'd need. Well, I mean to say this page would catch fire if I quoted even a part of his three-alarm rant. Whew! However, we reconciled when I told him he was in on a real five-star scoop, which the Chief himself had approved. The man became happy enough with that—now all I had to do was make good on my word.

Well, we didn't make the papers that day but by half past whatever we had noodled the text as much as we could and then celebrated as the last specialty type character was set in. We sat for a moment, dazed and dieseling, as we'd done all we could do. We'd boiled the theory down and chose to emphasize explanations of what was occurring on Jovia, predicting significant radio interference, and a spectacular northern light display. Oh, we made few other predictions regarding further changes, some eye-poppers there, but we downplayed them to be safe and still cover our bases. At last, when the copy editor we'd been working with brought in the final text, I held it up for all to see and wearily asked, "This explains the current phenomena on Jovia then outlines more?" The student and his professor blankly nodded. W just smiled and that was good enough for me.

The professor added, "Of course we exercised some caution and limited ourselves to the portions we understood in the main. What you've written reflects that but it is still, essentially, speculative. Nevertheless, there will be some serious solar flare effects here on Eard, so, I've no doubt, that alone will get someone's attention and your story will be worth the read. Annoyingly, the final section uses figures most commonly found when describing gravimetrics, and some of the embedded terms are so fantastic as to be unbelievable. That's why I included something about heavenly displays of light and, of course, the radio effects."

"Are you saying there is a danger?"

"I don't think so, else the man would have said something in plain English. I'm only speaking for what those parts we understand, even though I disagree with some of that. Until we know what some of his symbols mean, we are, as I said, speculating and that only goes so far."

Chaffing a bit under the glare of his cold, gray eyes, I nodded. I had gotten what I wanted, and I was going to go ahead with it. "So, I wouldn't be laughed off the presses?"

"Hardly. The worst you'll do is excite debate in the combative realms of astrophysicists. Oh, it's dangerous stuff." He smirked then chuckled.

"Okay, well, it will be in tomorrow's morning edition. I'm going to get a front-page leader too." They didn't get the import of that and let it go.

"I must thank you, I am glad to have been of help; I think that goes for both of us." the elder man said, nodding toward his student. "It was the kind of math investigation one is rarely challenged with and it was refreshing to work through such a puzzling puzzle." He sounded cheerful as he gathered up his materials saying, "I'd like to know what comes of it, to be sure,"

"Sure," I said, "Maybe we'll get some bounce on it."

"Please, I'd appreciate discretion."

"Sure, no problem; no harm, no foul,"

We looked it over one last time. Our assessment: we had a good story. I could not be in better spirits than if I'd bottle partied. The professor, the student, and W took the story down for the morning edition while I caught a few winks.

An hour later, I woke with a start, ran out of my office as if I was on fire; I had to make good on my promises! I nearly ran right into the Chief. We both said, "I was looking for you, but I got the jump on him and began selling him on the once-in-a-century-lead story so hard and fast that he was blinking back. I finished by telling him that if he gave me the whole enchilada, a front-page header, full page inside, a co-byline for W—and the story did not deliver— I'd work six months gratis. Now all this time he'd been giving me his dour, grumpy poker-face. When I paused he grudgingly agreed, adding, not only would he do all I'd asked but, instead of working gratis, he wanted a share in my investment portfolio. I was taken aback, almost ready to say yes, when he busted a gut laughing. He told me W had introduced him to the professor and they'd talked all about it. He'd been convinced and cheerfully said I already had everything I'd just asked for.

Well, you could have knocked me over with a feather. The world looked mighty good right then. He asked if I wanted to join them at The Highlander's, or at Two Jack's, and hoist a few but I declined. I was beat out of it and still something of a teetotaler. There was nothing more to do so I went back to the now-empty office, snatched up my hat, and went home.

I was fried and refried. I gabbed a cab. I was sure the story would catch. Even the cabbie was full of himself, the expert talking on and on about the NASA story on Jovia. He said, "…sure them guys is smart, ya' know, but I can call a bluff as well as any card man can. I think they run up against something they don't know nuts about…" When I got out I tipped him well, went up to my apartment and, for a moment, stood there dazed.

My phone rang; it was the Chief. He was at Two Jack's and so actually cheerful; it was all a go, he said. Nice writing, he said. It's gonna be big time, he said. Sensing opportunity, I told him I wouldn't be at home, or anywhere else I could be reached; I needed sleep, and he was fine with that. Take the next day off; he said.

Now, although I don't lie, much, what I said was true. However, I was going to be just two flights up with Jana. She was the woman who had found me and helped my find myself, even as we found one-another. No one at work knew her, her number, or address, for that matter, well, save W. When we cocoon, we don't talk news, radio, and, most of all, not paper. She doesn't even subscribe to any, and that's been a point in her favor since when first we met.

Fully ready for rest, we slow cooked one of our cooperative dinners. I made vegetable soup, she put together some avocado and mushroom-chili quesadillas and we shared making a Greek salad. We talked about friends, movies, or things we've read; it was very nice. That night, we crossed a delicate threshold; we joked about children. Do you ever sometimes wonder if a woman knows you're planning to propose? I do, but I didn't.

In the morning, she let me slumber on but when I came to I heard her talking on the phone arranging for the sale of one her commissioned works. She heard me shuffling about, looked over, smiled in a knowing way as she hung-up, "Oh, you have joined the land of the living."

"Don't be too hard on this old body; it needs all the help I get for it."

"That wasn't your line last night."

"So? I go through changes, especially around you."

"Don't blame me for everything; it takes two to tango."

"Hey, am I awake? Mom said, 'never stray with an artist.' "

"Ok big guy, are you going to make with the breakfast?"

"I will if we use the melons you got cooling for a fruit puree, then I'll make some biscuits with cream cheese and brew black tea."

"I'll go to the deli; it's my turn. I've a treat in mind." She left promising to be back before I burn them.

I was just checking the biscuits when she rushed back in looking harried, with only the bakery bag and—a paper. I gave her a questioning look as I nodded at the paper. "What's wrong? Forget some money; there's some in my wallet on the counter."

"Your job has finally made an entrance into this apartment" she declared somewhat over dramatically, waving the paper at me mischievously. She said, "Take a look." as she held it still enough for me to grab.

"What am I, 'Public Enemy Number One'?"

"Well, maybe—or you might be yet, take a look."

I snapped it open and looked; this was a special edition with a single word, Jovia, making up the top third of the front page. She told me Old Charlie G told her he'd sold out his first delivery in twenty minutes; he'd only given it to her when she promised I'd sign it and send it back and that was cool. While I was scanning the lead story—mine, but with a number of comments and updates—she described the brouhaha brewing down on my floor. When the elevator had stopped there she peeked out, because of the noise, only to see cops interviewing neighbors, a pair of grim-looking suits, and more. I stopped ogling my copy long enough to focus on her as she mentioned that, in the foyer, there were reporter-types, a couple of cops, a guy in a gray suit loitering around, not to mention a three other, more sinister types, not-so-discreetly cooling their heels outside, each standing next to a black limo, all of which were idling expectantly. I loved her so much I almost told her, in my own sweet way. Instead, I grabbed her phone and called in. As it rang she cuddled close in to listened. I just love that.

"Hello? This is the News Dispatch, Editor's staff; may I help you?"

"Yeah, Maggie, …"

"Hold on," she said loudly before continuing in a whisper. "We've been waiting for you to call. It's like way hot over here; that story got a global bounce and … "

"What … "

"Well the probe is lost and some of the things in that story are starting to come true, except … well … where are you … are you safe?"

"Yes … "

I heard the old familiar sounds of switching, then the editor, himself, "Ralins?"

"That's me."

"Where the hell are you? I've got the police, NASA, MI7, half a dozen papers, along with a 'baker's dozen' of eggheads, all wanting to talk to you-know-who. How fast can you get down here?"

"Isn't my protégé there? He should be …"

"No one's seen him. He might'a been arrested for all I know …"

I doubted that. "I'm not far away but there's plenty popping over at my place, from what I've heard tell …"

"You should see it over here."

"I can imagine."

"Listen, one of our boys, Dan Rather, is at your place on the sly. Work up a slip, make a false pass—you know the routine. Get out of wherever you are, meet him, and get over here – without being accosted. I want everything you say only I want it first, see?"

"No problem, tell him to meet Jana at the D's, … DelRio's Liquor store. I'll have her… "

"Who's Jana?"

"Keep your hose out of that socket," I said to him, winking at her as she gave me a squeeze, "She'll recognize him."

"Where are you … never mind."

"Leave it to us; I'll see you in twenty."

As we stuffed food in our mouths I told Jana to look for good-looking, quite tall, Einstein-type of guy. A few minutes after she went out our plan went bust. Oh, I was on my way all right, but instead of sneaking into a cab or something like that, I was in one of the black limos getting the full siren treatment with a motorcade yet already. On the car's seat, I saw a competing paper, which had, apparently, shaken down the old professor. Their headline read: "Jovia Gets Hot." While, on the radio, a pseudo-expert, one of those who'd made a nasty habit of exchanging written arguments with me, was enjoying a moment of notoriety until he was embarrassingly schooled by an impatient NASA scientist who, fed up with the man's simple-mindedness, plainly demonstrated just how wrong he was, much to my amusement as well as that of one of the men with me.

By the time I arrived, in just about 20 minutes by the way, word had gotten out. There was a crowd in front of the paper's office, the street was jammed with cars, and a police line guarded the entrance. My entourage shouldered their way through the unruly throng as cameras flashed and questions were barked out amid a cacophony of cheers, jeers, and catcalls—the like of which is usual for a big story hubbub.

When we got into the pressroom it was a different story. After its weighty doors closed, the editor bellowed to squelch the chitchat, gave me a hard look, and told me to start talking. In a couple of minutes, I gave a synopsis of what had happened up until I was taken for a ride and brought in. I told them that the man they needed to hear from was little more than what might be an assumed name, for all I knew. I offered my notes to the editor but they were snatched out his hand by a grim grunt, if ever I saw one. He strode off to a nearby table and spread them out so groups of like individuals could crowd in to take a look-see and snap their micropix. A couple of the secret agent types got on the horn as a pair of gumshoes left quickly. I couldn't help the poor shlub who wrote that letter but I had a hunch that he had brains enough to outsmart them. I was about to start taking questions, when the doors were pushed open and two cops were being forced back, losing in their attempt to restrain Maggie. The chief bellowed for quiet and, trusting her completely, asked her what she wanted.

"It's Lovedraught, Jack; he says he'll only talk to you." This made for a bit of an uproar, and so it was my turn to shout them down. "Hey, hey hey! This is the man you'll want me to talk to, the author you've been yammering about or for." Well, they let me through to the phone. I was sure someone was listening in. When it rains, it pours, I guess. However, all they heard me say was "uh-huh" "Sure, sure" and a final "No problem" before he hung up.

I told everyone he'd be at this building inside the hour. He would make himself known, wanted access to media, and would explain his theory. In half an hour, several networks had installed their equipment, there was a lectern with a chalkboard, as per the man's instructions and we waited.

The man's appearance was in no way special, for someone who seemed to be in his eighties or nineties. However, his eyes were bright. He had a clear, vibrant voice. When the cameras went live, I gave a brief statement, before introducing the man who wrote now-famed Letter About Jovia, all the while I was wishing W were in attendance.

"The theory, being proved out for all to see, is the only important thing. It is why I'm here; I am not important, and the theory is that of my father, and his before him, who began the work. They'd be happy if they could be here, it is a rare moment, after all, as you shall see. Humanity's future will be changed by a sequence of events so distant from, and yet quite intimate with, ours. This solar system of yours is producing the first of four offspring…"

An uproar of confusion, questions, and shouting made his next minute or two unintelligible, but he did not stop for the uproar, rather he proceeded unheard until everyone just put a sock in it. From then on, all that could be heard, besides his voice, were the anxious scribbling of pens or pencils on notepads, the whirring of the cameras, and the shuffling of feet.

"…so much for the theories you currently hold regarding stellar initiation. History is being writ in the heavens, as you'll see. With the initiation sequence of Jovia, you'll observe and learn a great deal. I'll then clarify how each of the larger outer planets—Sitara, Urabne and Nosferatu

— will themselves go though an identical process at in the future and what that means."

"You already know Jovia generates heat, but cannot explain the other chaotic effects, which the first portion of our theory explains. As a planet approaches its optimum mass there comes a point when it evolves. What's happening now is just the onset of a change signaled by the fluctuation of Jovia's magnetic field and gravitational gradient, which coincidentally began as the probe arrived. The evidence from the fly-by provides proof of my ancestors' theory. The final result of this process is stated in the more cryptic, final portion of the theory."

"Explain that!" Someone spoke for all.

"Yes, what happens next is Jovia will begin to brighten as its temperature increases and the planet collapses. As this happens its magnetic field will increase in strength while becoming seemingly erratic and chaotic. Because of a reaction triggered by the incredible pressure at its core, Jovia is transforming. What you're seeing, at first, is the planet, a fuel source, being consumed."

"This, in turn, sets the stage for the next phase, the development of a stress point in the substratum, the fabric of the continua or aether. When the temperature and pressure pass a critical point, the substratum loses coherence and a temporal rent opens between the two continua. Through this rent matter and anti-matter react, and, as this reaction proceeds, Jovia increases in mass, size, and brightness."

"During the first brief moments of this reaction, Jovia's magnetic fields grow in strength due to an effect of the energy interchange between the matter and anti-matter continua, which is akin to friction. As this reaction proceeds Jovia will appear to fall away from Sul. This will be because, at that point, as a burgeoning stellar body, it will be fixed to its rift, and so maintain an absolute location relative to the gravitational affects of the rift and, to a lesser extent the relevant masses in both continua. During that time, Sul will still be moving in accord with the local and conventionally recognized influences of this continuum."

As Jovia's mass increases, so does its gravitational force and so soon the rent, being fundamentally unstable, will collapse and the two stellar bodies will soon settle into a binary arrangement orbiting about a mutual center with the normal rules of gravity coming into full force between the two stellar bodies. We'll then be living in a binary star system." He then shushed the murmuring and chatter "Hold on, I'm not even half way done, the best is yet to come."

"Oh, there will be some chaos out there to be sure; the shock waves from Jovia's reaction a will affect its moons as will its increasing distance from Sul. Some of those moons will stay with the planet, albeit at greater distances, others may be lost from Jovia, only to be taken up by old Sul or its remaining planets. It is possible Jovia may take a smaller outer planet with it, who knows. If all goes well, we'll see a new solar system created." There was a serious murmur but anyone speaking was shushed.

"How did your grandfather have any idea this would happen?" Someone shouted out what I—or everyone wanted—to ask.

"It was not so hard to figure the mass of the planet and come to understand that it is, in essence, a fuel supply awaiting a trigger for its core reaction. Jovia is simply big enough to do the job. More important will be the rupture of the substratum, which may only be a few cubic decimeters in volume and last but a matter of minutes. I do not know how my ancestors knew about the breach, the reaction, its intensity, or brevity; I only followed on with their work. It is this rent which allows a full-blown Matter/Anti-Matter reaction, unleashes vast amounts of energy, which immediately devolves into the most basic form of matter, hydrogen. Thus Jovia becomes a stellar body."

Our little professor took a drink, and then added, "The Aurora Borealis on Eard will be most spectacular."

Clearly there was more; everyone waited. "This new system will relate to our own, much as a parent to a child. Both bodies will have a common orbital center but the impetus, provided by the initial reaction, will give this new binary system enough inertia to sling it out of this galaxy."

"You have speculated that the universe began with a rupture in the continuum, where matter anti-matter reacted creating what you called The Big Bang, this same reaction still happens only on a vastly smaller scale when a star is born in the fashion we're about to observe.

"The bigger picture? All stars age. They eventually run out of fuel to sustain their reactions. When a star dies, it releases the matter it is made of into the void, where, as dust, it reforms into planetary bodies, which can, eventually, as we see with Jovia, go stellar. Every celestial body takes part in the cycle of mass accumulation and distribution."

"Any danger?" Someone called out.

"Oh, there'll be some heavy solar flares. I suppose when those happen folks who are inside shelters on Eard will be luckier than those who are not and comets and meteors will be chaotic. All Jovia's moons will be up for grabs too. "

"Your system has three other offspring yet to be born—Sitara, Urabne and Nosferatu. However, for them, the process will go much more quickly. You see, even though intergalactic space has less material, there's no competition for the that which is out there."

"Now, I want to get this done with. Please observe the blackboard." He turned to it, placed a dot on it, and said, "Your sun, Sul," then, an inch or so from it, he drew another saying "this is Jovia, its first offspring." He added a third dot, to form a triangle, saying, "the Sitara sun, and here, here, and here," He drew three more dots, each relating to one side of the first triangle, to form another triangle. "These are for Urabni, Nosferatu and the first grandchild." To this drawing he added six more dots, again each was placed so that it formed another set of triangles using the pairs of peripheral dots already drawn for their bases. "The next round of solar bodies—each of which will relate a pair on the previous ring, to form further triangles. Please understand this diagram is only an analogy, a two-dimensional model of a three-dimensional progression." Next, and more rapidly, he added further rounds of dots to each previous periphery, saying "These are the future generations if you will, grandchildren, or great-grandchildren."

As we watched, someone called out, "It looks like a pinwheel!" Another, "The pattern of water going down the drain."

The man continued on. "As you can see, by the tenth set, the pattern is similar to that of a spiral galaxy, not unlike the one we'll be departing from, or the one old Sul is the germ seed for."

He waited for a long quiet moment. "I can tell many of you have gone on adding more rings and can see what this means. However, there is more. I do want to finish." I wondered, as did everyone else; pencils stopped, everything stopped.

"One more thing has to do how life evolves, into, or toward, or through consciousness. As you know, your planet developed at an optimum distance from your sun, allowing life to evolve, but there is something else just as important. You can think of it as neural vector excitation. As we stand here on the surface of Eard, we revolve around its axis. The planet, in turn, orbits its sun, which goes about the galactic core. Then, your galaxy moves in concert with its local community and that moves in concert with its regional string, which moves in accord with its companions. All of these vectors have a cumulative impact on the manner in which electrons behave in a neural system, due to their special relationship via, to, or through the substratum."

"Without going into details, it is this set of vectors which creates, and/or enhances, the potential for consciousness. Your sun is within the bounds of the galaxy's own circle of life, where the vectors present support the development of intelligent life. This, too, is implied in the formula. What will happen, as your new galaxy forms, is there will be new factors, or vectors. First, because of your central position in your new galaxy, there will be a new balance, and/or counterbalance with all the others. This will affect the harmonies or resonances of the other vectors. Thus, will your descendants be fortunate beyond your wildest imagination. They will prosper in ways you cannot now imagine, and do so for untold ages to come. It could be that, in some six thousand of your years, there will be at least two habitable worlds within a few light-months of your Eard, as you may still measure things. Although the number of habitable worlds and their relative distances will grow over time, your compensating technology, or inherent abilities, will develop even faster as your neural systems continue to evolve in an environment free of the previous set of constraints. Your increasing awareness will dissolve the illusions that currently divide you from one another. The old will give way under the pressure of your development. There is no stopping this."

We waited for a moment, until we gathered he'd finished. There was a clamor of questions, ridiculous demands, or offers. During this pandemonium, he sidled over to me and said he would answer any of their questions, if he and I were allowed to take a quick break, in private, to talk first. Needless to say, once the boss man understood his request, it was granted, and the crowd would have to wait for a few minutes. The crowd, having no choice, stood and waited. We went into the maintenance manager's private office and closed the door.

"Well," I started, "how does it feel to shake their roots, not to mention everything I've ever heard of?"

"It's done now, here." He gave me a small packet of papers folded up in a complex origami-like fashion. His hands trembled as he gave it to me and he seemed unsteady, tired.

"What's this? Another formula?"

"I cannot stand this strain much longer. These notes contain the translation of the terms in the formula, as well as a few certain surprises, which, if you handle them right, with W in mind, should make you both embarrassingly wealthy; I believe your wisdom will grow with it. Not that the translation of the formula, and all its implications, will leave you a pauper, by any means."

"Why are you doing this; what's going on?"

"I said I wouldn't answer questions as regards myself. I needn't say anything."

"True enough and fair enough." I humbly admitted. He briefly added the note was more than a key to the symbols; it also had a description of a secure means to contact him.

He seemed exhausted. The excitement and attention were clearly too much. He'd lost what color he'd had. His voice was now a hoarse whisper, quite in contrast to the self-assured style he possessed just a short while ago. I put the packet in a pocket, took out a notepad, and turned to the table to write down my info for him but I heard the door close and turned to see he'd gone. I rushed over, yanked on the door, only to see quite surprised W about to knock.

"Did you see Lovedraught?"

"No."

"Wait; he just left." I said, glancing every which way.

He said, "Well, I just came from the back door and ..." thumbing in the direction of the pressroom where the crowd awaited, "there's only one other way he could have gone."

"I guess he wants to take some questions after all."

"Well, it seems pretty quiet out there to me." W said.

I nodded. "By the way, they're looking for you."

"Which is why I got here via the subway." He referred to the little known subterranean connection between the paper's main building with its annex across the street, ages ago it was a pneumatic tube station. "I'll bet we don't see the good doctor again."

Puzzled, I looked at him for a moment but let it go. "Well," I grumped, "I have to face music but you don't. You can hide and I'd advise it. I'll need someone on the outside." He nodded, we shook hands, and he padded off around the corner. I thought hard for a moment, shrugged, and strode valiantly back to the chaos however I was truly shocked when my man was nowhere to be seen. I waited nervously until the clamor settled down. I told them he'd asked me to be his interlocutor, agent, or representative. Again, I waited until they quieted. I began to improvise, to give my friends time to get away, but it wasn't long before they clamored for him and him alone so I said I'd go back and get him.

Two tall, muscular men shadowed me until I dashed into a different office, locked its door behind me, and slipped the packet in an old-time pneumatic mail chute. Wasting no time, the men shouldered into the door and it soon gave way. They were big loud men asking loud, hard questions but I stalled them until they got my number, understanding what I'd known all along, that the man had skipped. They hoisted me off my feet and hustled me back, giving me a few choice words to mull over. They handed me off to, what else, suits, gorillas in suits, even as a number of others scattered on a desperate manhunt. Feeling safe enough, as I was in public, I stood mute, no matter what was said, asked or by whom. After a couple of minutes, I was whisked away—into a supply room—patted down, frisked and, embarrassingly, quite a bit more. However, they didn't know about the packet and I still figured on getting it later from the so-called subway. It was easy to not tell them about something they weren't aware of and so I believed I was keeping Lovedraught safe.

Soon stellar events unfolded, pretty much as predicted, yet nothing could be found of the man. I imagined they'd be looking for him until hell froze over. I never once thought they'd find him. W was going to be disappointed, he surely wanted to talk to the man, as did I, at least once more.

Two weeks later, I was released. That whole long time I had a sick, depressed feeling because I'd heard how thoroughly the whole building was being searched. I mean everyone had been absolutely thoroughly examined before they were allowed to leave; there were forensics, microscope scanners, and readers, the whole nine yards. When I heard they'd found the subway I hoped my man had assumed the worst, bugged out, and was long gone. Then, even if they found the folded note, they wouldn't be able to find him. On the other hand, if they did somehow miss the note, and I was able to miraculously get it back, I feared it would be useless in terms of contacting him, for the exact same reason. I also worried about using the information as he'd intended. The only good news was there was no mention of my man or the note.

We arrived a home a day after I did; he'd been found and rousted a bit as well but he'd had even less to offer than I did. We both assumed our place was bugged, so while it may have sounded as though we were talking business deals, we were, in fact, using hand signs, notes, and more to talk privately.

In that manner, we discussed matters. I began giving him the lowdown regarding the note, and how I wished I'd placed it somewhere else but that stupid little room was only place I could get to with time enough to lock a door behind me.

In a coded fashion he replied, "Oh, before I forget: I'll be wanting to get back on that debt I owe you."

Puzzled, I stared as he cheerily messaged, "I hope to make for a very merry unbirthday for you" whereupon he slid the small packet of intricately folded papers across the table to me.

Then, in code, "I appreciate your thoughtfulness."

"It's the thought that counts," he coded.

"Now that's the most understated understatement I've ever heard," I signed. He nodded and, as he handed me something added, "And just think, it's only the beginning."

It was a simple note, less than fifty words. "Well," I said, "All I can say now is that other understatement was absolutely and wildly understated —and we're at a whole new level of understatement"

Tale, the Eighth: It Must've Been Moon Glow

This was 'it' for her, though she could hardly believe how quickly it had come about. Yet, here she was, going through the parcel she'd purchased and heading toward her discovery. It was a shame she had to be patient. While she knew the engines and life support of her vehicle would allow her to make the journey in a single go, she had to guard against the increased risk of inattention to detail, procedures, readouts, or simple drowsiness, any one of which could be fatal. In the early years of the moon's second colonization, a series of accidents, which would have been comical—except for their fatal consequences—made colonists aware of what they called time-drift. That's why she planned to drive only for ten-hour shifts over the course of three days. On the second day, she was well into her parcel, and determined to complete the journey after she started out the next morning.

Her Explorer had one non-standard piece of equipment mounted to its roof, a message rocket-launcher. She didn't want her backers or supporters to go unapprised nor did she want everyone on the Moon in on what she'd found. Message rockets were used when businesses wanted to 'go quiet' on a find. On the Moon, you could never know who might be listening, where that someone was, or what kind of a slip might sink a ship, so to speak.

Twelve standard days ago, she was happily exploring her newly bought tract of territory. While everyone knew this Moon was chock full of rich deposits, the first mines had all been located in or around deep craters, which had made such sense that this became a hard trend for the industry. She, in contrast to those who had gone for such low-hanging fruit, had staked her claim in a rare kind of up-thrust formation, between a set of large craters. While this had made for slow exploration, she'd already found workable deposits of a few things such as iron and copper but there was also silver. She was smug about her gamble paying off. She believed that thinking outside the box was going to make her fortune.

On a simple routine sweep she made her discovery and then quickly abandoned the remaining portion of the survey to beeline it for Terra-Crater —pausing only to get readings on a nice uranium find. Once she was back in town, she hastily set up meetings with a few well-chosen banking houses and investor groups. No newbie to financing, she sold off shares using the assessed valuation of her tract along with reasonable projections for a set of juxtaposed properties all based on the partial, yet very good, data she'd collected. She worked all the angles and the angles on those angles by setting up a shell company, run by the silent partners who controlled several parallel subsidiaries. These allowed her to lock down a majority of the shares, which were secured by a reserve based on promissory notes and extended to herself "ghost-capital" from another company she'd formed. She knew her secrets wouldn't last but when the money started rolling in her house of cards would become a mighty redoubt.

She knew all this sudden activity, referencing a single area, would be rare and that those who watched trade boards had her on their radar—this was to be expected. Oh, she misdirected, as was par for the course, and so, all to soon, and with only a small portion of the total at risk capital, she was ready for the windfall. She quickly fitted out a newer, larger Explorer and booked out before the proverbial dust could settle.

Needless to say, there was speculation as to what made the parcels so valuable. While she was publicly dismissed as one more gold-rusher attempting to bite off more than she could possibly chew, she also became the kind of person the more cerebral, observant types were keen to watch, perhaps reconnoiter, or more.

When such a person rushes off, well, it is to be expected that the curious, the adventurous and or avaricious, may well follow on. It could also be added that there would be a subset of those who were, let us say, more than curious, far too persistent, clever, and resistant to harmless hints. These became suspect of harboring unsavory motivations. Creatures such as they had to be taught proprietary law in a manner that would disallow them from ever violating her or anyone else's privacy again. Then too, and needless to say, a woman who is an engineer, explorer, and veteran of over one hundred space runs, knows how to arrange for unwanted trackers to have the kind of accidents that are all to common on the Moon and which happen, every day.

She awoke happily on the third day. As she hungrily prepared breakfast, the ciffex percolated in the autopot. She ate and sipped looking over development agency maps. She had approached her property from an unusual direction and used a difficult route through tough terrain in order to weed out the incapable or clumsy. As she sipped she calculated that by adjusting her route she could be at her discovery in less than seven hours.

Before pressing on she suited up and went outside to a signal dish she been setting up each night and alerted her DroneMaster at its station point above her. Then, from about as many directions, came a dozen GuardianWasps, each on loan for a thousand of as-of-yet unearned credits and using fuel like God knows what. She wanted to check their footage directly, on the sly. She gave a grim smile when she saw they'd stopped at least two casket-crawlers, of all things, after they'd entered her property and destroyed three hard drones. She smirked at as she watched a clip showing the demise of one unlucky Joe, on foot, imagine—who was crushed by an unfortunate avalanche of rock destabilized by one of her drones. She then reset the priorities of their mission parameters and loosed them to vent their fury upon any subsequent trespassers. These well-crafted devices, in the right hands, could be repurposed much to the demise of trackers, aka predators, and our sweet little gal was a marvel at tinkering with her toys.

What she had found on this Moon looked like a road, or rather one end of one, anyway, just inside her property line, which is why she'd had to secure those adjacent tracts. It was level, jet-black and, if not a road, well, it still meant builders, their remains, or ruins. Any of those eventualities suited her just fine.

There'd been puzzles. First, the roadway had an odd appearance. It wasn't just dark but absolutely pitch, as if it were an absence. To her eyes, the whole of it seemed to waver ever so slightly, as a mirage does—though to her gloved touch, it seemed solid enough. Still there'd been no way she could affect it materially nor would it read accurately with instruments or sensors.

According to the drones she'd sent to track it. The roadway went along the bottom of a deep, nearly straight, fissure for some ways. The drones had to navigate using the rock faces to either side because the roadway couldn't be read. Then too, the readings sent back were irrational. Despite their long flight times, none indicated going farther than a tenth of a mile. Worse, all of them crapped out, no matter how she adjusted their settings. Frustrated, and out of her store of drones, she'd cobbled together something that would race along the ground with a view-cam strapped on. She guided this by microwire. Although it also crapped out, before it did so, she caught a tantalizing glimpse of the prize, something unbelievable: a wide verdant valley with what looked like a quilt work of farmland, under blue skies. It was as unbelievable as it was real. The satellite images for the region were indeterminate, of poor quality or missing, no surprise there.

This time around, she was prepared to reconnoiter herself. Her vehicle could take anything—rockslides, radiation, you name it and, when she had some evidence in hand, the message rocket would safely get the word out even as the free ranging security units would keep her, and her claim, safe. Once back, the whole nine yards of financial jiggery-pokery would be triggered, and she'd set herself up as queen. Although she didn't know whether the road began or ended on her parcel, she knew fame and fortune awaited the one who discovered where it went. She was certain the parcels she had snapped up were where the find had to be. She was wily enough and darned sure nobody could deal her out of this game during the interim between fame, and its attendant power.

One could hardly say the drive was arduous, for the vehicle, structured like an oversized van, had all the comforts of home, a single bed, food unit, air recycler, and a stereo, which, even now, played Berthaybhim, as interpreted by one of those new computer musicians. All this belied the proximate environmental dangers outside the van's almost invisible Maxi-Plex windows. The pinkish atmosphere, which hardly occluded the stars even at high noon, was deadly in and of itself, not to mention being far too thin to keep anyone warm. It was no matter how innocently the occasional dust-devils appeared. She had stocked her vehicle with high-end food, the only luxury she allowed herself in anticipation of a prosperous future. Of course, she still maintained the surgical cleanliness of the mess, lest any particle of food or droplet of porter or wine set in any unlikely place, to spark a malfunction.

After about six and three quarters hours, she began noticing the gap in the echoes of the frequency signals, the kind any vehicle throws off and receives. This had been phenomenon, which led her to the road in the first place. Yet now, even after all her plans, hopes, and musings, she was unexcited. She stopped her vehicle and, for a reverent moment, stared at the dark strip leading away into the narrow defile and out of sight.

Confident, she set out. The mountains soon towered over her and she was in the absolute dark of the deep crevasse barely able to see the roadway, no matter how brightly she set the lights. She guided her course using the sheer rock to either side and sent out six variously reconfigured and reengineered drones, though only one sent back a fragmented video. Again, and for only a few seconds, she saw the valley overspread with farmlands, laced with roadways, and, sparkling in the distance, what looked like crystalline pyramids overtopping a distant tree line of jungle.

It wasn't long before she began an ascent and then the roadway leveled off. Moments later, she saw a brightening ahead. She noted the data conflict showing that, although the odometer read over thirty miles, she'd hadn't gone a hundredth that according to satellite readings, which fluctuated from near zero.

She stopped, to have a celebratory meal. She ate a chicken salad sandwich, some RealFruit, and MixyJuice. At first, she ate hungrily, then paused because of a slight savory flavoring in her sandwich. She put it down and grabbed a second, ham and cheese this time, but it too had the same flavorful accent. She opened both to examine their contents. They looked as though they'd been sprinkled with pepper, which was odd. She used a magnifying glass and, upon this closer examination, saw the spots were a varicolored mould or fungus. This was not supposed to happen to Moonfoods products. Disgusted, she wrapped both of them up for evidence, and chucked them in the freeze unit. Fortunately, everything else stored there was just fine.

She sighed, decided to drive on, and soon came into the open. She was glad to catch sight of the moon's slight atmosphere sprinkled with stars, the neutral, off-gray of its soil, and the mystery road leading directly ahead to a slight rise, where she could see a much brighter bluish-white glow beyond.

She reached the rim of the great valley. The atmosphere below was thick and deeply blue. As she began to drive down through a cloudy layer, the cool gray-colored stone gradually became covered with a green patina. Farther down still, the green thickened into a mat and then was combined with outcroppings of what appeared to be coral in a wild array of colors and phantasmagorical shapes. When she descended below the clouds, she could see the varicolored verdant landscape, appearing much like her home world's farm country.

The glen she entered was lush with knee-high grasses. The aquamarine sky above occluded the stars. The road ended and she drove on slowly until, as she rounded a bend, she caught sight of a woman with two children, frolicking in a small roadside meadow.

They were wearing white smocks, barefoot, and dancing. They stopped as did she. The children ran over laughing. They pranced about the vehicle and delighted in the sounds they produced by rapping on this or that part. Their vocalizations, words it seemed, were nonsensical sounds; but their playful attitude was all-too-familiar. She looked up the woman walking slowly toward her vehicle. Slim and beautiful, she had a graceful, fluid gait. Her demeanor was calm; her look bemused. As she stepped along butterflies rose from the verge and became a distraction for the children, who gleefully ran off chasing them.

Feeling safe, she opened the hatch of her vehicle, sniffed fresh, wonderful air via her filters, verified it was viable and clean, and removed her helmet as she mentally recounted the universal first contact protocols.

In a moment, seemingly, she was face to face with the strange woman and, uncomfortable, took a step back to then stand stock-still. The woman held her cupped hands together and made a motion, as if offering something. Puzzled as to whether the woman was attempting to communicate, or making a symbolic gesture of greeting, she watched only. Then the woman's palms began to glow. In them, out of them, a glowing blue sphere took shape. Parts were marbled green and grey, others a misty white. The colors moved or swirled. Transfixed by its beauty she felt no fear of the woman who held it aloft above as they both looked to it.

However, in an attempt to regain self-possession, the would-be-queen began to purposefully blink as she examined the woman's face. It was classical, eternal. The beautiful woman began humming and the queen looked away from the woman's radiant face and utilized every trick she knew to clear her head and calm a mounting excitement, even as she began to feel very comfortably warm and drowsy—as if she'd been drinking wine. As if in a dream, she was again enthralled by the woman's musical murmurings, looked her way, and became entranced by the colors of the woman's dazzling eyes and the indescribable beauty of her skin and facial features. Then, suddenly face-to-face, they searched one another's eyes. It was all love, all clear and simple. The woman continued singing as the once hard businesswoman, now saddened as forgotten, unwanted, memories up-welled for the now melon sized globe had become a fount of long lost memories.

She heard the wind come up. The distant tree line was in slight motion and beyond was a gem like brilliance. The two children clutching bunches of wildflowers came running back in dreamy slow motion. They held the flowers up to her and from the bouquets a few bees lazily flew off in the now heavy, languid and redolent summer air. Then the woman turned to sashay away continuing to hold the globe aloft in one hand. She, who would be queen, dreamily followed on. The woman then stopped, turned, and stared as she let the globe rise slowly, as if a balloon. There was smell of sweet grass in the breeze, the laughter of children, and then the sky about the globe blinked into a deep black even as she reached through a memory of the woman's face toward the beautiful sphere. Her outstretched hands failed to reach what it became, her home planet's blue, cool beauty. Then there was a rushing sound as if of ocean waves—was it wind tearing through grasses? There were flames all over her and a blinding flash.

Helmetless, she died quickly and fell, making almost no sound. During her last spasms of pain, she turned on her side reaching toward her vehicle only to see it rapidly crumpling into itself as small points of light and shadowy spots danced all over it. It was just a few steps away. She was in a tiny crater, not even a half acre in size. Its steep sides surfaced with those colorful corals so beautiful. She saw their colors change wondrously.

Now, the soil, on the other hand, was activated as never before. In a matter of moments, the harvesting of materials was well underway. She and her vehicle were quickly reduced and repurposed. The bacterium-sized members of the collective worked from the both inside and out of her and her machine. An observer would have seen that, gradually, both seemed to descend into a thickening carpet of dust, or multicolored ground-hugging mist.

That night, there was happiness in the most unlikely of places. In what would seem to off-worlders as something very much like medium-sized shallow pond, holding a picturesque, yet distinct, illusion of quilted farmlands on its gently rippled floor, where, in the tiny misty forests overspreading the periphery, brilliant jewel-like pyramids overtopped the deep cool green. There, in their beautiful tiny little sky, were brief minuscule flickers of light, akin to what a firefly might produce, fireworks some might imagine, winking here and there. There was also sound, not unlike that of fragile wind chimes, as they might be heard in a mid-summer night's dream.

Psalm 875 "Outlast"

outlast the stillness of frozen air on a dead world
glistening dust forbidden to the touch
around me the hills of the "new world" ripple the horizon
this was not the world we sought

outlast the ageless void all about
for as far as can be seen
even the naked stars seem to draw the heavens close about
confining me intimately

outlast
those first few minutes
lucky to be in a suit when we hit
and able to build the hut—as I call it
by sealing a ruptured fuel tank
furnished with scraps from the ship
parts and pieces
carried by hands and muscles swelling up
skin breaking open   being burned by the cold
the suit not made for this kind of work
outlast the heating and air circulation units
and the abundance of stored food
enough for a thousand for two years
all well preserved in the absolute zero
outlast the bubble I live in
outlast the rocks black with burnt wreckage
outlast the horizon and the quiet
outside my heartbeat
outlast
the time I have

Tale, the Ninth: A Farewell to Arms

It was a Thursday afternoon. As he drove home, he was looking forward to a sweet little three-day. He and his family had arranged a camping trip to spot a little north of Big Basin. They wanted to explore a portion of the area that would be new to them, perhaps sign up for the naturalist tour of the coastal forest, or do the crest trail again.

Before he'd finished work, his wife had called asking him to get a few things at her brother's store in Glen Park. She was still preparing for the outing because her day had been disrupted by a call from her mother. It seemed every time a new educational technique, method, or device was in the news his wife, Alice, would get a call. Although it would start out innocently enough, often it would devolve along familiar chaotic lines. It was fortunate her family was not within visiting distance.

As to their trip, being talented planners, they always made allowances for delays and chaos also, as he was coming back into town and planned to make that stop, he decided to swing by Café Bouef, where they'd met. On a whim, picked up a kitschy souvenir as a surprise for her, a small crocheted heart. It was similar to the one they used to leave around the apartment to surprise each other when they were first married—cute. He knew she'd love it.

He and his wife were successful, and lived in a home they'd bought on the west side of Twin Peaks. Although he was originally from Colorado, he'd been disaffected from his family ever since he moved to New York City in order to study public interest law. Now, living in San Francisco for the last twelve years, he was enjoying his success and that of his wife, who was a city supervisor and investment counselor for non-profit organizations.

They'd met at the cafe on a rainy Saturday. He'd gone into work to clean up files and case notes left in disarray by a notorious partner in the firm he worked for at the time. Back then, he wanted to "show his worth" to the firm and move on up in it. Feeling tired he'd stopped at the café to get a Giant's espresso to go; it would perk him up for the drive home and, in the unlikely event that someone should ask him out, he'd be up for it. When he walked in, however, he saw the local jazz legend Daniel Hefez with the renowned Nova Jazz sliding easily along through a great old standard. He gave his regards to them all and decided to stay on. He couldn't believe the place wasn't crowded and then, when a couple of men offered to buy him a drink, he went to join them.

Back then she'd been working at Bird and Beckett, a bookstore in Glen Park, only a short walk from the Café. She was a regular there but that day she walked in with a couple of her women friends. They came right over and joined the two men. Although he had been surprised, he quickly understood that this meet up had been pre-arranged and he was good with that!

In the years since, they gradually told each other the whole story. She'd been somewhat embarrassed to admit she wasn't very interested in him, at the time, because her friend, Joyce, had set her up to meet one of the others. He told her he'd only been invited to sit with them because someone hadn't made it. Also that he'd been very attracted to Joyce. At first, he used their friendship to get to know Joyce. As it turned out she had little interest in him and, when she moved to the East Coast, Alice became more and more interested and interesting—a long story there. After a time, both of them found in the other the mellow, soft-spoken kindness and deep-seated caring that each had been seeking in a partner.

In the three years preceding their son's birth, he'd been joyfully surprised at the stability of their relationship, as well as their capacity to meet each other's needs, and handle difficulties; many of their friends could not say the same. They both knew how to converse over a wide range of topics, each in their own way, which made for long enjoyable discussions. They were also interested in theater, dance and, when cooking together, they shared recipes. They derived satisfaction from involvement with their community, the arts, their library project, and with educational issues. He had always been an avid reader but this was one of the areas where she surpassed him; it was also she who organized and managed their private library, for fun and profit.

Their first major disappointment was discovering, shortly after their son David's birth, that she would not be able to have more children. Both were disappointed as they'd intended to have four or five. For a time, Alice became depressed and he thought she feared he would leave. They found help, recovered, and soon their relationship was as healthy as ever.

They underestimated the impact of caring for a child. Each of them learned to reorganize their professional and personal schedules. By the time David was two people were usually moved to remark upon his precocious ability to communicate, question or comment, and his musical talent was praiseworthy. As he continued to reflect back, he smiled at how hard it was for him to believe David was now nine and already giving ample evidence of his own tall, lean body shape, while David's rounded face, high cheekbones, dark eyes and luxuriant black hair were a credit to his mother's French-Iroquois descent.

Pleasant as his reverie was, he became annoyed by the snarls of traffic he had to work through and was stressed by the time he pulled into the market's parking lot. Then he had more discomfort because he didn't look forward to an encounter with his cynical, archconservative brother-in-law. Luck was with him, however, as the man's son, Aaron, was the one behind the deli counter. They exchanged pleasantries, he asked after Alice, and then went to make up the order.

He was embarrassed to see how easily, nay, automatically, he'd lied to the son, just as he would have to his father. There had been a change in Alice. He had been noticing a sometime reticence and quietude and believed it had something to do a party a few months back, a celebration for Joyce, who had just come back into town. He noticed, on that day, how she was quieter and did not fret about the usual things—how she looked in this or that, or if certain pieces of her outfit went together—as she usually did, when expecting visitors or going out.

Then, after dinner, just as the coffee and cake were served, Alice excused herself. After a while, he wondered what was taking her so long so he excused himself and went upstairs to their bedroom, where he found her weeping uncontrollably into a pillow. She said she had no idea what brought it on. She said she'd kept quiet about being uncomfortable, even depressed the whole day. There was sadness or ennui, yet she didn't think this friendly occasion was the cause. She had excused herself in order to avoid making scene, which might have the guests wonder about their marriage. He asked her if she was concerned about Joyce but that only made her laugh, which he'd taken as a good sign. She had him go back down and tell everyone she'd made a phone call and had lost track of time. He felt assured that, for the moment, she was all right. Later, after she rejoined the party, the celebratory mood of was restorative and everyone left smiling. However, when, a week later, one of her long-time friends, mentioned Alice's quietude and another brought up a bout of her crying at work, it was clear that something was going on with her.

He began to pay closer attention and saw a pattern of moodiness that evolved into a behavioral complex during which she'd appear tired, pale, and her expression was flat. In such a state, she was hardly conversational. These moments began effect the family. He noticed her sleep was disturbed from time to time and saw that this was a sometime precursor to her mood swings.

They discussed the matter, though these talks yielded mainly descriptions of effects but not their cause. They came to see patterns in the distress. The most common was an onset of ennui, combined with growing sense of futility, which he'd notice when she'd unexpectedly put aside whatever she was doing and go off by herself, quietly, without giving notice. Alternately, there were periods of near manic excitement, as if some great event was about to happen. Sometimes, there were physical symptoms; she'd say it was if she had butterflies in her stomach, complain of chest pain or aches, as if she were in mourning. No matter how an event got underway, at some point, she'd decline into a languid attitude that invited sleep. If such rest did not relieve her symptoms, sadness would then predominate as a precursor to, upon occasion, the uncontrolled sobbing. It would sometimes take a few days to recoup altogether. Counseling provided some relief, in that they learned how to cope better but the cause remained elusive. Neither of them was interested in drugs.

However, fortune intervened in these affairs when David, in the course of describing a school assignment, had his parents organize a camping trip. The family's outing was to Alpine Lake up in Marin County. They enjoyed it so much, they began to go out for day trips during weekends, and camp every few weeks. Though bouts of moodiness persisted, there was now a counterbalance of truly good times. She could return to happy mode and their lively discussions, now including their son, were the best ever.

He was brought out of his moody reverie when Aaron called him over to pick up his order and he was soon on his way.

As he pulled into traffic, he tuned on the news. It was bad, as usual. Japan and China were finally discussing internationally disputed claims to the sea floor, though in angry tones. Both agreed to let the U.S. mediate which, apparently, surprised everyone. The Muddle East, as he called it, was still consumed by interlocking or overlapping wars involving almost every nation in the region, one way or another; however, it was all relatively low key. In the middle of a story about treaty talks he switched to an innocuous talk show.

What with the errands she'd asked him to do and the traffic, it was early in the evening and clouding over by the time he got back. He wondered if they'd be rained out. Alice was very pleased with the gift; replacing as it did something precious that brought back fond memories. She was glad that he'd remembered the anniversary of their meeting. He hadn't, but took the credit for happiness' sake.

They chatted amiably as they carried supplies to the car. On the last trip, down he brought the charcoal and tent, she the sleeping bags, and David the lantern. When he opened the trunk, he saw another bag of charcoal and more boxes of dried food and concentrate. Puzzled at this unseemly and substantial stash, he asked why she sent him to the store if she had all this already. Before his eyes, she grew pale, and her whole posture slumped, as if she were terribly tired or suddenly ill. She offered quietly that nothing would go to waste and there was room for what they had.

He, suddenly chilled by this change, put on a cheerful air, and said they could keep the extra in the car, it would make the next trip all the easier to prepare. When she smiled, even if it was somewhat nervously, he was relieved. David, seeing a chance to chip in, mentioned how, with the way prices go up, she'd been a wheeling-dealing smartie-pants. She brightened and laughed heartily. Later, on the sly, he gave David a high five for the save.

As he finished he'd arranging things in the back seat and trunk, she brought out their treasure chest, a deceptively small jewelry box containing over half a million dollars-worth of valuables, as of the last assessment anyway. She said she wanted to bring it along because some things could use a cleaning. Although this was not part of the plan, he told her it was a great idea, but added that he hoped she'd go on some of the hikes, and she said she would. Everything was fine again. They turned in early to get a "zero dark thirty" start.

Driving along the next morning they played "themes." Each took a turn naming a theme and then everyone would take a turn singing some portion of a song matching the prompt. They also played word games and twenty questions to pass the time. They stopped at Alice's Restaurant for brunch and looked over maps of the park to pick a campsite.

They arrived about noon. She began to prepare their first meal on the hibachi, while he and David got the tent up and arranged all the essentials inside. They all played "What's My Question," a family tradition. Each person crafts a secret question and the others, by making statements, mentioning names, dates, places, or objects, are entitled to a yes or no response—depending on the relevancy. Then, by virtue of the data gathered, the "puzzlers" as they're called, come to know what the question is—but more often they don't, still its fun. Soon they all enjoyed her veggie kabobs and hearty pea soup. After dinner, they played cards until the sun went down, then talked or told stories.

Alice and David went into the tent first and let him stay up to police the camp, and take some time to watch the fire and the night sky, something he enjoyed in particular. It was a calm, clear night; the smoke rose directly up showing not a trace of wind. He wasn't sleepy. He enjoyed the quiet and the occasional cool breeze, through the still, warm air.

After a while, he went into the tent to tell Alice he was going to back to the car for some supplies. He was completely blindsided by her drawn, teary-eyed and morose expression. It shook him badly, and he must have shown it, because she told him she was fine, really. They hugged sincerely, although he was very unsettled and thrown for a loop. As he left, she suggested he take his time. He said he'd return after a little bit; she murmured that he could stay up if he wanted, but not to forget the hike they had planned for tomorrow.

By the time he reached the car, he decided to go for a drive to settle down. When he hit the highway, he turned north toward San Francisco, but soon was quite alarmed when he saw an exit sign for Highway 92. He hadn't thought he'd gone anywhere near that far, but what far stranger than that was the absolute lack of traffic on both sides of 280.

Next, as he was blinking back sleep he got the fright of his life when his headlights glared back at him from a wall of fog that seemed to have a glow to it. He pressed the brakes slowing to a crawl and drove cautiously into the fog straining to see clues or signs for the next exit. He became worried that he would be worrying her. To check the traffic, he turned on the radio and received, amid bursts of chaotic static, someone reading a list of cities: Buffalo, Chicago, LA, New York, as well as a few others he couldn't make out. A moment later, when he rounded a curve, static overwhelmed every station so he turned it off.

Moments later, he hit the brakes and swerved to avoid a vehicle that had been left athwart two lanes and seemed to have been abandoned. He didn't get it at all—it wasn't damaged and if it had run out of gas, why hadn't they coasted to the side of the road? He pulled off, got some flares out of his trunk, and placed a couple in front of the thing. He still planned to go back, yet didn't want to abandon what could be dangerous situation.

After some time with absolutely no traffic in either direction, he tried but could not move the car. He lit another pair of flares and drove on into the fog, but it grew progressively opaque and he couldn't be sure if he was passing exits or not. Then, of a sudden, the roadway was choked with abandoned cars. He set out his last three flares, one for each lane, and went back to his car. He turned on the radio only to hear static all up and down the dial.

Curious, he walked into the massive pile-up. Many were not wrecks; they'd been abandoned and some had been vandalized. He went further on, wondering why no help had arrived. He was startled when saw the first bodies strewn about. He looked back to his car for reassurance; it was still there with its flashers on. There wasn't much he could do; he headed back to it.

He was close on to it when he heard what had to be a large, angry-sounding mob, approaching from the south. He hurried to his car and was surprisingly out of breath as he clambered in. Just then the first salvo of stones and bottles landed all around him. He started his car, turned off its lights and drove slowly. He wanted to get back to his camp and avoid the mob. He drove on to the open meridian to get onto the southbound side and crept along as the fog was thickening quickly.

A sudden blustering gust of wind shook his vehicle terribly as it cleared away the fog. He saw what must have been a hundred ordinary looking, but very angry folks advancing his way, they charged, as more objects hit the car. He panicked; hit the brakes, as he looked for a way out. He froze. Some bottles smashed near his car. When two of them burst into pools of flame, he was still indecisive and unmoved.

Then, jolted by two gunshots, he feared for his life. The mob, having spread out across both sides of the roadway to block his passage, now began to converge on him. All he wanted to do was to get out of there but couldn't decide. They took advantage of his caution. Some jumped up on the hood and roof; another smashed the driver-side window and tried to wrest control from him. Someone tried to open the door. In his mind, he imagined this wild, crazed mob attacking his wife and son. The windshield shattered; something heavy hit him in the face. He couldn't see well. There was a sudden fierce, stabbing pain in his shoulder, and then his upper arm. Nearly blind and in a rage, he put it into gear, floored it, and the car jumped forward. He couldn't swipe his eyes clear as he drove through the crowd.

For what seemed like minutes, the car jostled over what had to be bodies of who-knows-how-many people while, to either side, others, violently slammed aside, screamed in pain or with rage before he raced off swerving wildly. It couldn't have been long before he was slowing down on quiet empty pavement. After some minutes, he pulled over, cut the engine, and stood outside to get a hold of himself and clean up a bit. The night was quiet. He steadied himself by checking a few constellations, but the ones he knew were in their right places at least they were OK.

He got back in and drove but it was odd; how very quickly he was back in the park without remembering much of the drive. He parked the car, locked it up, and went in haste to his family. He was exhausted, trembling from the shock, rage, and fear. But there, inside the tent, was his wife, so beautiful in sleep. She began murmuring one of her pet names for him and, as he slipped in beside her, she cooed softly and embraced him so sweetly; he happily blacked out.

He woke up inside the tent, forgetting for a moment, the trial he'd been through. There was no slash on his arm or bump on his head. There was no pain. He could hear his wife humming outside as she put together breakfast. The radio was softly playing classical music. He got up, dressed, went outside, and told her he was going to check the car. She nodded, adding that breakfast would be ready by the time he got back. He had to be sure the car was all right. If it was, then everything was. There was a history of sleepwalking in his family. The dream had been incredibly detailed and vivid. He was glad to see the car was undamaged and right where he'd parked it yesterday, when they'd arrived.

On the way back to camp, he recollected his dream and wondered about the symbolic meaning of the drive, the thick, glowing fog, the congestion of cars, the bodies, the crowd of mad, frenzied people from whom he had to escape, and why they were all dressed as if for work.

The smell of bacon was in the air when he came back. Instantly, he was aware of his tremendous hunger. The breakfast satisfied him, but he was distracted throughout it, as he mulled over the dream. He was sure David and Alice noticed, but thankful that both were patient and allowed him some quiet time to sit, eyes closed, relaxing in silence, as they finished eating.

David broke the quietude, asking to explore the stream near their campsite. Alice gave her permission but warned him not to go in beyond mid shin depth, for the water was swift. David walked off along the pathway following the stream. After he had been gone a few minutes, they put out the fire, began washing dishes, and got to talk. Of course, he began to talk about his dream as he dried the plates. He laughed at the absurdity of the whole thing but when he turned to hand her a stack of dried dinnerware, her pale face and shocked expression told him he'd said something significant; although he knew intuitively this was not the moodiness he had come to know so well and dread.

"What's wrong, did you see something in my dream?"

"You didn't mention about the cities?"

"What cities?"

"Buffalo, Austin, Chicago, LA, on the radio, you know, before the static."

Now it was his turn to be shocked. He sat down at the picnic table she had just cleaned. She sat next to him and told him, as he'd begun to talk about the dream, it was as if she could see the whole crazy scenario on a movie screen in her imagination, except the part about the cities had been left out in his account. She went on to say she hadn't been sure until he told her about the escape he'd made, the jostling of the car over so many people. That's when she knew it was a reoccurring dream of hers, and one that she'd been having for some time, which she hadn't been able to consciously recall until now. She believed that she'd kept it buried, because she'd been unable to reconcile her love for him with the murderous intent she'd seen in him in that dream. He asked if there was anything else and she mentioned the two Molotov cocktails. There was a moment of silence before she, in a moment of insight, said she knew the dream had been a presage to her mood shifts; she was sure it had been the cause they'd never found. Then, oddly, they both said, "a war is coming."

They looked into each other's eyes; it was a strange moment—the quiet day, the sunlight on her face, with the soft touch of her hands on his. They decided to go back to the city. She went off to find David while he decamped. He was sure he could get a couple weeks' worth of vacation. Alice, not willing to waste even a moment's time, challenged David to a footrace to get back to the camp. It was good to see them both smiling. During the drive back, they told David about the cattle ranch and farming operation his cousin in northern Wyoming had and their new extended plan. He was very excited. The uneventful drive back went quickly as they worked most all of their plans.

When he came home late that night, he'd secured sets of emergency supplies, two months for vacation, and she'd parked the Winnebago she'd rented in front of their home. As a family the finished packing it up with everything, and they had plenty of space for the precious books and microfilm library. They set their alarm for four-thirty a.m. to avoid the traffic on northbound Highway 1. Before they turned in they both looked in on David.

The next morning, they were quick and quiet. David was difficult to wake, as usual, so they bundled him up and put him in the Winnebago, where remained fast asleep. They tucked blankets around their beautiful sleeping son, and swept his silky dark hair off of his untroubled forehead. They were ready to go, when, annoyingly, Alice remembered one more thing. He smiled widely when she came out bearing their oversized family album.

As she locked the door behind her, he remembered how they'd stood there years ago waiting or the real estate agent and appreciated their slight view of the ocean. That view had been something they both enjoyed as they had breakfast and was a factor in selecting the place. She held the album to her as she descended the stairs. He stood by the Winnebago as the idling vehicle's exhaust drifted off in the slight breeze. He looked at her lovingly, as she stood facing him. They looked into each other's eyes, for a moment, before taking hands. "John."

It was not a statement, nor, for that matter, a question. He didn't answer, save to hold her hand a tad more firmly. In her eyes, he could see the reflection of this young and beautiful city stretching out toward the sea, under a smooth, still, silver-gray overcast. They sighed as soft mist began to slowly drift down. As he looked at her face, flecks of it settled into her dark hair and twinkled. She put down the brown leather album as the sirens began. They had a precious moment as they stood now side by side looking out to sea. For a moment, a dear precious moment, as a tear brimmed at his eye, they pretended, musing as if it were the sun brightly piercing the distant overcast to brilliantly illuminate the Farallones and then the whole of the Pacific. They closed their eyes, turned toward each other, as a warming breeze came on, strengthening with each heartbeat, each thought. They embraced as they kissed themselves goodbye.

Psalm 13 "Gone"

Into this ancient city the sands have settled.

Up high in the night's sky
The broken moon   hangs
As if waiting for a cloud.

Under its cold light
Drafts play in the dust
Between empty buildings
Which glare through darkened doorways
Or jagged misshapen windows.

There are still people here   hidden
A sparse few
Of the once millions.

Who sees this shadow
Moving back and forth
Among the ruins
A solitary figure
Indistinct and furtive
Long after evening has turned into night?
Lonely   only the sky tells the hours now
At the calling of a lone bird
That shadow turns   with its man
Cold branches
Are picked for their combustive potential
Though this place will not be home
It is finished with people
The vast array of buildings and streets
Is quieting
Whispering its very last breath
It is   a city of sand
With a grief as vast as its silence
Someday – soon
No one will know of it—no one will do the telling
Or ask to hear its song

Which is why the figure is as mute as its shadow
And chooses to wander
So long as choice remains not choosing
Thus, there is no home in this city
Fast by the great peaceful sea
Only ill scented drafts – touch
What has now become a stranger to hands
Where the curling whistle of wind
Sometimes seems the only calling
Of what might be a name

Armageddon   comes in
on little cat feet!

Psalm 435 "There are ages"

Which come and go
Lands that vanish   with their peoples
When seas wander them over

Time does not speak to us of these creatures
Time   does not speak to us at all!

It has heard   we are deaf

It would signal
But it has heard   we are blind

It would do a song and dance
Give us the whole nine yards

But it has found
We are not at home anymore   on this world
And Time knows it

That's why Time is going its own way now
Leaving us   to ours

If we were wise   we'd take heed   ask after it

But we aren't   wise that is   and so we won't
And it's not as if   we haven't, for the longest time
Seemed to care   one teeny tiny bit

And so now   well, now   time has run out
And it is all on us
Oh, by the way
Do YOU hear that fat lady singing?

Tale, The Tenth: At Your Service

My name is Dermann and I will tell you, at the outset, that I am contented, fifty-four years old, and in an untroubled state, both because of my well-deserved position, as for my health. Before I began working for my current employer, Sachrosan and Dowr, some four or so years ago, I worked for the respected Drehd and Graves of Manhattan. I left my promising situation there, as I had no taste for vicious office politicking, or continuous infighting; not to mention the slow pace of advancement, which was an anathema to one as superbly talented and vigorously intelligent as I.

Once I began with my current employer, my advancement was rapid, thanks no doubt, to their quick attention to, and reward for, high quality work, such as that which came to light when I played the starring role in a major anti-trust corporate litigation, the renown Tom Dooley portfolio. From my dedication to that case, I built a reputation, which led me to the position I enjoy.

In the business world, my career has reached an acceptable plateau from which I can easily survey the orderly routes of certain ascension to the lofty peaks of rigorous portfolio management, thence to the gentle vales of contemplative partnerships, and onward into misty vistas of transnational currency exchanges.

Being well placed in the upper echelons of the formidable company for which I work has its rewards. I could afford the classic renovation of a two-hundred-year-old farmhouse in my company's village, just outside Dwighton. I love the place; however, I'm not yet a year-rounder. But I will tell you, the autumns there are the best, the cozy valley ablaze with gold and red, not to mention, the stellar hunting and fishing. The jewel of the holiday crown is Christmas, the one holiday I always spend there, visiting my neighbors as we celebrate the bonus season, as we call it. At that time, the populace reverts to the use of horse drawn sleighs as a practical alternative to the almost useless autos—captured as they are by snow drifts which often mound garages, easily erasing distinctions of lawn, sidewalk, or street.

The town, in stark contrast to this pastoral winter scene, boasts a completely modern airport, capable of accommodating the jets executives use to keep in touch with the frantic, outside world. For the most part, the town has kept to the easy, rural ambience of visiting, community house-raising, and such like. By common agreement, the relationship of the town to the valley harboring it, is one of respect. You see, only a very few persons are allowed to settle in ever; oh, it's quite exclusive all right, absolutely the top drawer!

My fondest memories are of my childhood days along the bank of the Crissom, the creek meandering through the valley, where the town and the few others, were founded on gristmills –some of which still operate as a legacy-businesses, as well as tourist attractions. "Up the Crissom" takes you to an isolated plateau, covered by a rich, vibrant virgin forest, where, in Five Springs Canyon, the Crissom has its source. That is also where the company lodge is set, a center of robust masculinity; camping trips begin or end there. While you may argue as to whether the fishing or the hunting is better, I think that's comparing superlatives. I very much enjoy the fact that there is always some kind of hunting going on. This is why everyone wears bright orange jackets when visiting the lodge. Why, just last month, Franz, the agent who used to work the territory I've taken up, was killed, and his manager wounded badly. Oddly, neither had had the proper gear on; it seemed they mistook each other for game. Poor Franz, he had been living there for just two months with his new bride. Of course, she was taken care of—so beautiful, but that's not the point.

Such is the town I hope to live in when I retire up, or "arrive" as we call it. When I am there, I pursue my own forms of leisure, the constructing of finely detailed, electronically controlled, models of historic steamships with hand made engines. The practical side of the hobby is selling models, except my favorites, at craft fairs, or in the tourist shops of the mill towns.

My only other passion is the study of card play. I may boast of a reputation so terribly proficient that I rarely play any locals or company men. I must prey on visitors or tourists at The Cloverleaf, the town's only inn. If any of them should naively boast of his or her skill at Keane's Saloon, the regulars there, who enjoy setting them up, will finagle me into a game whereupon I old school them much to the glee of onlookers. However, the main reasons I play are, first, my enjoyment of figuring probabilities; in this pursuit, I can exercise my considerable mental acumen. Second, as I learn to read my opponent, my intuition is tested and last, there is nothing like contesting the limitations of human capacity and what better way to sharpen one's wits than by pitting them against the cold laws of chance and the chaos of raw human nature? As I see it, the profitable results are a measure of my ability to circumvent odds and to read my opponents – valuable skills in the insurance trade, believe me.

One other thing, my secret talent is hypnosis. I can determine when someone is prone to susceptibility, not everyone is, but I've become very skilled at initiating and clever in my commands. Therefore, when I can use it I do so and to near magical effect betimes.

At the moment, I'm far from my quaint, handmade stone hideaway outside Dwighton and on a road assignment. This will be my second trip into Franz's old territory but my first into San Francisco. It was a nice Tuesday afternoon on a brilliant, postcard perfect kind of day and I am enjoying the drive south on scenic Highway 101.

I will admit I like money, admit it easily. My desires in life have always required a substantial amount of the gelt. I find the pursuit of wealth quite fascinating—the ways to earn it, or manipulate it once you have it, seem endlessly variable. Therefore I, in point of fact, have a difficulty sympathizing with those unable to attain the means of their own subsistence, who wind up impacting their family, or becoming a burden, hanging off the teats of society's underbelly, but they, or their issue, are of no import to a self-made man such as I.

I calculated I'd be in the city at just before nine, drop by the office, and be able check into my suite by ten-thirty or so. This will give me time to make certain arrangements and place the usual discreet ads in local papers. I'll have plenty of time to do all that before for my first appointment, a luncheon at the Hyatt Regency Gold. However, the salient business of this trip will be the completion of old affairs, to be specific, those of Mr. John Temple.

The man has turned a ripe seventy-eight years old and lives as unobtrusively as anyone in my sort of business could want. He's retired from his rather successful real estate firm; however, as with most self-made men, he prefers to keep his hand in. His history is simple. He was the only offspring of Lorne and Mya Temple and has lived his whole life in the city of his birth. He believes he has a special affinity for the town. According to Franz's notes, if you ever get him started on this topic, you would be fortunate to make your next appointment—even if it was on the following day. The basis for Mr. Temple's mystic connection is that all of his grandparents were immigrants that arrived in San Francisco by misfortune and that his parents were both conceived in the chaos following the '06 earthquake. Then, although his parents grew up in the neighborhood of Lotta's fountain, fortune played its hand, by bringing them into each other's lives when they were arrested at Chinatown's infamous underground speakeasy in the basement of Li Po's bar and grill, back in the day.

Mr. Temple has always been strongly independent and, never content to live in his father's shadow, he joined the Marine Corps in 1967, chomping at the bit for military action. His career was quite the success. I ought to mention his capacity for leadership and bravery was complimented by his perseverance. These factors led to decorations, as well as field promotions, culminating in a captaincy.

When he came back home, the family business was distressed. He and his father came to terms and thence to one of our banks for a loan. We, of course, sent out an agent to arrange the requisite insurance policies, which made sense at that time.

Mr. Temple soon proved to be the brain of the outfit. After repairing and redirecting the family business into a lucrative carpentering and interior work firm, they expanded into contracting before venturing into various real estate investments and developments. It was this last, which proved to be the man's making and is the source of his current fortune.

My main interest in his affairs focuses on two points: one, a recent examination revealed a congenital heart defect, which has become noteworthy of late, and, two, he has never has been covered for personal assault. The latter is not an oversight. At the time of the policy's last renewal he was forty-six years old and still in the habit of extremely rigorous exercise, participating in marathons, wrestling clubs and addicted, or so it would seem, to self-defense training. According to company files, he thought extending the policy to areas wherein he could well look after himself, was an insult to his independence. Ah, the man has pride. To my immediate predecessor and myself, Mr. Temple's most consistent characteristics were parsimony, stoicism, and pride.

"All these years," I said to myself, checking the rear mirror as I switched lanes on the Golden Gate, "and he hasn't bothered to deal with a little clause so now, now, he is seventy-eight. Well, well, well." I know I was smiling; it was just this kind of detail that caught my quick eye.

The man himself was, according to most intelligence reports, in very good health; however, as this was now in question, my strategy in the affair was, to some extent, predetermined. A simple investigation of his apartment to examine his papers, to do a bit of revision, rearranging or replacing, would clear the way for real profits. This wouldn't be a problem; after all Mr. Temple was a man of schedules.

I stopped by the local office to get updates on my intended and picked up files on a few others I could also close out during this swing through the Bay Area. I checked into my hotel, went to my room, and gave the paperwork a once over making mental notes. There was no real news as far as Mr. Temple was concerned. He still resided at the building his grandfather bought before the turn of the century, 3075 Oak Street, a stately white and blue Victorian—a classic of the pre-quake styling. For him, the place must represent continuity; it has always been home. As an astute only child, he must have understood he would, by inheritance alone, always live comfortably, as did his parents. He now rented out the lower two floors, after a recent and extensive remodeling, to persons who required professional workspace. Although this presented some unfortunate complexities regarding plans, there were work-arounds; there always were.

Mr. Temple usually slept until ten, when he would be awakened by his clock radio, always set to a classical station or soon thereafter by his apartment's buzzer—the postman always rang twice to signal incoming personal mail and but once if there was none. This was the only area in which his meticulous weekday routine seemed flexible. My client was of the opinion, and I agree, that classical music soothes the nerves and makes the transition from the slumberous depths to waking easy, gradual and engenders a contemplative disposition, much suited to the kind of man Mr. Temple fancied himself as being. According to the file, his tastes ran from Ravel to Liszt. After rising, he then calls the office to confer as needed with its management. My client leads a calm life, as is his wont, in privacy.

While Saturdays were variable, Sundays were not. On that day, he sleeps precisely until noon before taking a walk in Golden Gate Park. For some reason, he always visits the Children's Playground; this last bit seemed evidence of sentiment, for my client had never married—a salient point, which invites lovely little options that would otherwise be off the table. After walking, he returns to his suite, opens all the windows and, while several powerful fans thoroughly air the place out, engages in ritualistic practices, a program of isometrics, and calisthenics, all of which were integrated into fighting styles and practices. Next, he observes his physique in a full-length mirror mounted on the wall near his bed. As often as not, he takes up a handheld mirror to examine the qualities of his aging facial physiognomy. This process of self-examination complete, he showers, dresses, and then breakfasts on fruits and his notorious homemade bread.

By description, he is six feet five inches and weighs about two hundred pounds. He was, due to his regimen and diet, slim and sleekly muscled. In the photo I have, his face appears calm, even sedate; his brow, however, did not suggest excessive intelligence, nor were his gray eyes particularly bright. His face was drawn. Although one could see the foundations of a strongly featured man, one would never say he was handsome. All together, he appeared ordinary, even simple. Only his half-smile gave any hint of success, yet it was but a half-smile. There was no indication that the man was cunning and clever—his trademarks in the world of business. The social affairs to which his status entitled him were studiously ignored. This was the man "in a nutshell".

I closed the file for a moment. I had been reflecting, if this was a typical case, how rich a territory this must be. Again, I thought of Franz's untimely death; were it not for that, I would not have this great opportunity.

I looked over the files currently requiring service on this tour, such as Mr. Temple's. I could see why Franz had been awfully busy and well regarded. My new stomping ground had many possibilities. I was so lost in a reverie of calculating the estimates of my future income that I would have forgotten my appointment had not my wristwatch alerted me. I quickly secured my briefcase and left for my appointment.

I mentally checked the schedule for next day as I walked along, mulled over the advertisements I had placed, and developed a few ideas for Mr. Temple. I was so pleased with myself, as usual, that I hardly scowled as I waited to be seated with my appointee.

I was taken to a table in the main dining area, near the fountain, an open location, yet one that would certainly obviate any eavesdropping. The man, a Mr. Davidson, had taken the liberty of ordering fruit salad, hot Earl Grey tea along with melba toast and a small reserve of wild orange honey and a sliced lemon. I was pleased he'd taken the time to gather accurate information regarding my preferences. I like an eye to detail. Our talk was amiable. Over our salads, I apprised Mr. Davidson, in detail, of the loopholes in Mr. Temple's policy, described the pattern of his habits, as well as the wording of the ad I had placed. When I had disbursed the foregoing intelligence, I was complimented as to its precision. I related how it was not I, but one of our operatives who had observed Mr. Temple, in preparation for my visit. Mr. Davidson nodded before requesting some clarifications on certain details thus indicating he was a man with good follow-through. When I, in tones of closure, asked if he had any further questions, he only recited some salient points regarding Mr. Temple's outdoor activities and wanted to be sure he had them aright, or if anything else that came to mind —an excellent workman he.

We agreed that the Sunday strolls in the park were the most reliable and most easily accessed window of opportunity. Here, for the first time, Mr. Davidson smiled. He said he'd have the applicants chosen by the afternoon. I told him that would be fine. I asked if he thought the whole case could be wrapped up by this coming Sunday and I was assured, given the accuracy of the provided intelligence, the correction would be in place by that afternoon. We finished our meal, shook hands, and parted. He, having connections with the management, took the check.

"How pleasant," I murmured to myself as I mused on the several appointments I had, each with their forms of built-in flexibility, so to speak. Thus, I was in a cheerful mood. If this was the man to be my counterpart in this territory, I could look forward to a productive relationship.

As expected, my liaison man, Martin, was waiting in the lobby of my hotel when I arrived. One of the ads I had placed had been meant for him. It was I who told him of Franz's death; although I could tell he was not in the least concerned, though he uttered a few pleasantries, which were dutiful and respectful. He was a stocky man, focused on practicalities, who just wanted to get the job done. We talked while we went over to an interview room Davidson had setup in a motel in a seedier section of the burg. At two p.m., our first man entered and, by four-thirty, we had our team. I was assured their training would be accelerated to accommodate the timeline. Of course, they were pre-screened for mental manipulations and, once under my spell, nothing they'd seen, heard or were told would stick with them. As for blowback or collateral damage, any such would be obviated by the paternal relationship they had with Mr. Davidson or his family not to mention the dossiers held on each applicant—the usual triple lock.

After the interviews, I went on to tackle the appointments I had made for this run. The first was a somewhat dramatic example of human error or frailty. One of our insured had been devastated by the death of his wife in an auto accident. He was in need of consolation—and a policy review. My plan was to insinuate myself into his affections with a dramatic show of my consideration and concern then allow how sincerely I regretted presenting myself after his recent difficulties, that I knew how it was, and so on. I would mention Franz, if need be, and have my tear juice ready. Actually, the unpleasantness works for me, as there really is no better time, in terms of client receptiveness, than to insert oneself into a client's intimate affairs during a period of unprocessed grief. According to our eyewitness accounts, and authorities agreed, although it seemed some kind of simple mechanical failure had occurred, it was not possible to determine any cause from the burnt and ruined remains of the auto. Driver error was therefore cited as the primary cause, which mightily mitigated our outlay. The man's wife died in a loophole, as it were, again thanks to Franz. So far, this case, as a whole, was small potatoes. It was projected to generate about seventy thousand dollars. Now, I liked Franz, always had but was a bit annoyed because it seemed to be typical of him, going for such low-key approaches as a default.

I timed my arrival at the man's home to be just after the dinner hour, when most people are most agreeable. I introduced myself, empathized with his loss, and decided to doubled-down on his reaction by letting him know, I too, had lost someone, my dear friend, and his insurance agent, Franz. As we cried on the man's doorstep. I was prepared to lie should he ask for details about Franz, however, he did not ask. In a matter of minutes, I had him suitably entranced, engaged his trust and we were sitting in his kitchen talking-story. To an observer it would seem he brought up his of his role in the liability and asked me to go over his policy then and there. I was tactfully heartfelt when I told him it would be best to learn from this tragedy and protect his loved ones completely. The whole affair took less than an hour and a half. I actually had the annoying little man thanking me for my concern and sincerely grateful for all I had done for him. I managed the meeting very well. He signed policies for himself, his daughter, and son. Each contract had some pretty clever turnkey elements, if I don't say so myself. Later, I would have the firm's accountants schedule the conclusions of these cases. I looked forward to a hefty appropriation procedure, which would more than make up for the day's paltry take, when the time comes, one must needs be patient.

Next was my opportunity for one solo performance. This was a sixty-seven-year-old woman, an invalid, who was living alone. She needed various kinds of coverage, despite her relative vibrant health. By the time I had returned to my hotel, I had closed out the file on her. She was immune to my charms and there had been no compromising. The ensuing fire not only eliminated any responsibility our company had; but garnered a net, only some five figures really, so it was hardly worth the time.

After I got back to my suite, I showered, shaved and I called to see if there were messages. Mr. Davidson had called. I got in touch with him and was pleased to understand the Temple case would be wrapped up early Sunday. This meant I could get the papers in order ahead of time. I told him I'd have the relevant data to him, by messenger the next day. Also, on Friday, Mr. Davidson saw to it Mr. Temple went out for the evening. As he went out, I went in, rearranged his paper work, and secured banking and ID information, before faxing the revised documents to the home office. I had a brief, very nondescript phone call with Mr. Davis and all was set.

Thus, by one o'clock, the next day, most all the business on this part of my tour had been concluded and I looked forward to a night on the town. I went to various places in North Beach, and managed to strike it lucky, picking up an impressionable and very susceptible, twenty-something-brunette, well that's what she said her age was. In exchange for drinks and dinner, I had everything I wanted of a typical night on the town. I utilized one of my favorite personas—a recovering retiree who has reformed and was fortuitously ready for a reentry into love. She, I think, actually enjoyed my conversation and the persona I had used often enough—she said so a number of times. Her reaction would have been effectively engaging, even flattering, had I been the person she believed me to be. This unusual factor not only added to the sensual delights we shared, but also heightened her distress, deliciously enough, when I dumped her after a sumptuous breakfast, leaving her with the exorbitant tab for the meal as well as the hotel. What made it all the sweeter was the shocked expression on her face not to mention her tearful offers to make things up somehow. Still, her sincerity was a surprise; it was as if we'd had a relationship or something. I guess people still take marriage proposals and cheap, plated rings seriously in this modern age—how hugely sad.

I drove off to San Jose in a jocular mood, happy as a clam in rich black Mississippi mud, with time enough for another couple of appointments.

San Jose was a quick success as were the two Oakland appointments. I was driving through the wine country, Sunday morning, when I thought of Mr. Temple. As a matter of practice, I often visualize my clients in their demise; it's my way, allowing me to feign compassion, as needed, in any follow-up procedures.

If all my arrangements had progressively harmonized, Mr. Temple, John, would have woken up to a familiar, quiet scene in the master bedroom of his home, the room where he'd been born, after all. In its confines he had, memories, continuity, nostalgia, and, in all probability, romance—his father's, if not his own. It would seem to him an ordinary, predictably beautiful, Sunday with every reason to take his constitutional, as it might be called.

I saw, in my mind, his prodigious capabilities in the art of self-defense and the passionate hate with which he'd regard his assailants, chosen with that in mind, of course. I had bet Davidson that he'd fend off or disable, the first two, those who'd drawn the unfortunate lot to approach him frontally. I could see him splattering their flat noses, smashing in a mouth or two, before delivering practiced, crippling body blows and maybe finishing one of them off with a calculatedly murderous kick. However, we do plan well. He'll have no time to defend against the person coming from behind; they'll grapple him off balance and get him to ground. It was a set performance piece, you see, no matter how successfully he defended himself, there was a fourth in waiting, who would then finish the business and or see to it no one talks.

The reports would read he was dead at the scene. The witnesses, as could be expected, will hardly give chase to the youths who will pile into a waiting car, which will then speed away only to be discarded and found some time later, or not. The police will have no way of making an arrest and the stolen car will be a dead end. Our man, John, had neither relatives nor anyone directly concerned with the disposition of his properties. The police would, therefore, only do the usual. The nice touch was that one of the youths would be seen losing money, a nice sprinkling of fifty-dollar bills. This will serve to distract any who pursue the youths and cover certain bases. Mr. Temple was known to be a man of substance and those dropped bills would only serve to emphasize this inconvenient fact.

At four p.m., I got word the case was closed, with all the loose ends tied up and buried. I figured to net fifty percent of the fiduciary investments, which had been made with the premiums, as is usual with our accounts. That could be as much as six hundred thousand dollars but the big action— the company's hold on the estate—would net ten times that.

My last stop in the area is near Sacramento. A client there has had trouble with fires in his paint store, two in the last eight years so I figured one more wouldn't garner any real attention. After that I'll lay out a covert operation, which will work him into a financial hole. I expect to wrap up a real gain out of this paper loss after only a few months time. There would be proceeds, from what would then be an unclaimed estate and it would be my department, which would benefit handsomely, very sweet deal.

Postscript

Well, you have to "go figure"—the man in Sacramento was not susceptible and a bit stubborn, as Franz would put it; however, the take was a whopper, some four hundred thousand in cash, hidden just where my expertise would find it, in a wall safe of all things. "Whodduh thunk it" as they said in the old days. It was with this case that the light went on and I came to understand Franz's approach. What I had thought was a simply formulaic, or chintzy, style of default processing, was actually a quite efficient method for plowing through the sheer number of cases he had available for processing. I did underestimate poor old Franz.

I flew out of Sacramento and was soon on familiar highways driving home to hearth and kin. It didn't diminish the joy to have a cool fortune in the trunk of my car; I felt great. Once off the main road, I went along the two-lane, calling ahead to let them know I was coming home, and yes, I bragged just a bit. Then, oh then, I was told, oh sweetness, I could just drive through, that I was, expected, that they looked forward to my…arrival. Yes, the man used those two key words, arrival and expected. I was made!

With about five miles to go, I could not have been happier. I picked up my voice recorder to dictate ideas for a new kind of holding account and then I left a message for the Syrianan Group, telling their secretary I would like to schedule some fairway time as soon as I got in. I told her which approach I was using and my ETA so she could streamline my entrance procedure; I wanted to breeze on through, just waving to the guards. I felt I could use a good round of golf, get a dinner in, and soak someone at cards, before imbibing some high spirits.

However, something in the rearview mirror caught my eye; it was a company rig, a diesel truck, hauling a large propane tank. The idiot driver was closing so I sped up to put some distance between the swarthy, brutish troglodyte and myself. I was pulling away but when I glanced in the mirror again it was to see a flashy, red sports car pass that truck—sheer madness on this winding mountain road! When it flew past me, the driver, a stone-faced woman in a Hindu headscarf, was staring ahead fixedly; her silvered sunglasses reflecting only the road ahead. I thought of my wife and how I miss her so. I thought I saw someone hunkered down in the back seat but I couldn't afford give more than a glance as they sped on by. Then they slowed as they approached the well-known hairpin. I too let up on the gas and tapped my brakes

Then, rounding the next easy turn, they gave it the gas as did I, figuring to get the license number and report them. I could see the gateway of course but to my surprise, an old motor home came around the last curve in the road; its brakes squealing as its driver, weaved alarmingly, desperately trying to slow down. When he swerved into my lane, we both slammed on the brakes and barely avoided a messy collision—the bloody idiot! Quickly, we both began to maneuver, I backed up to give him room and he turned sharply to his right to get his lumbering behemoth back onto his side of the road. Very impatient, I looked ahead and saw that the red sports car had pulled onto the overlook in front of the gate. I heard laughter —her laughter.

That's when the tanker truck smashed into the rear of my car jamming my font end into the motor home. I hammered my fist on my horn and screamed at the jerk as I signaled to him to back away, but then that damned monkey-of-a-driver, in the mobile home, stupidly shifted into reverse and suddenly lurched my way—I don't know what he was thinking. I screamed at him as he screamed some garbled swarthy Indian gibberish at me.

I swore—the idiot was still blocking my way, his motor sputtering; its gears grinding and clunking. Then, the tanker truck behind me, backed off however its bumper, locked with mine, caused my car to pivot so my front end lifted up and faced the edge of the road. I shifted into reverse and floored it. There was a roar of growling gravel as smoke and dust flew out from under my back tires. I heard the squeal of metal straining on metal. That truck driver backed up breaking off my rear bumper. Royally enraged I fumbled at my safety belt and began to open the door. That's when the truck lurched forward, slammed into my car, and over I went, falling into the thin clean air. My car and I spinning as we fell. I had time to see the company logo on the motor home. For a moment, I could also see the red car and my wife waiving at me. I had no idea who was standing next to her but I knew she was going to be very lucky, very wealthy, and suddenly available.

Tale, The Eleventh: The Wake-Up Call

Of course, the young man was asleep at three-thirty in the morning; thus, he did not hear them enter. When they flipped on the light it was quite the shock; for a time he was disoriented and couldn't see. As his eyes adjusted, he saw six men surrounding him guns drawn and showing badges. They were silent. One, with an earphone, said, "We're good to go." Another grabbed the man's clothes off a nearby chair, casually tossed them onto his bed saying, "It's time to get up. No talking. Zip it."

The astute young man dressed quickly, his intuition telling him they men didn't know why they'd come for him or where he was ultimately going. To them he was an ordinary man in his early thirties, an office worker in downtown Nova Francia—very single, easy going, quiet and nondescript, well, except for being six nine.

They took him outside to a waiting car. As soon as he was inside they handcuffed him and at least two kept their guns on him at all times. He didn't talk. He noticed two identical near the one he was in; one soon took the lead while the other followed. The young man was groggy, for he had spent himself wildly at a party. He had totaled his teetotaler body, or nearly so. He guesstimated he may have had an hour or so dead sleep. When one of the men held up a bottled of water he took it and drank of it greedily. He was going to ask for a second but as soon as he began to move his mouth he was gagged and completely restrained. He had no options or moves. One of them said, "We'll remove the gag only if you agree to remain silent." The young man nodded vigorously and the gag was unceremoniously taken out. They gave him more water, some pretty good breakfast sandwiches, and great coffee.

They drove to he city's park and onto its equestrian field, where a helicopter awaited, rotors turning. He was given over to another set of men, apparently with the same orders as the first. As soon as he was secured in a windowless compartment, they took off. Minutes later they landed at an airfield where he, along with twelve other new men, boarded an unmarked airliner. They went on what may have been be a cross-country flight; however, all the windows were closed. Hours later they touched down for a layover and a new set of men replaced the others—again they flew off for some hours.

When he finally deplaned, it was at an abandoned landing strip, which was nothing more than a long stretch of weed-ridden, poorly maintained pavement and, off to the side was what must have once served as the field's office building but which would pass for a large one-story ranch-style suburban house were it not for the set of decrepit gas pumps out front and the large, poorly maintained, and oversized barn-like building covered with corrugated tin in the rank field behind it. The setting was about as rural and nondescript as one might like. This facility had clearly stood unused for decades. They walked him over to the small boarded up office and entered through its unlocked door as the sun was coming up.

There was a jolt of motion underfoot and sudden noise as the floor around us began to descend and went down more than a hundred yards until a doorway appeared to rise up in a nearby wall and, when it was fully exposed, the movement stopped. They all just stood there and dumbly waited.

When the door slid open it exposed a hectic military headquarters in full operation. He was baffled and evinced confusion though he wisely remained mute. It seemed his presence caused a buzz but it wasn't a happy one. As his entourage walked by they ignored the unwanted attention. The young man saw some stop what they were doing to stare their way, others, clearly exhausted and bleary-eyed, looked his way impassively while small sets, of the hard-boiled variety, muttered amongst themselves in a manner reeking of cynical antagonism as they cast hard looks his way. All in all, he was glad he had no ability to read minds.

He hadn't broken the law, at least not to any extent making this scenario reasonable. They led him out of that room into a long corridor, boarded a kind of open subway car, and rode it for half an hour. He was quite at his wit's end, resigned but patient. In his mind, there had to be some soon-to-be obvious, yet humorously improbable error, in which he'd been taken for someone else.

They disembarked from the subway. He was transferred into the care of just one man whom he followed silently across a deserted concrete landing. Together they walked into a small concrete room with a single, ancient light fixture dangling from the ceiling. Silently, he was directed to sit on a plain metal folding chair in front of a bare steel table and that man then left.

Not a minute later three other men entered silently and sat down across from him impassively. They, too, seemed weary and were somewhat disheveled, appearing as thought they were running on fumes, as they used to say. The men looked at one another and or towards him and their disappointment was as clear as their disgruntled disposition. One frowned shaking his head.

The tallest cleared his throat and tossed a photo of our confused young man out on a table, "We know who you are, it's ok to talk here."

Hesitant, the young man replied, "Apparently."

The young man studied his companions and waited. The man who tossed the photo on the table, looked past him, signed to some unseen person saying to that person, "Get ready."

He then looked at the young man. "Believe it or not, we are following your instructions; you'll continue to be silent now and follow directions."

Then a gravely voice behind him said. "Diacritical emblematic introspective hyper-awareness." Instantly the young man slumped into unconsciousness. Then, after a moment, he sat erect clearly in a hypnotic state. The same voice added, "You will close your eyes and then stand. You will follow the men; one of them will guide you." He felt a heavy hand on his shoulder and complied with the directive.

The young man believed they were soon in another chamber because it became quite cold and there were echoes with a notable delay. The young man snapped his fingers, timed the result, and wondered all the more for there was nearly a four second delay. They went up some stairs and waited a moment before he heard a groaning metal door open. They continued on until he was told to halt. He did.

"Very well," said the tall man, who seemed to be in charge. "Now, in a moment I'll give you the command to open your eyes. When you do you will only look forward at what is in front of you and read the text to yourself, silently. Open your eyes."

In front of the young man was an open metal container with some kind of intricate machinery and complex wiring inside. Apparently, someone had etched his name and address on its open access plate along with a brief set of instructions which, as the tall man had said, they'd been following. This was why he had been brought here. One of the men turned to him "You get it now?"

"Of course. Please … had there been any other way … "

"We got that," one of them growled.

One of the others said, "You got in there, ruined the guidance system of this missile, fused some components, and rendered it inoperative. Yet you were not physically present here. Well, you got our attention."

"What about the money? The ten billion in credit, that's what I said."

"We got it arranged and, however much good it will do you but you'll have it once you make good.

You know," said the third, "I'd thought the whole idea of psychic arts to be that much bullshit—I mean praying to move the lesser moon, or deflect a satellite's orbit, all that crap. The only reason you are alive is you said others can do what you can do."

"I got that. Yes, there are; however, you'll never find them; even I cannot. We are not happy with things the way they are. We feel it's time for a change, if you'll look at the inscription, for example, you'll see it's not my handwriting but I was here, so to say, and recall watching the letters burned into place and dictating some of the instructions."

"I won't ask how it is done,"

"That I couldn't tell you, for the life of me."

"It may come to that, soon enough, but I have no say in anything. So, you can knock out their warheads?"

"Of course, I've that kind of range, I can take out every darn one of them."

"You could do this now if we asked it of you?"

"Sure."

"Why the offer, I want to know," said the only man who had been silent all this long time.

"Someone has to win this stalemate but without a war. We only want order and peace. We, those with my talent, can make a difference; we have chosen you to be the winner. We thought this the best way."

The tall one said, "let me make a call." He stood, walked to a door, opened it, went through, and was gone for about less than a minute. When he returned, the young man was saying, "… that part of the directions was the most important. I had my own programmed instructions. You see, I don't really know how it works, so I had to cover myself. I redacted and suppressed memories in order to create a complete alter ego that would decompose after I heard the key phrase. If anyone had made mention of a fission device or fusion device, I might have visualized one and set if off by accident; it's very tricky, you know…"

"I've the okay from the highest source; here is a map of the locations, per your instructions."

"Are you all ready?"

"Anytime."

The young man told them he'd need complete quiet, and so everyone just sat and waited. It was a several minutes before an officer hurriedly walked in, went over to the tall man, and whispered. That man blanched, sighed heavily, slumped back in his chair and covered his face with his hands.

A moment later he growled, stood, reached across to the young man to shake him out of it but the young man was deeply unconscious and completely unresponsive. The man shook him harder and slapped him twice. The others pulled him back as the young man's body fell onto the floor in a heap. The tall man let the rest of them know what he'd just been told. "All the nuclear reactors in the world were in meltdown and the world's arsenal of nuclear weapons had either detonated where they sat or were well on their way toward targets.

In the following long, long minutes, during which the world, as they knew went up in nuclear flames, they sat absolutely stunned in their very secure room. They could not, did not react. Rather, they sat looking down at the young man, who remained as impassive as stone. There was nothing to be done. Everyone in that simple concrete room was in a state beyond grief.

In the greater world, billions of lives expired, were expiring, or expected to expire, as there the three men sat, staring at an antique wall clock as its second hand swept over numbers. Things would never be the same. Finally, the young man came to with a start and, realizing some kind of error had occurred, let out a sigh. He knew it would all improve, eventually but, more importantly, he wondered if he would leave the room alive.

Psalm 313 "Long after time – what is?"

Long, long from now
When all that is now   is forgotten
More than simply buried in the mind
Or the earth
More than simply covered up
But gone
Truly dissolved through the immense passages of time
During which the Earth has completely reformed its surface
And is done turning under its continents

When every human thing has vanished
Beyond all hope of ever being found
When no living thing recalls our peculiar smell or fear
And life has recovered all that was lost.

When all that is now
Is absolutely gone
Beyond anyone's knowledge of what once was
Is or might yet be –

Long after time
When there is no forgiving
Or forgetting
When the quiet world simply rests
Through its long horizons
And the moon casts down innocent light
Where winds are gentle
And the forests have come back into their own
Long after
Long, long after all that we've dreamt of
When even the greatest of our myriad possessions
Have been broken down into the smallest of grains
And so, have become part and parcel to the earth
And each is simply moved by the wind or the water
And all has been absorbed by
And recycled millions of times
Through plants and animals
* The living carpet that life is upon this world*
When there is no evidence of any kind
When matter is so purified
Until purity is no longer a relative term
And all is well.

Long after time has gone
When it is no longer a measure
When measuring is no longer needful
When counting is as forgotten as numbers
And sense is a term applied
Only to the eyes, ears, tongue, nose or touch.

Long after time   what is?
What will be?
When peace itself is the only thing
And nature is let to do what it does best
After the recycling of all that we once were
Has erased all the details

Leveled the playing field
Once and for all

Long after
Long, long after time
What is the chance
That the Earth will decide to try once more
To weave spirit into matter
Manifesting such illumination
As brings consciousness into life
And if not in human form…
Then certainly with a prayer that this time
Its promise will be kept!

Tale, The Twelfth: The Journeyman

In this country, we tell a story about a magician and a journeyman. The magician, as might be expected, lived in a quite ordinary manner unworried by need. His humble, but comfortable, dwelling was near to a friendly village and it was common for the inhabitants there, and those of the neighboring farmlands, to consult with him. You must not have any grandiose notions about magicians, for in those good old days of the last age, the requirements of the people were simple. He could tell the weather in advance, knew the stars, herbs and roots, and could make medicinal treatments in concert with the wiccans. Further, with access to all manner of books and the rare ability to read, he had a practicable knowledge of many crafts. His library allowed him to consult on most any project or problem that arose. Yes, he was no miracle-worker, by any means but he was still well worth a visit. Then, to top all that off, he would often barter for good food, handiwork for his home, chores, and wine, of course. Then too, so many folks came and went there that his place functioned as the community message board and post office. Also, because a number might be seen sitting there a spell in the shade of the sentient trees about the abode, he or his place, were the local source of gossip and news from the greater world. He also enjoyed matching up goods for services between his friends and neighbors; these arrangements of magician with a given county were quite common in those halcyon days of yore.

It was just before Burning Man, an annual gathering of magicians and musicians. A particularly jocular journeyman, seeking work in the aforementioned village, happened to pass magician's place near mid-morn. The gay young man, being trained in the art of glasswork, couldn't help but notice a collection of glass works on display in the front window of the magician's house. Intrigued by what appeared to be a master's work, he did not hesitate to present himself in order to become acquainted or, better yet, known by his lights and common ground.

It is said the magician opened the door before the man pulled on the polished oak knob to signal his presence. In any event, the young man, taken aback for a moment, announced his name, his trade and, as was the custom with countryside magicians, the elder asked if he could be of service.

The lad did not mention the purpose of his visit but rather, in the old-fashioned manner, asked about the prospects for his trade in the area. There ensued a leisurely talk over some invitational tea, which the young man accepted only on the second offering, of course. After some easy conversation, the youth acted as of to notice the dozen very excellent glass pieces on display and asked who had made them.

When the magician indicted he'd made them the young man, in exception to common courtesy and custom, gushed with questions as to his methods, as his mind raced, excited at the chance to apprentice with such a great master. The youth was disappointed, as the explanation did not make sense. The works hadn't been made in the ordinary fashion. Seeing disappointment in the lad, the magician offered to show him how they were made.

Imagine the delight of the journeyman as the magician then clarified, in some detail, the process for making these gently delicate vases, containers and glass ware, simply by placing some finished piece, as a catalyst, usually called the "tutor piece" under his pillow, along with a piece of Trillian crystal, and the material—a lump of furnace glass for example—from which a new piece would be made. Then, explained the magician, he could direct the shaping of a piece in a dream. In the morning, the creation would be complete. Needless to say, the young man saw his fortune made before his very eyes and wanted nothing more than to try it out. However, to make up for his prior rashness, he said only he'd be interested if there was time.

The journeyman arranged to spend the night with the magician after proffering a respectable measure of coin, which the magician accepted—out of politeness, even as he silently resolved to make the usual charitable arrangements in accord with the custom regarding community windfalls. The young man was certainly no slacker; in the remaining portion of the day he went to the village where he crafted a few samples in a demonstration of glass making done in the customary way. Primarily as an introduction but he sold a couple of pieces and came back happily with some gold and silver change. That night the journeyman followed the magician's directions for the evening's dream work.

Immediately upon waking the young man searched for the new piece under his pillow. There he found the magician's tutor piece and another, his own creation, a thumb sized flower vase, made entirely out of emerald—that being the seed stone he'd chosen. He could not believe the beauty of the piece. It far outshone anything he'd ever seen. As he held the small, slight vase up to a window the light streaming inside brought into view the complex and subtle designs which appeared on it or through it. They put him in mind of a breath of spring air, redolent with a floral scent. Why, one almost heard the humming of bees, just looking at it. However, as the gem had been quite small the miniature was extremely light and fragile. He was quite surprised when it shattered as he ran his hand over its lip. He was disappointed but only for a heartbeat as he thought of the admiration he'd get once he brought his new talent back home. Why he'd be able to propose marriage to the renowned Gloryanna, support a family, and become a man about his bergholm.

When he breakfasted with the magician, they talked of the method. The magician then chanted under his breath and the young man's mind was flooded with memories from his dream and the detailed instructions the magician had given him in that state. He couldn't contain his questions; the magician only smiled, instructing him to finish his meal and to take rest, in order to allow much more to rise into his mind.

The journeyman went to sit at the in the broad shade of the most ancient of the Bardic Oaks, a much-respected resident whose presence there had preceded even that of the magician by an age. There, as he dozed, he recalled the many instructions given him. There was much to remember. He decided to hire a scribe, which is what he went and had done that very forenoon. With the document in hand, he returned to the magician, who was glad for the young man. The magician checked the notes making additions and markings. He explained some changes and soon they were both satisfied he understood the crystal seeding for fine glassworks.

Early the next day, with a new and beautiful work in hand, the young man thanked the elder, who would accept no praise saying, curiously, the art of the heart had to live on, that it would belong to them only as long as they shared it. The youth, however, had to work hard to cover his shock and revulsion at the very concept. He did not want to share the skill and didn't want the old fool to share it either. Still, he put on a happy face and chatted, even as he drew nefarious plans.

Then, of a sudden, the magician seemed to tire and apologized for a sudden dire need to retire. More mysteriously, as they clasped hands in the farewelling ritual, the elder forbore to meet the younger man's gaze even as he unceremoniously hastened the ritual along. In hiding his own intent, the journeyman didn't note the elder's change of mood, his unseemly actions, nor feel the doubts fluttering about his own heart overrun as it was with cold mental calculations. Both the youth and the elder wanted to part ways, but for starkly different reasons.

It is often difficult to ascertain character. Then, as now, people of even the most remarkable rank or station will err. So, it was on that day, when an age of ten thousand years was not uncommon for magicians, and their wisdom great, this one made something of an error—in judgment of all things—imagine!

Anyway, the story goes on. The journeyman spent the next night in the village, where he rented a cart and horse. To everyone, he spoke well of the magician and told anyone who would listen that his journeyman days were over and he was going back the king's city to set up a shop. They, in turn, were very happy for him and a bit proud that their magician had done such good work, as always. In fact, the young man was so cheerful about everything to everyone that this was remarked upon and the local bard crafted the song from which this story arose.

Although we cannot know what the young man thought, we do know what he did. After the magician retired for that night, the young man, nursing fantasies about his new life, stole up to the simple dwelling and made off with all of the magician's pieces and a few books, including the one about glassworks. One assumes he wanted to ensure complete mastery of the skill.

When the magician woke, he saw his works had been taken and was annoyed. Not long after, when a neighbor came by asking a favor, the magician, also found a few books missing. He was, for the first time in ages, unable to be of service and so became quite distressed all the way around. He asked his visitor about the young man and was told what everyone in the village knew; he'd gone off, bright and early, heading for the highway to the royal city. The theft wasn't, out of common courtesy, mentioned.

The journeyman hadn't traveled far along the road long when, on the second night, he decided to recreate a vessel that he had, as an intemperate child, broken in a fit of vengeance. He used several gold coins for the new work placing them along with one of the magician's vessels, for a tutor piece, and a Trillium crystal under his head roll. He slept fitfully before waking with a start, believing he'd heard someone walking in circles about his camp. He called to no avail. After a time, he slept, as if drugged.

To his surprise, he only dreamt the ordinary dreams—as he had all through his life. There was no magic until he saw himself sleeping and was cheered. This was how glassmaking dreams started. He saw the gold form a foggy cloud all about his head roll: this too was right. He saw the tutor piece soften as if made of jelly and liquefy to form a small pool. Then, for a frightening moment, he saw a horrifically anguished face in it. He was so disturbed he nearly woke and struggled then to regain his place in the spell.

He relaxed, however, returned into a slumber and began again. This time, in his dream, he heard the sound of wind, turned, and saw the gold haze carried off, which was strange. The pool from the magician's vessel started moving about, which is what it was supposed to do as part of dream process. He uttered the words and sang the chant he had used for his first vessel, though he got caught up when he had to figure out how to substitute the phrase for gold to replace that of emerald. He clearly saw a memory of the vessel he'd broken and the misfortune, which had flowed from that one intemperate act. These memories obfuscated the process. He became distracted with that memory unaccountably and fell into reliving that fateful event. He was not happy with how he saw himself. He tried, fitfully, to complete the spell but, off and on, he forgot what he was doing. Finally, he slept.

Before he awoke, he felt bright sunlight on his arm, pleasant for a moment before it became burning hot. Alarmed, it seemed his arm was on fire! He woke with a start and was horror struck to see his good right hand covered by mass of hot, hard glass, enclosing the skeleton of his fist. Worse, the glass was crawling slowly up past his wrist, burning worse than hot oil as he looked on.

He ran to the near stream but dousing his limb there made it far worse, if one can imagine such. The man's whole body convulsed with pain; he lost consciousness. When he awoke, the glass was between his elbow and shoulder. All the rest was gone!

Having no choice, and driven mad with pain, he mounted his steed and, abandoning all else, rode swiftly back as he prayed into visualizing a meeting with the magician, who would then help him. In his extremity, it seemed as though he had only gone on for a short while before he met the magician at a fork in the road.

Jumping off his exhausted steed, he stumbled and fell to ground whereupon he began to supplicate, howling stuttered apologies, and confessing all he'd done. He crawled toward the magician reaching out as he did so but the elder, wisely avoiding his slightest touch, quickly stepped back. The young man collapsed, clearly exhausted and began moaning loudly.

The elder said he could help. He then held up a lucent pea-sized green pill telling the journeyman he should place it under his tongue. The elder tossed it over to the young man who snatched it out of the air and placed it straightaway. His pain diminished even as the pill melted. His face transformed from one of sweating, twisted muscular agony to a drowsy, dreamy calm. The incredible relief from the unendurable caused him to slip into a profound, if fitful, state of unconsciousness.

The young man and the magician communed soulfully via the mystical mind meld. The magician forgave the journeyman, adding that he'd come all this way to prevent any untoward event. The wise man let him to understand that there was no way to stop the glass from consuming him, or the further consequences for which there was no remedy, but at least he would not die. He did not add that the young man had engaged a poorly crafted, yet quite powerful, spell, that the only possible cure had to be concocted at the magician's dwelling and, since the horse had run off, there was no practical way to get there him in time. The young man thanked the elder for his kindness and was soon overtaken by oblivion.

The old man sat nearby observing the rapid consumption of the man. There was a quiet hissing sound as a while plume of steam rose from the place where the hot glass dissolved flesh and bone. When the process was completed the glass separated into two pools. These, in turn, formed into two beautiful although very dark, semi-translucent vases. If one were to hold them up to bright noonday sun, one would be able to make out the final facial expressions of the glassmakers each contained.

The magician went on to find the cart, chanting as he did so and, as sympathetic fortune would have it, a man leading several horses happened by. Being neighborly, this man helped the magician get to the cart, recover his belongings, and assisted him further as needed.

Psalm 14 "Swami PranhaBondsAnanda"

If someone about you is tearful, do not laugh.
You cannot be full if someone about you is hungry.

There cannot be peaceful bliss when hate quakes the earth or
Thunders through the sky.

You cannot be cleansed in filthy water.
There are no names.

We cannot see God through religion;
God cannot see us through religion;
Religion cannot see God for all our perceptions

Our temple   our self
Our world   our time
Nothing is without these
For us   to be   will always be.

Mystery, magic, meditation, metaphysics, monotheism,
Mentalness – all useless without motherhood.

When trees die they provide for others.
When rocks crumble soil is made.
Air is in everything.
Water gives and takes.
It is called the universal solvent.

The lesson is obvious.
Thus, today is the strangest day of your life.

Even the best magicians use no books.

Prayer requires no word   no book
The worst thing to do with scripture is to just quote it.
There is no perfect human teacher.
To err is human to forgive, humane.
If the past teaches anything, it is hindsight.
Today is slipping away; tomorrow will soon be as well,
Beware   it will be all you can make of it.

It is no use asking questions that you yourself
Must ultimately answer for.

There are no steps or paths for that matter.
No thing is holy. Respect and veneration have their place.

To never say anything and will not
That is acceptance of what is and justice.

God says nothing; our lips speak volumes.
God needs no home; we house images.

God lives and loves with human spirit alone, if need be.
There is nothing greater than all there is.

That we have not found our place, is our discontent,
Our scourge, as well as a resource for its cure.

There is only one land, one language, one sea
Above them all the stars wait for us.

After the Tales

Disappointment

The simplicity of the stories disappointed Paz – after all these were supposed to be something monumental. Paz trusted the wisdom of the process, in which sets of stories were tailored to each candidate and these, being part-and-parcel to the citizenship process, helped them all ensure the blessings of life, liberty, and justice for themselves and to their posterity. Yet, to Paz, the selections were depressing, ordinary, or horrific. More important, however, was something else – a mystery, for want of a better term. There was something unsettling that nagged and disturbed but it was vague. It wasn't the fact that the mythological First Earth was central to three of them, which made the collection unreal, despite Paz's long-time interest in that hoary legend. Nor was it the apparent facts that human kind had made such errors, nurtured such villainy, or produced individuals with heretofore unheard of and wondrous powers.

Paz did some rereading but the heartfelt unease did not diminish. Over the course of a few days, Paz did practices and meditated but these also provided no relief. Research provided no illumination either. Although the other stories all bore a good deal of commonality in style, theme, or perspective, ironically these tantalizing hints, or commonalities, did nothing to clarify the essential matter. At heart, Paz became convinced that there was a vital aspect to them all, which remained elusive.

Paz called for an advisor, a privilege allowed of all new citizens. A few moments later, one entered. Apropos of the severity, this man dismissed the social niceties.

"You have finished reading your set of *The Tales*?"

"Yes, but I am unsettled; there's something unsatisfactory, missing or…"

"Do you have a question?"

"Yes, well, no. I am discomfited because I sense each tale is connected, a part of something grander, and I don't mean the other tales. I believe they all point to something essential and very simple – yet it escapes me. I call it the unity factor, which is the puzzle. My desire is to understand what I have not yet understood. Because of this I am prevented from regaining equanimity and balance. I would be very much pleased to be relieved of this discontent. I hope you'll be able clarify."

"I see. Be assured this is not at all rare. You must know that some tales are sourced from First Earth. These were included for you that you might fully grok what it means to be human in the current context of collective history. Part of what *The Tales* show is how choices, even simple personal decisions, or behaviors, have ripple effects, which increase in force over the ages, contrary to what one expects. It's uncomfortable, I know; we all here know."

"Yes, and although I understood that, hearing it said is helpful. Thank you."

"What you want to know, what will help it all make more sense, or begin to make the stories whole with you is if you are taken to the source."

"Yes, I'd wondered about that."

"It is best to have you meet the author."

"Please, I am ready."

"Yes," he said somewhat sadly, "You may well be. Please stand next to me. Hold my hand."

On a world, abed and dying

There was a moment of darkness accompanied by brief a disorienting moment of vertigo then weightlessness but before Paz could react there was a flash of light, a view of a planet from a low orbit and Paz heard the counselor's telepathic comment, "This world is uninhabited save for one and they who care for him." Before a further thought could form, they found themselves in a nondescript hallway facing a closed door.

The building was an ancient structure apparently made out of a single large mass of rock and the door was of heavy wooden planking. The advisor's voice reached into Paz's mind. "The person, the source of all the tales, is inside this room. He lays abed and dying. We will see him, although, he will not be able to see us. This is for two reasons: first, he is failing in health and is largely unaware of his surroundings. Second, we're in a time bubble, so we'll appear as a minuscule glowing gilt point, smaller by far than any mote of dust. This is how time travelers appear to those they visit. He will speak, and in so doing, requite your needs."

"I am thankful. How will I know what he says?"

"Just as you hear me now but know that he's assisted in this." Then, as if walking through the wall, they entered a small room where an all-encompassing golden light, as wondrous as it was bedazzling, blinded and confused Paz who then heard, "This light is a product of the many trillions of time travelers present in this here and now. If you focus on the man's face," mysteriously the man's face swam into view, "and maintain this perspective the brilliant surround will become peripheral and inconsequential."

The man's features were ordinary, a commoner. He lay under light cotton covers with only his face and right hand visible and seemed asleep. The entirety of the room was lost in the golden glare and so the color suffused the bedding, the man's flesh—everything took on one shade or another of it. When the man's eyes opened, even they presented no other color. The silence was solid. Everyone was here for the man's silent recollections

All His Children

When I was young, I once heard that if you say a word, over and over, during the course of a minute or so, you'll become estranged from that word and it will sound foreign, mysterious—even alien. This is what has become of my name, Weldon Tanner, which is now only a set of sounds, a collection of auditory bits, having as much to do with who I've become as the farthest star, or most ancient bit of icy rock, has to do with the salsa on my avocado this morning. For a while that may have been my name but I am not of it or through it any longer. I am become that which I cannot describe.

Although this happened long ago, memory, being timeless, makes such distance of no consequence. I've learned how the simplest of choices, on the most ordinary of days, however innocent seeming, ripple into the widest ranges of the universe to the influence of all. This may well be the point of my life, as well as the reason I tell this, my last tale, which, I hope, will serve as a petition for the amelioration of my cause, the making of full restitution and amends for all my effects. In this telling do I present my petition for release from form into freedom.

A chorus of voices gave Paz to understand there was approbation and approval. A voice said, "Speak that we may find for freedom."

I was just forty-three, way back then, a youngish specimen of homo-sapiens-galacticus, looking forward to a long and healthy life. Now, I'd always been lucky, and that's how this story begins. I met a friend, coincidentally, as I was shopping, of all things, one unexpectedly free afternoon. This person, in turn, hooked me up with local labor counselor, from General Services Administration. She was holding court at a nearby unity house. My friend's intuition was spot on. When I arrived not ten pips later, I found they happened to be filling a berth aboard the recently refitted, and much touted, Queen Elizabeth Gold. Not only did I have the flight hours, I also had service aboard her, as well as other relevant experience such as scouting. Call it kismet, synchronicity, fate, or luck of the draw, but soon enough. I was in the hiring hall for the Royalty Lines.

Everyone has heard of their flagship liner, The Queen, which was reputedly owned personally by a legendary member of a royal family, back on Earth itself. Now, I won't go on about how a bit of judicious Irish bragging whisked me through the screening process because, these days, I pull my weight and more, which is the way you do when you're part of a crew. I'm confident sure, yet being quick of study and good with people is what carries me through day-to-day—in every way. That's a life lesson, sure.

I remember walking her decks after I boarded—dazzling! There was red carpeting, statuary, as well as real potted plants, gilt fittings, chrome fixtures, soft lighting, not to mention servants of every class, each having their own color-coded monkey suit. Mine happened to be red with a gold trim and more buttons than a stuff-shirt Rear Admiral. It even had epaulets for god's sake—and I was just a steward, second-class. Looking around her that day you'd never guess the Queen saw active duty in the Dravis Cluster, when she ghosted in taking part in the rescue operation for the "Lost Army" of Veyan Jet Knights stranded on Dravis Two.

That was after everything had gone to hell and damnation for me, twice over. I was on board at the time as a refugee having lost everything and everyone I'd ever known. At that time, below the main deck, only the major bulkheads were still in place, making it what we called an airship, meaning the down below was empty of air because it wasn't expected to hold any. All that room allowed them to store of an army's worth the great killing machines from that era. All the levels above the main deck were open wards where rows upon rows of the suffering or dying stretched for a couple thousand yards fore and aft from where I was stationed amidships, on deck twelve. The whole place had a smell that would curl burnt bacon.

I tended those who'd look at me, yet not see, hear and not reply, or speak without being understood, and who, although alive, had odds stacked against them ever recovering what keeping their lives had cost their souls. The Dravis Conflict was the last war we humans ever fought. It was because of the wanton destruction of planets and genocides that the Galactics, in contravention of their prime directive, intervened in human affairs. Thanks to them peace has reigned since. I always thought it was fitting; after all, according ancient human lore, war had been the invention of heavenly beings so it wasn't all-to-strange to have something very much like that bring an end to it, and they sure did.

But when I boarded her to start work she was all primped and spruced up. As a total service vessel, she was "full" when hosting just three thousand clients on one of her touring runs. Her crew, however, was about five times that—this was because of The Queen's famed selling point: its one-on-one, all-day, all-night personal service at every client's every whim, beck, or call.

I remember, it was a few years later that this, my last tale, began. The cause for the relevant decision point occurred as I was on my way to a gambling set-to arranged by some good-buddies of mine, the bottom line of which was, win or lose, I'd win. Now, I don't mean I was going to fob-off, nor that I was so roundly lucky as all that. The plan was for me to "just happen by a game" and make "only to look on." However, my friend, my co-conspirator, would talk me into playing, which I'd seem very reluctant to do. The real point was to introduce myself and in so doing, snag a few clients for my specialty, groundside adventures, shore leaves, and tours of the most lucrative kind. Like I say, win or lose; I'd win.

However, as I turned a corner so did my luck. A woman who was absolutely schnockered, or as we're direct us to say, intentionally intoxicated, was having great difficulty navigating the broad, clear, well-lit corridor and accosted me for service. I couldn't slink back once she'd seen my monkey suit. I put on a glad-to-help-mam game face and responded. It being of no import that I'd just pulled a long double shift, was beat out of it six ways till Sunday, and had a promise of easy lucre beckoning yet already.

That all said, she was a looker for her age. In addition, the authenticity of her translucent glitter dress, accent, tanned skin, and blonde hair, led me to think she was not only wealthy, but hailed from one of the core worlds, maybe even Earth itself. Thankfully, she had enough self-possession to see she needed help, since whatever she'd ingested was having its full incoherency-inducing effects and she absolutely, positively was unable to find her room, nor tell me her name clearly enough for me to understand it.

Oh, she was high and tight alright and spunky enough to give more than a few hints about all the fun she'd been having, how she was up for more, and wanted to know if I could help her find "artistic outlet" she kept on saying. She laughed beautifully, throatily as she stumbled off balance. I caught her when she tripped lightly on her feet—fantastic. She was a number, sure. You know, I wouldn't have said anyone could slur a wink but she sure could. Her hands were friendly too and got friendlier with each over-acted stumble. Since I didn't know what kind of networks she was tied into, I played the obsequious, all-to-delicate, man servant as I mumbled my way through our so-called small talk. Surreptitiously I signaled for an easy chair, code pink. Moments later, as my embarrassment mounted, the cushy vessel hove into view with an even younger, more handsome, and more tightly-clad manservant; as her eyes got big, I got forgotten.

I then hustled to punch out, still hoping to make the game. However, as long as I was suited, I was vulnerable to further such delays. I hurried along the grand balustrade overlooking the Ballroom Plaza, amid ships, risking an open short cut to the purser's office.

As I hurried, I couldn't stop up-welling memories. Three days after she rescued me off a derelict cruiser-turned-yacht, The Queen was attacked by a set of Harridian scouting vessels. They couldn't destroy or commandeer her, of course. However, as berserkers, they could wreak a great deal of carnage, which they sure had a bloody good talent for. I'd no choice but to fight for my life, which I nearly lost more than once. That's why, although I could never be a Jet Knight, I am accepted among their number for I had gone a'shielding, as they phrase it while protecting a number of them, as patients, from unholy ends. And now, every once in a while, when I note one of them onboard, we make time to talk-story, share the grimmest kind of gallows humor one might imagine, and laugh at how we each made it through the dark fog of war, lit only by the lights of faith, courage, and hope.

I avoided eye contact as I made my way intent on my objective. I adopted a purposeful, determined stride, as I signed to other suits so they'd deflect further requests as I closed on the purser's office.

I was in the queue waiting to be served and thought about the game, figuring, even then, what I'd do if I could get there. I was willing to sit in as a fifth wheel on the odd deal, if it came to that. After all, my man told me, it was the proverbial lead pipe cinch. We were going to take bunch of "fat babies"—rich, old, overweight men all new to space—of the kind who think they know fact from reading fiction. All I had to do was play well enough to stay in the game long enough to pique their interest in what I had to offer. Then, later, we'd take 'em all for a ride.

It was a pat plan, since Queen was on an "easy tour" of the fourth galactic arm, and I had lots of choice worlds to choose from. There was Morisston's for fishing, Galvenston for the dinos, Plexus for the Blue Ruins and The Underworld, New Nero and the Bloefeldt Series for inebriation and hard partying. I tell you, on this run, I'd always found my sideline profitable. Even my walking groups came back with tales, which became taller in the retelling.

But, as they say, "the best laid plans of mice and men" which means that pretty little gal's delay really knocked things all callawumpusly. I was in line waiting to punch out when I was beeped with a level two. I almost lost it but went to the briefing knowing full well my chance at easy game was officially toast.

We assembled at the Cine-complex. To accommodate the six thousand of us, they'd opened all the moveable walls. I was way in the back and wondering what in the blue blazes would call for this kind of talky-talk. I heard someone nearby say the ship had been running silent and deep for a while and another who mentioned he'd heard there'd been a directive for ghosting. I was about to ask them for more data when the first mate piped all quiet.

First, she reassured us the ship was just fine and that the reason to proceed with all due caution was because a set of wilders and roustabouts—Bryanite-Darwinists, for want of a better term—had been making a mess in the region. The Galactics had humans dispatch several dreadnoughts to "talk them down." To me, it looked as though the captain was just erring on the side of precaution, attempting to avoid undue attention. Nothing to worry about, was the conversational consensus of the murmurs around me. She went on to add, should passengers inquire, we were to say that the Queen is simply complying with temporary traffic regulations applied to the region of space being transited. We were to confidently guarantee the overall schedule. Last, to distract everyone or ease discontent, there would be a full-on masquerade ball. Then, with a wink and a nod, she added there'd be top scaled overtime-and-a-half for any crew so disposed to cash in on some easy party money. My thinking was that this was to be the means of reducing the inevitable requests for shore leave.

That is one of my pet peeves. Shore leave is granted when any delay eclipses a passenger's right to reasonable requests for disembarkation, in accord with their contracted scheduling at the time of embarkation or even booking. This was always honored, yet this annoying vestige from ancient seafaring days now gives anyone the right to disembark, for any reason, should their vessel's course change enough to inconvenience them even by a matter of hours. It's of no import to management how many a smellfeast takes advantage of this when the itinerary happens to change, no matter how insignificantly, or slight the delay. Many see it as a perk. Then too, there are those who need to have time off ship. I've seen it all.

I went back to my cabin after being allowed to clock out. Just as I knew there'd be a few nitpickers aboard looking for some kind of freebie, I also knew I'd be called, because of my sideline.

Now, no one disliked babysitting more than I, except maybe Jason Lourdes Marque, Esquire III and so, of course, we got slated for that shore leave expedition. I was given time for shut-eye, before he and I had to meet at an assigned ready room, off one of the shuttle bays. The com gave us a launch window. I agreed to be the security and safety officer, in exchange for more snoozyness. While I did that, he made the arrangements.

By the time I came to, we had twenty-three requests. One of them was a pip of a pip. A Mr. Henry, who had suggested Lastro's World, submitted a plotted course, and offered advisements, yet already. We noted he'd responded with all this data in a matter of minutes, after the notice had gone out. Clearly, he'd had all these things worked out in advance—how else could he have pounced so quickly? Mr. Morgan Henry, the 24th, was an Earther from one heck of an established family. His data profile showed him to be demanding, prideful, self-centered, and a well-known fount of tirades and complaints, a grade A, number one, PITA, pain in the ass.

Jason sent notices out for the assembly as I prepped the shuttle. We were surprised when only one woman, a Barbara Vee, demurely entered at the assigned time. She was painfully shy, saying only, "I'll wait quietly until the others arrive, if you please." We offered some refreshments, which she mutely accepted. Then sat some ways off and ate, before meditating, or that's what it looked like to me.

Having nothing to do, we cooled our jets. Then, just as it got uncomfortably close to launch, the rest boisterously came in with, Mr. Guess Who, the PITA, Mr. Henry, in the van, brashly bragging to all as to how he'd seen to the arrangements for the trip and, as their spokesperson, would guarantee they'd be treated well. Before he got too full of his big blowhardy self, Jason took the wind out of his puffery by asking for a reference number, something that did not exist and then, as he pretended to look over the chart, for the first time, mind, asked a couple of technical questions only to cut the boob off mid-answer as he turned his back and appeared to be listening intently to a set of headphones, which did not work, and half mumbling something about a clearance approval, then an issue with the captain's office regarding part of the safety check on the selected shuttle, and a signature being needed, wholly fictional. He made a frantic gesture indicating I was to approach him. I then made a tedious show of checking readouts and pretending to talk to someone and then arguing vehemently favor of our PITA's plan. Jason could be quite the duplicitous chain-yanker when he wanted to be and I knew we'd be yukking it up over this one when we hoisted a few afterwards. Abashed, maybe for the first time is spoiled life, the man was put back. He sat and frowned as he slumped into his seat. As for those who'd been cowed by him, his supporters, they cast doubtful looks his way and some began chatting happily.

As Jason's act wore on, and since they were all quiet enough, I spoke up as the security and safety officer. "Lastro's surface is barren, much of it is covered with old volcanic fields; there are wide-open tracts of barren rock, as well as some regions overrun with sand dunes. The ocean, such as it is, is quite shallow; however, it covers more than eighty percent of the planet. There is nothing to speak of there, so to speak. However, Lastro's is a transition world having as it does the potential for life evolving, after its initial atmospheric transformation. For this reason, and in accord with safety regulations, we'll be wearing static field generators to protect the environment, as well as ourselves." Then I held up the small device. There was the hubbub, of course, and I was about to clarify, when Jason showed his thumbs up.

He turned to them all and said, "Ah, yes, Mr. Henry's plans have been approved, however there are caveats. "We must all use those units," he said, "if we are to land on the planet. They only weigh a few ounces but project a powerful closed field, which can filter gaseous molecular compounds, in this case the planetary atmosphere, your breath, and microscopic detritus. You'll have to walk about in full skin suits but you'll be able to breathe the air, which is within tolerance. You'll get to enjoy sunshine but your static units must be operating at all times."

PITA then made a show of clearing his throat as he stood up tall and, taking a deep breath, opened his big fat mouth "I don't think such precautions are needed; I've been to world's like this before ..." I cut in loudly talking over him for a moment, eyeing right into him, "These are Galactic regulations, Mr. uh, uh … Henry, is it? Yes, and they are meant for all visitors to worlds, such as this, protected as they are under Galactic mandate. They have special surveillance and visitation protocols in place. Of course, if Mr. Henry, or anyone else, has another candidate destination, we are willing to begin making new arrangements." I gestured over to Jason, who smiled sheepishly. There was a stunned silence. Jason and I knew, that our PITA knew, there wasn't time to make any new arrangements. Our PITA shut his pouting pie hole and sat back down, somewhat deflated, but grimly eyed me when some quiet laughter burbled into the tense air.

I added, more for the others than he, "The reason for the precautions from the central thesis the Galactic Law. Any 'cause' for law, meaning a violation of The Common Accord, General Harmony, or writ thereof, must also have its equal and opposite 'effect' which is to say the absolute amelioration, redress, and full restitution for all parties of interest, or assumed interest, in, of, to, from, or for the cause for any finding to be just, fair, whole, and complete. Since we are in Galactic space, we are bound to their precedents and principles. To clarify via speculation, if anyone on this expedition were to be hurt, the individual, this company, the social support, and/or relevant regulatory agencies, all having interests, would have to make complete amends in accord with their shared co-responsibility for the event." I could tell some were unsure, and few stirred uneasily, so I mollified them.

"Lastro's world is being monitored for the development of life, and the precautions I spoke of will allow us to visit the world without contaminating it. I can't imagine the consequences the Galactics would apply to a violation of that order. The good news is we don't expect problems. The static field units work best on hard, flat surfaces and the landing site we've chosen is admirably suited in that regard. We'll also be near an ocean—a scenic plus. Please note, as long as you walk about in a slow, relaxed manner, the static units will easily maintain the necessary security." After they'd been briefed on the skin suits, static units, and essential safety protocols, we suited up, boarded the shuttle, and were soon touching down. I noted our PITA had his own specialized skin suit, expensive and full of backups and extras, which he bragged on.

The landing site was a featureless table of ancient, speckled jet lava and the sea was a beautiful blue and nearly motionless, while the sky, brightly colorful at first, gradually lost its predawn blaze as it slowly cooled into a beautiful azure shade that had a greenish tinge at its zenith. Some low clouds clumped along the ocean's western horizon. At first everyone just stood around, the only sounds being the slight breeze mingled with the nearly inaudible snapping crackle of the static units doing their jobs. Soon people began meandering about, in pairs or small groups, chatting.

When Barbara shyly asked if she could talk with me I was happy to oblige. She mentioned wanting to avoid our PITA, I glanced his way and he was staring our way. I shrugged and we conversed amiably as I kept an eye on everyone. I told a few humorous anecdotes about my work, which relaxed her a good deal. She had a beautiful smile. In the passenger notes she was listed as having severe situational claustrophobia, which she alluded to as we talked about her shore-leave request. She averred how this place, open as it was and being so stark, had ironically made her somewhat uncomfortable and so was thankful I was easy to talk with. I was glad to relax, enjoyed our conversation and told her so. I wasn't kidding about that, no sir.

There wasn't much to monitor. All was safe and secure so I was able to pay her attention. She was a breath of fresh air, compared to the usual run of folk on vessels like the Queen. We went through the little there was to say about the place, the weather, and began talking about our pasts innocently enough; when, lo and behold, if we didn't both mention Plank's —almost at the same time. We each had family there and each knew someone in the other's clan. Odd or weird as this was, as it rattled around in my mind, other things had been percolating up, such as romance. We swapped landholder jokes, though we kept our intense laughter discreet, lest decorum and protocol be edged, which was why I didn't hear my com until it had redlined.

I excused myself and looked about, then did a head count, and came up one short. When I double-checked, I was surprised it was Jason who was missing! He was supposed to be with Mr. Henry—he'd lost the toss and so had to chaperone the least-liked person I'd ever met. Well, Mr. PITA was about fifty yards away, looking down into a dark hole in the landscape, something that hadn't been there when we'd touched down! The whole place had been flat as a pancake, yet it sure wasn't now!

I hotfooted it for sure. Odd thing was, there'd been no temblors. When I looked over the edge, I saw Jason a few yards down, flat on his back. He signed to keep things private letting me know he had an upper leg injury, pain level seven or eight. I guessed he was essentially okay. I looked to Mr. Henry, who was steamed—livid would be the word. I wondered if something had happened between them. To be on the side of decorum, I asked if he was okay. I took his surly, curt spiteful curse as a yes.

Jason must have walked over a large lava bubble, which our landing had destabilized. Even a small crack would have allowed the heavily mineralized sea water it contained to drain as the tide went out. So, while the sensor reads had been correct during the approach and landing, things had changed afterwards. I alerted the landing party, directing most of them to board the shuttle while accepting a few volunteers to hold a line and lower me down to Jason. It was worse than he'd thought. He needed expert help. I alerted the ship, and the med team advised getting him into the vessel where I'd have access to supplies and the automed; with it they could monitor him and advise us.

Jason could barely stand on his one good leg. He had a back injury as well. I suspected there might be internal bleeding, yet I had to get him up and out of there. I tied myself to a loop in the line, hoisted him on my back and, as he held on to me, I held the line and the passengers pulled us up. We all helped get him inside. To his credit, Mr. Henry proved his worth; he sure knew his way around that med kit. The automed's readouts were relayed, and he was instructed as to which hypo-sprays to use, and which first aid to apply. We were advised Jason would have to be stabilized before we could risk his life in a lift off. They were sending a medical team who would transfer him to their vessel first. We were to keep him warm and comfortable. As the pain meds kicked in, Jason fell off into a profound slumber.

Everyone was okay with that plan, except Mr. Henry. He insisted we lift off. He was sure Jason would be fine even though the med crew disagreed. He surprised the heck out of me when he went and disabled the comlink. Then, in response to my objections, began arguing and just wouldn't button it, very annoying. Inconsistency be damned, he also wanted to stay on to explore. He argued he was entitled to shore leave and certain the emergency team could simply come take him back when they arrived. The others were arguing with him, against him, and/or amongst themselves- it was a chaotic melee, a brouhaha to beat the band.

I don't know what else I could have done. I forcefully bellowed to get everyone's attention, then, in a more reasonable, yet firm voice, told them we were following standard ops, I was in charge, and lift off was not happening. Then, to our royal PITA, I said, "Even if we were to leave. I certainly couldn't maroon anyone; you'd have to come along."

He retorted. "You can't force me to be a passenger, the med team can pick me up."

I countered, almost losing it, "The med team certainly wouldn't come all the way here, just to pick up someone who had decided, against protocol and procedure, to stay on. Their primary issue is Jason. Even if we took off, they'd only go so far as to rendezvous with us to get Jason and then head back to The Queen. If that happened you'd have to make your own arrangements, which would be expensive and might take some time."

He argued it didn't make sense for this small vessel stay on the surface, that I was endangering them all and dismissed the expertise on Jason's condition, as well as the seismic and Doppler readouts now indicating surface stability, the ship was on solid granite, bedrock. He wouldn't accept the idea that I wouldn't leave a passenger marooned. Without my adding another word, he went off. His frantic raving intensified. He threatened a lawsuit for just cause, and somehow became incoherently livid at the thought of my marooning him, which I didn't grok at all. I faced him, firmly stating, "If we lift off before he's medically fit, he could bleed to death internally. We'll leave when Jason is safe. Right now, with certain rescue close on to us, we go with protocol."

He reacted explosively with some serious name-calling, which he also spewed toward anyone who said anything from that point onward— even if they were sympathetic with him! When Barbara spoke up, he rushed over to her in such a towering rage as to have her screaming in terror, before collapsing into a full-blown co-dependent panic attack. No matter his intimidation or blustering threats, she compulsively talked on, begging for him to understand her, which only fueled his ire. For her safety, as well as his, I put myself between the two and tried to talk him down. When I hit my recorder, in case things went haywire, he noticed and made a grab for my com unit loosening its wrist band.

When I blocked his grab, he began one-sided fight taking some serious swings and he attempted to grapple me. Hoping to avoid harm, I backed off but when my back was to the open hatch, he pushed me out. As I fell, my static field popped and sizzled, signaling severe strain; it had to encapsulate me while I fell.

He went back for the control panel hollering at everyone to strap in. I got my wind back, tried to clamber back inside but he turned, rushed, leapt, and power kicked me back out. I was flat on my back and still recovering when he jumped out to come down on me with a power stomp. I rolled out of the way, causing him to lose his footing and nearly fall. I got up and we faced off, crouched in wrestler's poses. We circled. I glanced to my chronometer, the next few of minutes would be very long.

The function of his static unit could hardly be expected to cope with the kind of quick, gross motor movements he was making. I could hear his unit whine, sounding much like a mosquito in the ear. If it went out, he'd be as unprotected from the planet as it would be from him. This became the central issue as I kept my distance and my guard up as I hoped to resolve this mess.

I had to place a distress call to the med team and wondered if they were close enough now but the band on my com unit had worked loose. I had to keep an eye on him while stealing glances at it in order to code the sequence properly. That's when he jumped at me. He jumped! His unit squealed; its rapidly cycling pitch rose out of the human hearing range, which made that distinctive boinging "broken spring" sound. I guessed it had snapped out. He grappled onto me; we both lost our footing and fell to scrabbling in the dust. He got me in a chokehold; I head-butted him. He fell back. I coded, slapped the sequencer, and heard it send. We both stood warily; he was panting hard and unsteady on his feet.

He lumbered toward me slowly, uncertainly. I stepped back, reset my static unit to encompass us both, and he stopped, stood, breathing heavily and swaying slightly. We eyed each other in a tense face off. Then, he lunged and we struggled anew. The good news was that, while we wrestled, my unit could protect us both; the bad news, as a capable infighter, he was causing hard pain. I feared I was at risk for internal injuries. I pushed him off, then stepped in to keep close and so protect him. I did not know if I'd reset my unit properly but I couldn't take my eyes off him as, again, he came in swinging.

I had to end the fight. I crouched and then sprung up using my legs to power few deep body core punches. These crumpled him and he went down on one knee. Yet, he rose and tossed the very fine volcanic dust in my eyes. It was gritty, irritating. In a few blinks I couldn't see well at all. He closed in to working me over. I feared I would lose my sight, my eyes stung so harshly, rasping, it seemed, with each blink. I was wheezing, sneezing, and wracked by a cough that doubled me over and just wouldn't quit. Life endangered, I lashed out getting in a couple of full-on blows, culminating in a lucky uppercut for the KO. A group of passengers, with Barbara in van, ran outside to help me back in, as others wrapped Mr. Henry up in a blanket, tying it fast and placing another static unit on him as I directed. Everyone thought I was a hero; in their eyes, I'd done the right thing. I passed out before the med team arrived.

When I came to, I was in the shuttle protected by a containment field. Back on the Queen, I was hustled into isolation, as was Mr. Jerkaholic Wrecks, but I was held far longer as my eyes were damaged by the dust and my lungs had to be cleared.

We all logged legal statements. The initial hearing, which followed soon on, held no surprises. First, Mr. Henry was found guilty of reckless excess and endangerment, assault and battery, not to mention a wide range of other charges. However, it was no surprise that, in an absolute fit of near incoherent vehemence, he vowed revenge and had a full prep for the appellate process filed within moments of the finding. The Queen continued on tour, however and, soon enough it was same old-same old for everyone, except for Barb and I; we became wonderful together.

When the tour was over, the unending influence of Mr. Henry, whose wealth and social connections were alarmingly grandiose, would not allow any peaceable solution. Complex and lengthy litigations continued at his intemperate insistence.

Bad as this situation might seem, there were certain changes the Galactics had brought to human civilization. The first and foremost of these was a justice system absolutely worthy of that name. With a fair, accessible system of justice finally and firmly in hand, humanity had transformed quickly and beautifully. Although I still had to go through the wringer, the more Mr. Henry tried to get back at me, Jason, or the other passengers—for what amounted to our being sane and rational—the more wealth he threw away, and the more his precious family name became defamed, then sullied and, finally, mired.

Another change for humanity had been the gift of an independent informational media so my guess was that his family prompted him to give it up, which is why, after six months of fame and infamy, he suddenly ceased all efforts and directed his proxy representative to pay princely sums to all involved. He made handsomely acceptable, if not fully proper, amends. The grand total was mountainous.

In court, on the day the decision was read, we were flabbergasted by his final appearance, whereat he haughtily dismissed the court, its proceedings, and its findings. He incoherently rambled on for some time in what had to be a closing statement. I believe the gist was that he was happy he'd won. Then he walked away, strutting really, all puffed up and proud that he'd showed everyone just who he was and what he was made of, money apparently, and how little the mountainous pile he'd given away, mattered. He was blithely unconcerned at been faulted, by the Galactics no less. Some people were still that rich.

On the upside, Barbara and I had found the time to find each other. With our new love, as well as a handsome nest egg, we knew a good deal when we saw one, and deal with it we did.

Plank's is a beautiful world so, in short order, we had a homestead, began raising rimeweeds, breeding teletuks, brimson, and terraformed eco-blends. We were, as they say, rolling in clover, except there was no clover to speak of, EPA rules and all.

Well, some ten years went by nicely enough. We had a run of it, expanding our "milk" operations by hefty percentages every season. Our region of the galaxy was booming and we were in on the ground floor of all that. So, color me surprised when, during harvest season, Mr. Henry and the events on Lastro's all came back on an ordinary day in the form of a simple grey envelope.

Apparently, apropos of nothing, it seemed, I was summoned to the justice department for hearing regarding events I thought long done and gone. It said there were actionable developments as a result of the shore-leave incident. What's more, the notice mentioned representation had been pre-arranged, which sounded serious, ominous even. I was surprised, but then again, not. Although I'd gotten over my ill will toward Mr. Henry, I never thought he'd get over me, or us. Still, we were in the midst of our happy years and neither of us thought it was a big deal.

When I entered the courtroom, my mood changed and quickly. Although Mr. Henry was not in sight that snarky lawyer of his was. Jason was there, as was the captain of the Queen at that time and many members of the landing party. So, this was a big deal. After gavel rapped there was a moment of respectful quiet.

After the dutiful preamble, the lights faded out and we heard the unmistakable voice of a Galactic representative giving evidence of cause as a large floating projection of Lastro's world appeared above us. We heard thoughts that translated as follows: "This first image was extracted from the visual record of the planet seen from the shuttle during its approach at the time indicated."

Everyone stipulated to this; we'd seen it before. The voice continued, "The second image is from the exact same perspective taken by a research vessel responding to notifications sent by the satellites monitoring the planet. You can see there are differences."

That was a typical Galactic understatement. All along the shoreline, near to where the shuttle had landed, the sea showed various vibrant shades of green. In fact, the overall color of the ocean was not quite the sterile blue of the first image and there was a verdant patina along much of the seashore, again in the same region. The voice continued, "The monitoring survey satellites detecting these changes notified the regional evolutionary science team. They then dispatched an expedition to investigate an incident of early life evolution—creating some excitement in the science community. What they found, however, were strains of unicellular and bacteriological forms—all common to worlds in the fourth Galactic arm. They found Lastro's had been contaminated."

"As the shuttle from The Queen had been the only contact with Lastro's between the relevant survey dates, the source of contamination would, most likely, have to be from one or more of those on that shuttle, then under the command of Jason Marque, with the safety and security of the mission entrusted to Mr. Weldon Tanner. Both of them may well bear partial responsibility for the violation of EPA standards and the relevant Galactic codes." Then, after a moment's silence, the judge thanked the entity.

Well, I was floored. I gaped. My rep responded rapidly, accurately, and to several points. The judge, while accepting their relevancy, asked to ask me a question, I granted the request.

He asked if my static unit had failed. I said it had not but added that Mr. Henry's had. To this Mr. Henry's representative was willing to admit. Then he hastened to add that, although Mr. Henry had passed on, in view of the charges, his body had been exhumed and a comprehensive set of evidentiary samplings had been taken and brought in anticipation of their being requested. He concluded by saying the Henry estate stood willing to accept its portion of the responsibility and was at the court's service.

I then offered my own samples, as did everyone else—a drop of blood, some mucous, sweat, a hair follicle, urine, and a fingernail shaving—and they gave us each a skin scan, all slight things. After the evidence was taken away, we were under a travel restriction to stay on Plank's until the lab results were in and the case resolved. This kind of thing was normal for any serious case. Barb was brave about it all. We still talked of our plans even though, for us, time stood still.

Two days later, we were called to assemble. Because this was done in a routine manner, we took it as a good sign, yet, when we arrived, there were far more people present—scientists, EPA officials, the press, and even more folks from the landing party. Before court was called into session, everyone milled about snacking on a rather sumptuous complimentary buffet. We chatted in a manner more appropriate to a happy reunion—after all, many there had benefited heavily from the generosity of Mr. Henry, and I was still highly regarded.

Soon we were called to order, and the usual routines tediously gone through. We were all surprised to see hypno-casters brought in for a fact-finding phase. I worried, wondering if my attention to Barbara would be seen as contributory to the cause, and began to whisper this to her. She, appearing to have her own thoughts, shushed me. We held hands in a romantic, empathetic bond. I was very much relieved when I saw the time signature would initiate after we'd gotten Jason into the vessel, but before any fisticuffs had began.

We all watched the ghostly 3-D images played out the perspective views of each witness, from the selected time settings.

I was called, went up, sat down, and also blinked out of consciousness while the machine did its work. When I came to, the mood of the room had shifted. I was unhooked and went to sit back down. The prosecution motioned to forestall further testimony as the accumulated facts were sufficient to support a finding for the essential point, the cause. The judge ceremoniously asked if the prosecution was suggesting conclusion; they asserted as much. The judge, agreeing, signed to my man, clearly agitated, who made seven motions; each was dismissed as irrelevant, immaterial, or peripheral to the central thesis of the prosecutorial case.

"The court finds the Guardianship failed and, as a consequence, the protection of Lastro's world was violated. The pollution, the source of the vibrant, yet basic ecological system there, has been traced to Mr. Tanner's bloodline, his mitochondrial DNA, and a host of other life forms, many of which have specific links to the flora and fauna native to the ecosystem of his body. He is clearly the source of life developing on Lastro's world."

"The court finds this to be the most reasonable conclusion; per Mr. Tanner's own testimony, his conscious actions— the resetting or adjusting of his static unit—allowed unprotected moments to unfold during which he coughed, sneezed, and swiped dust off of his face, out of his eyes. However unintended, this contamination was affected by his conscious and purposeful actions. While the court will stipulate it fully understands the egregious extent of the considerable contributory circumstances surrounding Mr. Tanner's actions, the essential point is that he is responsible for life on Lastro's world."

"Further, the court asserts, in reference to prior findings, in the lower courts and ships' logs, that the actions of Mr. Henry were prerequisite and absolutely material to those of Mr. Tanner. Indeed, without Mr. Henry's flamboyant outrages and endangerment, we'd not be here today. For this reason, the court finds the estate Mr. Henry fully responsible for all damages." He looked to the lawyer who represented the agency holding Mr. Henry's estate. The man acknowledged consent with a signification using his left hand. I was relieved and smiled.

"The decision of this court is made in accord with Galactic principals of cause and effect. Mr. Henry's estate will be held in an active trading trust so allowing all its proceeds to afford Lastro's world, not only monitoring but oversight and management as it develops. Next, based on the precedent of guaranteeing responsibility of parenting parties to fully care for shared offspring, Mr. Tanner will oversee the development of his offspring, the life on Lastro's World. To this end, he will be committed to a Galactic facility, where adjustments to his physical person shall be made."

I had ceased listening, after being let off the financial hook, and been daydreaming but the loud buzz of conversation brought me back around. I was puzzled and looked to Barbara, who was stunned. I began to stand to speak—not knowing court was still in session. My man grabbed me by my belt and yanked me back into a sitting position whereupon he stood. "Your honor, my client, his wife and, I believe, those present would like clarification …"

"Yes, of course. Mr. Tanner, in order to fully address the cause, the evolution of life on the planet, you, Mr. Tanner, will become, as the Galactics are, which is to say, virtually immortal, in order to perform your guardianship. You will be provided a place from which you'll be able observe, monitor, and care for the world of life you've created. The Galactics will soon provide it a satellite moon, from which you will perform the duties of your office until such time as you are relieved in full by your charges. Mr. Henry's estate, capable of financing these essential arrangements, will be charged with all due diligence, moderated by sustainability, to make that so. You will have Galactic and or android assistants for your personal support. The court will hear you now, Mr. Tanner."

Unsteadily, I slowly stood, Barbara joining me as I did so. We looked at each other and she gave me a nudge and nod indicating I was speak for us. "If my wife wants to be with me, I'd ask for the court's indulgence in the matter."

"It will not be a prison, Mr. Tanner, so long as the moon is legally you sole residence, you may live life as you choose."

"I would like to be there with him," she added.

"That will be fine, you however do not have to make it your sole place of residence, you understand."

"Yes."

"One thing more, Mr. Tanner. As the only living 'parent,' and because there are no provisions from Mr. Henry, you have the right to rename the world as it suits you. This can be done at any time; however, you must know the choice will be final."

"I'll call it Eden."

"Do you wish to reconsider?"

"No."

"Eden, it is. This court stands adjourned."

With the rapping of a gavel, my life was thrown out of orbit. I was in shock as was Barb.

"As I recall, at first, it wasn't at to bad. We managed our affairs at a distance but over the years I lost interest in most of the things I used to enjoy. We reorganized our operations into an ordinary worker-owned cooperative and charitable action corporation and became silent partners as we lived off the interest of our proceeds; it was a very rich life. It's not as if we couldn't go visiting or have friends over, but my residence was on Eden's moon—and that was that."

"The worst part was watching my wife age before my eyes. We loved as ever we did; however, I was soon alone and, from that point, in one sense, I always would be. I regretted our decision not to have children but later saw the wisdom of that painful choice. "

"Ah, but that is long done now. Over time I was forgotten and lived in a private reverie giving up all but an interest in my charges, my children. Eventually, after the world of my creation took hold, rooted, blossomed and made fruit, I took a measure of satisfaction as my children's children's children, to the nth degree, disseminated. I hereby testify, and swear to the Verity that they are free, sustainable, and self-productive. I summation, I declare this is so and make this my petition for certain relief."

Paz felt an impossibly huge surge of happiness as powerful as it was brief. The man's voice came back. "I want to thank you for accepting it so readily and for allowing me the freedom to close. In conclusion, and by the grace of those present, I hereby exercise my allowance. Although I am now; I will not be."

The thought stream vanished. That was his last moment. His eyes remained fixed and, as the suffusion of bright gold light quickly faded, their common hazel color became visible, as did a very ordinary room. Paz waited staring down at an ordinary man, now at rest.

Psalm 9 "Light, light, light"

From the start of this universe   until now
There has always been the light
Clearly, it is an essential factor
For what else do we all come to eventually and a'right
But the light light, light?

No thing overshadows this
It's what moves this poor body
Causes my fingers to trace such moments as this
Councils the passion coursing my heart well
And what so enlivens my giddy soul tonight
But the light, light, light?

Terms cannot describe or contain this
Actions provide mere indications
Lyrics might bear it so long as breath bears them
Nothing temporal can truly be seen without it
And all things eternal are made only of it
What else moves us within so as to create without
Passing for inspiration's sight
But the light, light, light?

And so, in the deep, cold world of winter
When sullen, lifeless and leaden heaven
Occlude the hope of celestial bodies
When the landscape beneath
Is set in a monochromatic display
Yes, fish may still seize the day beneath their ice
Yes, furtive, burrowing survivors do abide
And the heart of an owl harbors its heated blood,

As it wings down silently after sighting its prey
Dark talons clutch the unwary or luckless
Where blood spatters on moonlit white
What else rules there but the light, light, light?

What muffles the tolling bell better
Than distance and time?
What rings it ever clearer to echo in the mind?
What's the message it means to send
All these years later?
What do I do by telling you this?

Why do such words as these make their way here?
What causes my spirit to soar
My heart then mind to quicken?
What makes a singular difference
No matter how seemingly slight
But the light, light, light?

When death is no longer that distant, dismissed threat
But present, promised and immediately certain
Your intimate companion, if you will
Waiting on you, so to speak, hand and foot
What will move still   until that very last?
What makes its essential difference felt?
What else is there   to keep in sight?
But the light, light, light?

Psalm 8,451 "Peace"

Create this once
And you've created it one thousand times
One million times
One thousand million never ending times
Peace is what is
Between any two thoughts
Any two breaths
Any two heartbeats   a stillness

Peace   is what is
Between the dreams
The wants and wishes a stillness

Peace   is what is
When nothing at all is happening
When the air is calm
As the gold of day settles into night's deepening hues there is

A stillness
Peace   is what it is
In this world
When the soul is unruffled
With a simple indrawn breath
Providing perspective before you simply react
When you look before you leap, as it were
And you keep   a stillness
Peace   is what it is
On a tranquil pond with reflections that mirror life
Until that first duck skids in   or a breeze wrinkles it
Creating an impressionistic collage of green and sky sequins
With a stillness

Peace   is what it is
When each step is a forward step
On the path that lay easy before you
With a gentle wind at your back
And you walk along with   a stillness

Peace   is what it is
When your quietude is like that of the new moon's
As you're inspiration's reeling to a lover's serenade
All on a lazy hazy summer's night
And each clear moving note
Is embraced by   a stillness
Peace   is what is
In harmony
It's the heart of the matter
And therefore of all matter
Of the universe   for all time   a stillness
Peace   is what is
When you create it
And   being that it is,
All there is
Peace is
A stillness
Create this once
And you've created it
One thousand times
One million times
One thousand million never ending times
Peace is   a stillness

A Word

The transition back to Paz's room was instant. The two of them were standing right where they'd stood before they'd left. Paz, unsteady, sat down as the elder waited for a moment before taking another chair. Paz's relief was intense and overwhelming. There was too much to be taken in, so they sat in silence. Each time Paz attempted to mention any one of the many pressing questions, comments, ideas or concerns, all the more came to mind. Paz could do little more than sigh, every once in a while, in frustration, as it was difficult to put some order or priority to the flood of thoughts. Paz was dumbstruck.

Seeing this confusion, the elder only nodded as he watched, before saying, "I know. I've been there. After all, my only assigned duty is to take persons to that one time and place. I've studied the scene many times, yet I'm almost always surprised at how individuals react."

"That person surely is unique." Paz managed to stammer, after some additional and uncomfortably long disquiet.

"Well so it would seem—although he isn't." The advisor began cautiously. "There is one other, such as he, who may be seen in a similar fashion, albeit at a time when he suffers great agonies."

"What?"

"There are differences between them. This other also had a true purpose and so affected many in his time and beyond, even to this day, as many will argue. Although he did not have a Galactic's endurance, he did have a number of their talents—all of which were natural, albeit inexplicably so, to him."

"I don't know if that's appropriate for me, for now."

"Oh, I couldn't; I didn't mean to imply …"

"Why did you tell me?"

"I did not want to take my leave whilst leaving you with a serious misapprehension."

"When do I see this other?"

"I cannot say, I don't read fortunes, nor make a practice of divination. Thus you, I, or the man we saw, everyone will come into the presence of that other being in their own time and in their own way."

"What …"

"I cannot say more as I've not been …"

"Can you …"

"Clarify? No, for now, you have enough to work through. Decide well, live long, be social, prosper, and remember … always remember … justice is longer than time."

Paz offered the formal farewell. The counselor stood, bowed silently and left.

Once the door closed, there was nothing—or everything to do. What would come of all this, was impossible to say. Speculation was useless, while time, time opened as it never had before, and so, Paz awaited inspiration, but was heartily thankful that the unease, discontent, and malaise were over.

Paz sat, relaxed, eyes closed, to let all the memories come and go, as the universal fate provided, and when, finally, there was a pause, a long fruitful pause, Paz focused on the new, long, long life, which was about to begin. Paz was contented and understood that, despite fate, the future could be written, and so it was. Paz then read this psalm and appended a note attributed to his pseudonym, Peter.

Psalm 1,001 "The Manifold Manners of Means"

Through a flower's flow of colors
And autumn wind's undone
And the still white of the winter
Under a sharp and glinting sun;

Through a meal with good old friends
All with family heartily bound
And the stories by the campfire
And songs that are pass'd 'round;
Through the smells of summer grasses,
Through the Redwood dells a' dawn,
After moonless nights, a' sunrise,
Where to gleaming shores we've gone;

Through the words we banter daily,
The common office jest,
Through the phrases that we know by,
That language we speak best;

Through the hearts on fire - and winging,
Through the thoughts that wing o'er the swell,
Through the spirit that comes unto us,
We know we're one as we

The community of the heart brings one
On tender, on above
To present the present to us
In the quietest ways of love

The quietest way   the quietest ways,

In the quietest way   of love:

With each breath we breathe
In each moment that we last,
Before our eyes, in an eye's blink,
We make the future and the past!
And so, it happens that each day,
Whether by chance or through an old song,
Opportunity will knock as you go -
To pass life's tune along.

Friend Peter's Rhymes,
As translated from the indescribable

This world's ending
Not so much a concern   as
What comes next...

Building a new planet
Just possibly easier   than
Fixing   this   mess

New Planet Recipe:

Begin with nickel iron
Bring to a boil
Add ice as needed

Serves ten billion ...

Yes! Give this book away!

When you give this book away, please initial it here and indicate where and when you handed it off. I'd like these to meander the world over and perhaps migrate back to San Francisco someday as kind of message in a bottle. I look forward to its MUNI debut, finding it at a garage sale or on a shelf in a used bookstore.

Initials   **City**   **Date**

____

____

____

____

____

____

____

____

____

____

Once this page is full, please use any other page—go for it!